PRAISE FOR LISA STONE

'*The Darkness Within* hooked me from the start. Once you start you won't be able to stop!'
Katerina Diamond, No.1 bestselling author of *The Teacher*

'This is a cracking good read that had me hooked from the beginning until the end. Full of murders, spiritualistic intrigue and just a hint of romance. It is quick paced, extremely thought provoking and full of twists and turns. I didn't want to put this book down.'
Amazon reviewer

'Fantastic book, couldn't turn the pages quickly enough!'
Amazon reviewer

'A well-written and extremely addictive novel that will stick in your head long after putting it down.'
Amazon reviewer

'I flew through *The Darkness Within*; it maintained a dark and gritty atmosphere whilst covering some rather disturbing subject matters. But despite there being some very emotive and hard to read scenes described, I raced through the pages desperate to know how it would end and I certainly wasn't disappoint⋯ ⋯ewer

the words just flow off the page and as the story develops it's a difficult book to put down as you want to know how it's all going to end.'   Amazon reviewer

'Absolutely fantastic, I could not put it down. Cannot recommend this book highly enough. You will become addicted to this author.'   Amazon reviewer

'An enjoyable chiller for the summer reading pile!'
                                        Goodreads reviewer

'I loved the premise, it appealed to the horror/sci-fi loving side of me. Lisa understands human relationships and the ugly side of people very well, and this shone through in her work.'   Amazon reviewer

ABOUT THE AUTHOR

Lisa Stone lives in England and has three children. She has always been a writer from when she was at school, with her poems and articles featured in the school magazine. In her teens she began writing short stories, a few radio plays and novels. She finally made it into the bestseller charts with *Damaged* in 2007 which she wrote under the pseudonym Cathy Glass. Since then she has had 27 non-fiction books published, many of which have become international bestsellers. Her first fiction novel, *The Darkness Within*, was published in 2017.

Books by Lisa Stone:

The Darkness Within

Books by Cathy Glass:

Damaged
Hidden
Cut
The Saddest Girl in the World
Happy Kids
The Girl in the Mirror
I Miss Mummy
Mummy Told Me Not to Tell
My Dad's a Policeman (a Quick Reads novel)
Run, Mummy, Run
The Night the Angels Came
Happy Adults
A Baby's Cry
Happy Mealtimes for Kids
Another Forgotten Child
Please Don't Take My Baby
Will You Love Me?
About Writing and How to Publish
Daddy's Little Princess
The Child Bride
Saving Danny
Girl Alone
The Silent Cry
Can I Let You Go?
Cruel To Be Kind

LISA STONE

Stalker

avon.

This novel is entirely a work of fiction.
The names, characters and incidents portrayed in it are
the work of the author's imagination. Any resemblance to
actual persons, living or dead, events or localities is
entirely coincidental.

Avon
A division of HarperCollins*Publishers*
1 London Bridge Street,
London SE1 9GF

www.harpercollins.co.uk

This Paperback Edition 2018
1

Copyright © Lisa Stone 2018

Lisa Stone asserts the moral right to
be identified as the author of this work

A catalogue record for this book is
available from the British Library

ISBN-13: 978-0-00-823672-4

Set in Bembo 11.5/15.25 pt by
Palimpsest Book Production Limited, Falkirk, Stirlingshire

Printed and bound in Great Britain by CPI Group (UK) Ltd, Croydon CR0 4YY

MIX
Paper from
responsible sources
FSC™ C007454

This book is produced from independently certified FSC™ paper
to ensure responsible forest management.

For more information visit: www.harpercollins.co.uk/green

Acknowledgements: A big thank you to my editor, Phoebe, my literary agent, Andrew, and all the team at Avon, HarperCollins.

Security cameras are there to keep us safe, aren't they?

Chapter One

He woke with a start. Eyes wide open and senses alert. Flat on his back.

Julie slept on beside him; blissfully unaware he was awake. She could sleep through anything, he thought – thunderstorms, the neighbour's dog barking, cats fighting. Out for the count. Although there were none of those noises now. It was all quiet.

Perhaps it was one of the children having a dream that had woken him? Or the urban motorbike racer? It came out of nowhere, completed a full throttle lap of the area and then disappeared back into the night. It was a pastime that seemed to be growing in popularity, according to the local newspaper and the outrage of residents. Didn't urban racers have to be up in the morning to go to work? Obviously not, Russ thought with a stab of irritation, but then how did they afford such powerful bikes? He glanced at the luminous digital display of the bedside clock radio. 2.10am. Damn. He was wide awake now.

He listened again for the noise that had woken him but the house remained quiet. Maybe it had been one of the children – Jack or Phoebe – having a dream and they'd now turned over and gone back to sleep? Or perhaps there'd been no external stimuli and he'd been jarred awake by his thoughts? Prodded to consciousness by a worry that hadn't been settled the night before. But he couldn't think of what. His mind was clear. Usually any unresolved issue or anxiety remained when he woke so his mind was already occupied with a half-formed rationale or incomplete sentence, but not now. There was nothing bothering him, apart from a vague reminder to return his mother's phone call, which he would do as soon as he had the chance. She was overdue a visit and Julie had taken her last three calls. Yet while he felt a passing guilt for neglecting his mother, it wasn't enough to have woken him.

He gazed towards the slightly parted curtains and the inky night sky beyond. No moon to wake him, no noise and he didn't need a pee. It was unlike him to wake for absolutely no reason. He'd check on the children to put his mind to rest and then try to return to sleep. Busy day at work tomorrow. He needed to be fresh and alert.

Easing back the duvet so he didn't disturb Julie, Russ noiselessly left the bed. Although their bedroom was in darkness, a small strip of light shone under their door from the night light on the landing. Plugged into the wall socket at floor level and mainly for the children's benefit, it gave enough light if any of them needed to use the bathroom in the night without having to switch on the main landing light and risk waking the whole household. He'd check on Phoebe first; at four years old she was the most likely candidate, calling out in her sleep or not wanting to use the bathroom alone because of the monster she thought lived there.

Barefoot, Russ padded silently along the carpeted landing to her bedroom. He placed his hand on the door and was about to push it open when the ear-shattering shriek of the intruder alarm pierced the air. His heart lurched from the shock and his breath caught in his throat as the hairs stood up on his neck.

'Russ? What is it?' Julie cried, coming out of their bedroom.

At the same time Phoebe's panicked cries came from inside her room.

'Mummy! Mummy!'

'Mum! Dad!' Jack shouted over the screech of the alarm.

'It's OK, the alarm's tripped out like it did before,' he called back, quelling his own shock. 'I'm going down now to switch if off. Mummy will stay with you.'

Russ began downstairs, the siren's ear-piercing screech painfully deafening, as Julie went to pacify the children. He couldn't have tripped the alarm himself; it was on the night-time setting – off upstairs but on downstairs and in the garage. Usually the last one to bed and first up in the morning, it was his job to change the setting and he did it automatically. Doubtless a fly or other small insect had passed by a sensor and set it off. It had happened before; a tiny spider running across the sensor or a lone fly shut in a room tripping the alarm in its frantic search for an exit. A small insect instilling panic in a house of humans!

Descending the last two stairs, he crossed to the alarm control box on the wall in the hall. The green LED bell symbol was flashing frantically, telling him the alarm had been activated. As if he didn't know! He quickly entered the five-digit code – Julie's birthday. Then silence – wonderful, peaceful quiet – although his eardrums were still buzzing and would do so for a while. He'd leave the alarm off and then check the sensors were clean tomorrow when he returned home from work. Otherwise, he was likely to spend the rest of the night in fitful sleep, bracing himself for the alarm accidentally going off again.

The hall was darker now with the alarm's warning light no longer flashing. He began towards the foot of the stairs; he could hear Julie's voice upstairs soothing Phoebe back to sleep. He took one step onto the staircase, and then a sharp thump on the back of his head. A cry escaped his lips, and he had a vague sensation of falling before he hit the ground. Then nothing. No sight or sound, no more thoughts; just an all-consuming darkness.

Chapter Two

'I came down and found him,' Julie said, tears springing to her eyes again. 'The police said there were two of them working the area. There've been a number of similar break-ins . . .' She was on the phone to her mother-in-law, having to go through it all again, but of course she'd want to know the details; Russ was her son. 'Yes, they levered the window in the study and were in the living room taking whatever they could find when the alarm went off, and Russ disturbed them. Pity he went down. We should have left them to take what they wanted . . . Yes, he's home now, in bed resting . . . Yes, four stitches . . . I'm just going to make him a cup of tea. I will. Goodbye.'

She returned the handset to its cradle, wiped the tears from the corner of her eyes and went into the kitchen to make Russ the tea. His mother had been right when she'd said it could have been worse. So much worse. Those evil men might have gone upstairs and into their bedrooms. She trembled at the possibility. Thieves knew that most women kept their jewellery in jewellery boxes in their bedroom, the police officer had said. So in that respect she supposed they'd been lucky, spared the horror of having to live with the knowledge that those monsters had been in their rooms while they slept. And in Jack's and Phoebe's rooms! What if the children had woken and seen them? Would they too have been witnesses that needed silencing? She recoiled at the prospect. It didn't bear thinking about.

Neither did the possibility that they could have killed Russ when they'd hit him with the metal crowbar they'd used for levering open the study window. A life without Russ was unthinkable, as were all the other more horrendous scenarios. Although she wasn't sure these platitudes helped. She felt physically sick, weak, and couldn't stop crying. It had truly been a living nightmare.

Filling the kettle, she switched it on and then leant against the work surface as she waited for it to boil. It was only 6.30pm but in November the evening was already dark. The curtains and blinds were closed, all the lights were on, and the study window had been repaired but it still didn't feel safe.

DC Beth Mayes' words rang in her head: that they needed to review their security. 'When it comes to break-ins, lightning often does strikes twice in the same place, sometimes more,' she'd said.

One house she'd been called to had been burgled three times in as many months, with the burglars waiting just long enough between their 'visits' for the goods to be replaced. A professional couple who'd lost their laptops, iPads and phones three times. New-for-old insurance meant the replacements had a higher street value than the originals so why wouldn't the thieves go back?

Detached houses in leafy suburbs were easy and rich pickings, she'd said. They needed to upgrade their security and possibly consider CCTV, which could be installed for less than the price of the average family holiday. Russ was researching it now upstairs on his old laptop, which they thankfully hadn't taken.

The kettle boiled and clicked off. Heaving herself away from the support of the worktop, Julie took a mug from the cupboard. It was too quiet in the house without Phoebe and Jack. They were staying with her parents for tonight at least, possibly for a few days. Her parents had collected them from the hospital in the early hours, which had allowed Julie to concentrate on Russ, and meant that the police could look over the house uninterrupted – fingerprinting; taking their statements; collecting evidence. From the muddy footprints on the patio it appeared it had been two men who'd come over the fence from next door. No sign of the crowbar they'd used that would have Russ's blood on it, no sign of a getaway vehicle on their neighbour's CCTV, and none of the neighbours had seen or heard anything. Not surprising really at 2am.

Glancing anxiously over her shoulder – every little noise spooked her – Julie took a tea bag from the caddy and tried to concentrate on making the tea. How long before the house felt safe again? She doubted it ever would. It wasn't so much the physical damage – the window had been repaired – but the psychological and emotional damage, as the police officer had said. Beth Mayes had given them a business card and said someone from victim support would be in touch. Wiping her eyes again, she added a splash of milk to the tea and began upstairs to their bedroom.

Russ was sitting propped up in bed with the laptop open in front of him, looking positive. Apart from the small shaved patch on the top of his head with its four blood-encrusted stitches you wouldn't have known anything was wrong. When the nurse had finished cleaning and stitching the wound, the doctor had said Russ could go home but to rest and take paracetamol as and when needed, and return to the hospital if he experienced a severe headache, blurred vision or dizziness. Russ was made of strong stuff and had only come to bed because Julie had insisted.

'How's the head?' she asked, setting the mug on his bedside cabinet.

'Not so bad. Could have been worse.'

'That's what your mother said – could have been worse.' She kissed his cheek and sat on the edge of the bed, keeping her gaze away from the wound, which made her flinch.

'And you still don't remember what happened?' she asked as he took a sip of the tea.

'No. Not after getting out of bed. I came to in the ambulance.'

'Lucky you,' she said. 'I'll never forget it.' Tears filled her eyes again as the images flashed before her. His cry, the front door banging shut as the intruders fled. Her running downstairs and finding him unconscious and bleeding from the head. Frantically calling for an ambulance as the children stood at the top of the stairs screaming and crying. Then the wait, seemingly endless although it was only ten minutes, as she held his hand and prayed he'd make it.

'Perhaps we should move?' she said. 'I can't imagine ever feeling safe here again.'

'Of course you will,' he said, squeezing her hand. 'I'll make sure of it. We've only just finished doing up this place. It's our dream home. They're not going to drive us out. Look, Jules, I've learnt a lot online about thieves, how they work and how to stop them. Come and sit beside me and I'll show you. I'll make sure we're all safe, I promise you, love.'

She went round to her side of the bed and propped herself beside him, resting her head lightly against his shoulder, his familiar warm smell now slightly tinged with antiseptic from the hospital. He took a couple of sips of his tea and set the mug on his beside cabinet.

'It used to be the case that burglars usually only entered unoccupied property,' he began, 'but apparently the profile of the offender has changed according to this. It's often not the old-style burglar making a living from breaking and entering, but drug users desperate and willing to risk everything for their next fix. Intruder alarms are no longer

11

considered adequate, even if they're linked to a police alert. Most thieves know that they have time to break in, grab portable valuables and easily disposed-of items, and be long gone before the patrol car arrives. And it's men and women, although female drug addicts are more likely to resort to prostitution for drug money.'

Typical of Russ to research in so much detail, Julie thought. If he embarked on a project – whether it was at home or work – he did so thoroughly, researching and reviewing all aspects before he made a decision. As he continued profiling the would-be intruder and then showed her web pages with various security options for protecting their home, she began to feel some of the tautness in her body ease and she started to relax.

'I've emailed three security firms to come and give us quotes,' he said. 'We'll get the job done properly by a specialist firm with lots of experience. This firm is my favourite so far.' He opened the company's web page. 'It's a family-run business, established twenty years ago. Plenty of five-star reviews. Don't worry, I'll be here when they visit, and I've cancelled my meeting in Germany next week. I won't do another overnight until we've got our security system upgraded and CCTV installed.' Closing the laptop, he set it on the floor beside the bed and drew her to him. 'It'll be fine, Jules. I promise you. I haven't let you down yet, have I?'

'No,' she agreed and snuggled closer, pressing her cheek against his strong protective chest.

'It was a dreadful experience,' he said softly into her

hair. 'Especially for you and the children. But the memory will fade in time. It'll certainly make a good after-dinner story.' He nuzzled her ear, kissing the lobe. 'I know a very good way to take our minds off it. With the children at your parents and us already in bed, it's an opportunity too good to miss.'

And as Russ's hand found its way into her bra and the first flush of desire made her nipples stand firm and erect, the horror of the previous night began to fade. 'Just be careful you don't bang your head on the headboard,' she whispered with a smile.

'There's a solution for that,' he returned; 'you on top. Now, no more bad thoughts.'

'No, big boy.'

Chapter Three

Derek Flint sat in his smart blue van bearing the logo of his company and, with mounting anticipation, surveyed the house and street. He'd already checked out the area on Google satellite map and street view as he did all the properties he was asked to visit – no doubt the thieves probably had too. The amount of information available on the Internet was astounding, and frightening if it got in the wrong hands. But it made his job that much easier, and very likely that of the thieves as well.

His expert eye noted that one of their neighbours had the full works from a rival security firm. A stylish alarm box on the front of their house, correctly placed CCTV cameras and two motion-activated floodlights. Their other neighbour had nothing beyond a 'Beware of the Dog' sign on the side gate, which could only be effective if it was a Rottweiler or similar dog, trained to attack, and not a house pet. When he'd driven down the road he'd also picked out dummy alarm boxes with fake CCTV cameras. He'd made a mental note of their addresses. Who on earth did they think they were fooling?

Derek checked his face in the van's interior mirror and smoothed his hair. It was important he looked smart and presentable in his line of business, but not suited up like an estate agent or used-car salesman. You needed to instil confidence in prospective clients; these people had had a dreadful shock and felt vulnerable. Calling his business a family firm helped, and so did what he wore: navy trousers and a light-blue cotton shirt under a navy sweater bearing the company's logo. Navy was the colour the police and security wore and engendered feelings of safety and dependability.

Picking up his clipboard and an information pack for the clients from the passenger seat, he opened the van door and got out. It was exactly 9.30am. He was a stickler for being on time. It was important not to inconvenience prospective clients by arriving very early; and certainly not late – that was disrespectful. He couldn't tolerate disrespect, lateness, slovenly or sloppy behaviour. It infuriated him. He upheld punctuality, accuracy, diligence, respect and accountability, much of which he felt was now lacking in today's society.

Opening the low front gate, he took in the two-year-old modest family car on the driveway – a middle-income family, he decided. He relatched the gate behind him and walked up the path, noticing the shrubbery that partially

15

concealed the sideway. It was a well-maintained house, only recently modernized, so they obviously had some money. He pressed the doorbell and waited. Doubtless they'd seen his van, as would most of their neighbours. A break-in, especially one with violence, was very good for his business.

He knew that the owners, Julie and Russ Williams, were a married couple in their late thirties with two young children, most of which he'd discovered from the Internet, together with photographs of their last family holiday, and the children's birthday parties held in the back garden. So he had a picture of the rear of the house – just like the thieves. If people only knew how accessible their information was they'd be more careful sharing it. Smoothing his hair again, Derek cleared his throat as the front door opened.

'Good morning. Derek Flint from Home Security,' he said, handing the man his business card.

'Good morning. Russ Williams.' A firm handshake. 'Come in. This is my wife Julie.' Derek made a point of wiping his feet on the mat – it was only polite – then stepped in and shook Mrs Williams' hand.

'A pleasure to meet you. I was so sorry to learn of your break-in.' His brow furrowed with concern. 'I wish I could have seen you both sooner but I was fully booked all last week.'

'Not a problem, you're here now,' Russ said. Julie threw him a weak smile.

'Please don't worry. We'll soon have this place secure,' he reassured her.

'You understand we're having other quotes,' Russ said.

'Yes, of course.' He gave a small self-deprecating nod.

'Would you like a coffee?' Julie asked.

'Perhaps at the end? If you don't mind I'd like to crack on. I've a very busy day ahead.' It was important they knew how in demand he was.

'I'll show you around and explain what we've got in mind,' Russ said. 'I've been researching what we need online.'

Everyone was an expert now with the Internet, Derek thought but didn't say. 'Excellent. It's always so much easier if the homeowner is well informed. This is for you.' He put the information pack firmly into Russ's hand. Clients were always impressed with glossy brochures. 'I'll talk you through it later after I've had a look around, if that's all right with you?'

'Absolutely. So this is the living room,' Russ said, leading the way from the hall.

Derek stepped aside to allow Mrs Williams to go first and then followed with his clipboard and pen poised.

'As you know from our telephone conversation,' Russ continued, 'the thieves got in through the study and then crossed the living room and attacked me in the hall. The alarm did its job but without cameras there's little chance of identifying them. So we were thinking of cameras at the rear, sides and front of the house.'

'Yes, indeed,' Derek said, making a note. 'I agree.' He followed Russ and his wife into the study.

'They levered that picture window,' Julie exclaimed, pointing, the fear returning to her eyes.

'The new ones can't be levered out,' Russ added. 'They're being replaced tomorrow.'

'Good,' Derek said. Russ had certainly done his homework. He nodded thoughtfully, looked around and made another note, then followed them out of the study, back across the living room, and into the kitchen-cum-diner that ran the entire depth of the house. All recently refurbished with yards of glinting polished granite work surfaces. Incredible how some people prioritized their spending. Forty thousand plus on a new kitchen but leave in a crap alarm system.

'You've got a lovely home,' Derek enthused.

'Thank you,' Julie said.

'So we need to protect it and keep you and your family safe from the scum who steal rather than work.'

'Exactly my feeling,' Russ agreed. Derek thought it would be.

He made a quick sketch of the downstairs and then asked to see upstairs. Russ led the way up to the landing and then in and out of the four bedrooms, the family bathroom and downstairs again.

'Lovely house,' Derek said again, ingratiating himself a little further.

Russ opened the door to the cloakroom so Derek could see in and then led them through the garage and outside, where he pointed out where he thought the cameras should be sited.

'I agree.' Derek nodded, adding them to the sketch. He then spent a few moments looking interestedly at the back of the house and garden while omitting to say he was already familiar with the outside of their house from the Internet.

'Excellent,' he said. 'Shall we go inside now and I'll talk you through what I have in mind – incorporating your wishes, of course. And perhaps,' he said, turning to Julie with a humble smile, 'I could take you up on your kind offer of a coffee? It would be most welcome.'

'Yes, of course.'

While Julie made coffee, Derek sat with Russ at the oak dining table at the other end of the kitchen-diner and set out the brochures and paperwork, waiting until Julie returned with their drinks before beginning. Women expected to be involved now.

'So this is an outline of your house,' he said, pointing to the plan he'd sketched. 'I'm proposing siting the cameras here, here, here and here – more or less where you suggested.' Russ looked pleased. 'These are the cameras I use.' He showed them the glossy leaflet. 'I always recommend spending the money on decent high-definition cameras. They give you excellent daytime vision and infrared at night. They are more expensive but the images are so sharp the police can use them to identify suspects. Not that you will be broken into again once this is all installed.'

'Well, that's a relief,' Julie said.

'I explained to my wife that the reason one of the other quotes was so cheap was because they used analogue cameras,' Russ said.

'Exactly. You are well informed. I'll run the external wiring in conduit.'

'What's that?' Julie asked.

'It's a hard plastic tube that protects the wires so they can't be cut,' Russ said.

'I couldn't have explained it better myself,' Derek said, flashing him an approving smile. 'It's the safest option otherwise a would-be intruder would simply snip through the wire and disconnect the camera. Most intruders carry wire cutters. It's a small additional cost to you but worth it.'

'Oh yes, we must have those conduits,' Julie agreed, shuddering at the recollection of their break-in.

Derek made a note. 'In respect of the monitor I suggest this fifteen-inch colour monitor.' He opened another leaflet.

'You wouldn't run it through the television then?' Russ enquired.

'No. It's the less expensive option but using the television as your surveillance monitor is cumbersome and ineffective in practice. If you have a separate monitor you just glance at it. I would suggest situating it in the hall.'

'We'll have the monitor you recommend,' Russ said. 'What about voice warning alarms? You know those that give a recorded warning message – *you are being recorded on CCTV* – or similar.'

'I can install one if you wish – it's not a problem – but I don't usually use them.'

'Why not?'

'They can be very annoying to neighbours and in practice they are more likely to deter your newspaper boy than a would-be intruder. I think the money would be better spent on additional security lights.' He paused for their reaction. He never rushed his clients.

'Yes, go ahead,' Russ said. 'We have one security light down the sideway so we can see our way to the bins.'

'Noted,' Derek said. 'And I would suggest another at the rear and down the other sideway.'

'Not at the front as well?' Russ queried.

'Not necessary. You have the ornamental down lights, which you leave on all night.'

'How did you know we left them on?' Russ asked, looking at him.

A slight hesitation before Derek replied. 'You seem sensible and it's a reasonable precaution to illuminate the front of the house rather than leaving it in darkness.' He smiled reassuringly and moved on. 'That's the external security taken care of. Have you considered having a surveillance camera indoors?'

'Whatever for?' Julie asked surprised. 'There's only us and the children here.'

'You don't ever use a nanny, au pair, babysitter or cleaner?' Derek queried, assured of the answer.

'We have a cleaner,' Julie replied. 'But she's been with us for years. Our babysitter is our goddaughter, a lovely girl. I trust them both.'

'I'm sure you do – as would most folk – but many of my clients who take this option are surprised by what they find goes on in their absence. I'm not trying to scare you into buying something you're not comfortable with, but I wouldn't be doing my job properly if I didn't suggest all the options. Think about it and let me know. If you do decide to go ahead I would suggest one camera in the living room. You can easily turn it off on the monitor so you don't have to keep seeing yourselves.'

'We'll think about it,' Russ said.

Derek nodded. 'Nearly finished,' he said, glancing at his watch. 'I won't keep you much longer. Now to the NVR – that's the video recorder. It records constantly and keeps the recording for thirty days and then resets. I'd like to situate it out of the way in the garage.

'That's fine,' Russ said.

'And last but certainly not least I'd recommend connecting your surveillance system to the Internet, so you can watch your home and see it is safe when you're out.'

'Yes, of course,' Russ said.

'You'll be able to access your CCTV on your phone, tablet or laptop. Here, let me show you my office.' He always gave this little demonstration although clients rarely needed convincing. Blokes especially were eager to sign up to the latest online technology and impress their mates and work colleagues.

He placed his phone on the table between them so they could both see it and tapped the icon. 'There's my office,' he said proudly as the image displayed. 'It's empty at present, as it should be; we're all out on jobs. There's the lockup where I keep the vans overnight. The system I have is the same as the one I would install here. See how sharp the images are.' They both nodded enthusiastically, clearly impressed, as most clients were. He allowed them time to savour the images as he zoomed in and out. 'And here's my home,' he continued, swiping the screen. 'Again, the same system I would use here.' Julie peered closely at the webcam images of the inside of his home.

'Do you live alone?' she asked, which took him by surprise.

'Why do you ask?' he said, and closed the website.

'Just wondered; me being nosy, I guess.'

He raised a polite smile and returned the phone to his pocket. 'Do either of you have any questions about anything I've said? Apart from my private life,' he added. He saw her glance at him, unsure if he was serious.

'I don't think we have; you've been very thorough,' Russ said. 'Thank you.'

'I'll email my quote to you this evening. Go through it, and have a look at the literature. Let me know if you have any questions.' He gathered together his papers, finished his coffee, and stood.

'If we were to accept your quote,' Russ said as they began towards the door, 'how soon could you do the work?'

He looked at them thoughtfully. 'Hmm, I have a big job starting the week after next at a building contractors. You obviously want this place securing as soon as possible to stop the same thing happening again.' He paused. 'I tell you what, this work here should only take me a day, so, if you were to give me the go ahead tomorrow, I'll have it fitted for you by the end of the week. How does that sound?'

'Very good,' Russ said, and Julie nodded.

'Well, nice meeting you both and thank you for the coffee.' They arrived in the hall and shook hands.

'Try not to worry,' he said to Julie. 'We'll soon have you safe again.'

'Thank you, I feel safer already.'

'Good.'

He'd be very surprised if he didn't get the work.

Chapter Four

'Very nice,' Paul Mellows said, as they pulled onto the driveway. For a moment Derek thought he was referring to him. 'The house . . . it's a nice pad,' Paul clarified.

'Oh yes.' Derek nodded and switched off the engine, silencing a wave of disappointment 'So remember, we wipe our shoes on their doormat before we go in. It's these little marks of respect that clients appreciate.'

Paul sighed. 'I always do, don't I?'

Derek glanced at him with an appreciative smile. 'You're better than many of my apprentices, I'll give you that.' Paul was an attractive lad with fair hair and blue-grey eyes, but at eighteen he was brash with the misplaced confidence of someone who thought they knew it all. 'Eight twenty-nine. Nearly time to go. Is your phone off or on silent?'

'It will be.'

'And remember, we address our clients by their title and surname, so it's Mr and Mrs Williams to you.'

Paul stifled another sigh. 'I know. And we don't accept the first drink they offer even though I'm gasping and didn't have time for breakfast.'

'And whose fault would that be?' Derek asked indulgently.

'Mum's for not getting up on time.'

'You're old enough to get your own breakfast. So you know the routine.' Derek opened his door. 'You stay in the van while I ring the bell and make sure they are all up and ready for us. And no shaking their hands,' he added, his lip curling into a smile. 'Who knows what you've been doing with those hands at your age.'

'Wouldn't you like to know.'

Derek looked away as Paul's phone bleeped with a message. 'Girlfriend?' he asked as he got out.

'None of your business.'

Derek left him to it. Despite his impertinence Paul was learning the trade fast, possibly a bit too fast. He'd had to keep a closer eye on him. He rang the doorbell. The Williams were up and expecting him. With a brief 'good morning', he returned to the van for the equipment they needed, tapping on Paul's window as he passed.

'Thank God it's Friday,' Paul moaned as he got out and joined his boss at the rear of the van.

'You want to count yourself lucky you have a job. There's a lot unemployed among your age group, and you're learning a trade.'

'So you've told me before.'

Ignoring his slight, Derek passed Paul two toolboxes from the rear of the van and locked the van doors. Mr and Mrs Williams were waiting for them in the hall.

'This is my apprentice, Paul.'

'Hello,' Paul said, giving his shoes a cursory wipe on the mat.

'Hi. Would you both like a drink before you start work?' Julie offered.

'No, thank you,' Derek replied. 'I'd like to get going, if you don't mind.'

'And you, Paul?'

'I have to do as the boss says.'

'We'll leave our tools in the garage and set up camp in there, if that's alright with you?' Derek said to Russ. 'Save us keep going in and out of your front door.'

'Fine,' Russ said. 'I'm working from home today so if you need anything I'll be in the study, and my wife will be around too.'

'We'll try not to disturb you,' Derek said.

'Anything else you need?' Russ asked.

'I don't believe so.'

'I'll leave you to it then.'

'Thank you.' He gave a little bow.

Paul stifled a smile.

In the two months he'd been working for Derek, Paul had learnt that the company was nowhere near the size his boss liked to pretend – indeed as far as he was aware there was just the two of them. He also knew that as well as being obsessed with good manners and politeness, Derek kept himself to himself, never went out socially and appeared to have no mates. He seemed to live for his work, and was meticulously clean and tidy to ridiculous lengths. Some days Paul felt he'd done nothing but clear up. Derek also liked to work in silence, only breaking it to explain something about the job, or to deliver a lecture. Lectures included the youth of today, lack of respect, the lowlife scum who stole from decent folk, and noise pollution – the latter delivered after Paul had naïvely asked if they could have the radio on as they worked.

'If clients wanted a radio blaring out all day they'd have one switched on, wouldn't they? It would be intrusive for them to have to listen to our radio just because we want it on. An infringement of their personal space. Never forget we are tradesmen in these people's homes, here simply to do the job they are paying us for, so don't overstep the line into familiarity.' Paul had been sorry he'd asked.

But his boss's work ethos seemed to be successful, for he received so many requests for quotations that he could pick and choose the jobs he wanted. After visiting some premises he didn't send an estimate, but an email apologizing that his work schedule was full, which seemed odd to Paul as some days they'd finished by lunchtime. Paul had no idea what the criteria were for accepting or declining a job. He'd asked Derek but he'd been vague and as an apprentice he couldn't press him for an explanation. Paul was never

28

allowed to go with Derek when he went to estimate. Derek said it would be an unnecessary inconvenience to the clients to have them both there, but added that if he took Paul on permanently he would train him in estimating. For various reasons Paul doubted that would happen.

At eleven o'clock they accepted the coffee Mrs Williams offered and drank it in the garage. Paul was also allowed to eat two of the biscuits she'd arranged on the plate; to eat them all would have appeared greedy, Derek said. It was then Paul's job to return the tray with their empty mugs and the plate to the kitchen, remembering to knock on the door before he went in, even if it was open.

At one o'clock they had their lunch break sitting in the van to eat their packed lunches. Paul found it uncomfortable sitting so close to Derek who often had tuna and mayo in his sandwiches, made by his mother. He had the radio on low and always tuned to Classic FM. Paul ate his sandwiches quickly and then left the van to use his phone.

At half past five, the job was done. Derek checked the place was clean and tidy and that all their tools were packed in the van and then told Paul he could go. All that remained was for Derek to talk the clients through operating the system, and he never left until the clients felt confident using it.

'I'm glad you're pleased with the quality of the images,' Derek said an hour later as he and Mr and Mrs Williams stood in front of their monitor in the hall. He'd shown them how to navigate the screen with the mouse, rewind to a specified date and time, download information, zoom in and out, and decide which images to display. They were now looking at their children in the living room watching television.

'Stop picking your nose, Jack,' his father called from the hall. They laughed as Jack looked up startled, wondering how he'd been caught.

'I've changed the default password along the lines your husband suggested so you can remember it,' Derek said, winding up. 'It's now rujuwi10.'

'I won't remember that!' Julie exclaimed.

'Yes, you will,' Russ said. 'It's the first two letters of our names and 10.'

'Of course.' She laughed, tapping her forehead at having not realized.

'Change it again if you want,' Derek said. 'But please tell me if you do. I'm maintaining your system – free for five years – so if there is a technical problem I'll need to be able to log in to sort it out.'

'Yes, of course,' Russ said.

'Now, I've loaded the website to both your phones; are you sure you don't want me to do the same with your tablets and laptops?'

'No, that's fine, I'll do it,' Russ said. 'Thanks for every-thing. I'll certainly recommend you.'

'Thank *you*. Please don't hesitate to phone or email me if there is anything further I can help you with.'

'We will,' Russ said. They shook hands.

Derek turned to Mrs Williams. 'Nice seeing you again. You'll sleep easier in your bed now you're all protected.'

'We will indeed.'

Chapter Five

'You're late,' Elsie Flint hissed the moment Derek walked in. 'Your dinner's ruined again. I had mine over an hour ago. It's thoughtless. But why do I expect any different? Like father, like son.'

'I'm sorry,' Derek said, going to the kitchen sink to wash his hands. 'But you know I can't leave a client until the job is complete.' He ran the hot water, squirted anti-bacterial soap onto his palms and washed them well.

Tutting, his mother took his plated dinner from the oven. She set it at the place she'd laid on the small Formica dining table covered by a faded tablecloth in the recess of the kitchen.

'Thank you,' he said, drying his hands.

She humphed and returned to the living room, sitting in her usual chair in front of the television to watch the soap he'd interrupted.

She was a bitter woman, Derek acknowledged, and watched soaps most of the day to alleviate the boredom of her own life. And who could blame her? Her life was meaningless, shallow and without purpose but there was nothing he could do about it.

He crossed to the table, and drawing out a chair sat down. He picked up his knife and fork, wiped it on his napkin and looked at the congealed ready meal on his plate.

'I've told you not to bother cooking my meal,' he called through to her with a stab of irritation. 'I never know what time I'll be back.'

'And I've told you it's a waste of electricity to cook our meals separately,' she returned, and upped the volume on the television to stop further discussion.

In the past he'd suggested buying a microwave but she'd refused on the grounds they were unsafe, and, anyway, she'd never learn to use one.

'I could teach you,' he'd offered.

'No, thank you,' she'd said in a tone that left no room for negotiation. 'We don't need a microwave.'

He took a mouthful of the cottage pie and chewed slowly. Another stab of irritation. He resented having to eat her overcooked processed meals nearly as much as he resented being put in the position his father had left him in. When he'd abandoned them, Derek had become solely responsible for his mother. He'd been just eighteen and his own life had stopped. He doubted it would ever get going again while she was alive. He'd had to leave school to get a job to support them both, and had become his mother's emotional crutch too – her lifeline. It was crushing and sucked the lifeblood out of him.

Then he felt guilty for thinking these things, and hated his father even more.

'Sorry, lad,' his father had said on the day he'd walked out, taking only one suitcase and never returning. 'She's not the woman I married. I've stood it for as long as I can but it's a loveless, sexless marriage. You're an adult now and can take care of yourself. I want something better while I have the chance. I don't deserve this.' But neither did he, Derek thought bitterly.

As the only man in her life, his mother took out her frustration on him so that over the years he'd grown to feel as his father must have done and could almost appreciate why he'd left. But Derek didn't have the option of leaving. It was unthinkable. She'd never survive alone, which was not a consideration his father had had to contend with because, of course, Derek had been there.

Having eaten half of the glutinous tasteless heap on his plate, he stood, went to the pedal bin and scraped the rest in.

'Wasteful,' his mother called from the living room. 'Throwing away good food when there are kiddies in the world starving. You should be ashamed of yourself.'

He didn't respond – he rarely did – but crossed to the sink where he filled the bowl with hot water, added a squirt of washing-up liquid, and washed his plate and cutlery thoroughly. Drying his hands, he returned to the table and, in a well-practised routine, removed the salt and pepper pots and put them in their place in the cupboard, folded the tablecloth and placed that and the napkins in the drawer in the bureau.

He poured himself a glass of water, left the kitchen and began across the hall.

'I'll be upstairs if you need me,' he called.

There was no reply; he hadn't expected one. He probably wouldn't see her again until the next day when she would be downstairs in her dressing gown making breakfast. They sometimes had dinner together, which was the nearest they came to interacting; otherwise he followed his routine and she hers.

As he neared the top of the stairs, his spirits lifted at the prospect of what lay ahead. It was his 'calling', his vocation, and what kept him going and made his life worth living. It created a feeling of being valued, of being in charge, and gave his life some purpose. Without it he'd be nothing, a nobody like his mother, but in this he knew he excelled.

Opening the door to his bedroom, he flicked on the light switch then closed the door behind him, sliding the bolt into place. The cheap outdated furniture, threadbare carpet, single bed (his since childhood), and faded curtains were of no significance now. His surroundings were inconsequential compared to the work he did – keeping people safe.

He crossed to the one piece of new furniture in the room, the pine workstation that stretched almost the length of one wall. Reaching under the desk, he threw the switch and then sat in his office chair and waited for the monitors to power up.

The expectation of what lay ahead was uplifting, nearly orgasmic in its intensity. Nothing else gave him a buzz quite like this. His desk and the monitors resembled a control centre. Houston calling. This was his domain. Here he had a god-like status: all-seeing and powerful. Omniscient, and looking down on the minions that were the human race.

Four screens; he might buy more, although he was already working flat out. There just weren't enough hours in the day. Each monitor was responsible for twelve sites, forty-eight sites in all. He would be stretching himself to take on more and he didn't want to let anyone down. He changed the sites from time to time. Updated the selection as and when necessary. If he got bored with one or if the client no longer required his service, then he replaced their site with another. He was never short of choice. There were always people in need of monitoring, guidance and assistance. It was just that they didn't know it.

The screen savers appeared simultaneously on all four monitors and Derek entered the password, then clicked on the icon to launch the software for the live images coming from his clients' cameras. His senses tingled with delight as forty-eight thumbnail images presented themselves and the screens were alive with little people scurrying around like ants.

He peered more closely, scanning each briefly, deciding who to visit first. This was often based on where he'd left off the night before when he'd had to force himself away from the dramas unfolding before him and switch off and go to bed. How his mother with her addiction to television soaps would have loved his work; if only she knew, he thought. Real people living out real lives; not actors working from scripts. So much better to have the real thing.

He was sure she would have appreciated it and it might have bridged their divide and brought them closer – united in a common pleasure. But she was far too much the gossip to be trusted with something so precious. A slip of the tongue over the garden fence or when she was on the phone to her sister. It was a pity she couldn't be trusted, for this was probably the one thing that might have made her proud of him. Might, but then again he wasn't sure.

With his hand resting lightly on the mouse, Derek concentrated on screen one and zoomed in to The Mermaid, his first port of call tonight.

Betty, the proprietress of the 'massage parlour', was the only one of his clients who knew he was watching and she appreciated it. He always tried to spend time with her and her girls in the evening. He'd done a deal with her to install their CCTV after one of her girls had been badly assaulted by a client who hadn't understood that 'no' meant no. Betty had wanted cameras in all the bedrooms to keep the girls safe, but his competitors had shied away from the work, saying it was probably illegal. He hadn't had the same reserve – far from it. It was what he did, although Betty didn't know that. So they'd done a deal. He'd installed the surveillance system at cost price on the understanding he could watch the girls with their clients whenever he wanted. Sensing she had found a kindred spirit, she'd suggested another deal and now gave Derek 30 per cent of the earnings she made from her website, where she charged clients to view the girls performing. He'd been surprised to learn how many clients were willing to pay to just watch. It made him feel less of a freak.

He felt he enjoyed a good relationship with Betty and considered her a friend. Often she'd give him a little wave or say hello to the camera if it was at a time when he was likely to be watching and she wasn't entertaining. She'd offered him the chance to experience their service first-hand, but he'd declined. He'd seen how the girls gossiped in their spare time, sometimes laughing about their clients. He'd only had sex with a woman once and that had been disaster. Doubtless it wouldn't be any different the next time.

This evening as he looked at the images coming from The Mermaid he could see that Betty was busy showing a new girl around. Three of the rooms were in use and he clicked on Sandra's bedroom, his favourite girl, and enlarged the image to full screen.

She was entertaining a regular client, a guy from the city who was in banking. Derek felt he knew him, he'd been there so often, and he certainly knew his little ways. He always treated Susan well – with respect – and was very generous in tipping. In a different life he could have been like him, Derek thought, had his father not left them.

He watched, his breath and heartbeat quickening as his excitement grew, mirroring that of the client's. Unzipping his trousers, he lowered the front of his pants and then took a tissue from the box and held it ready. Masturbating, he followed the rhythm of Susan and her client, never taking his gaze from the screen until the last moment when his eyes snapped shut in ecstasy and his body contracted into orgasm. A small cry escaped his lips and he relaxed. He needed that – the release. Much better alone than with someone. It was so much safer; they didn't laugh.

After wiping himself dry, he threw the tissue into the wastepaper basket, then tucked himself in and zipped up his trousers. Now to business. He looked at the other sites on screen one. Methodical in surveillance as he prided himself on being in all other aspects of his life, Derek had arranged his clients in alphabetical order, using the first letter of their surname or that of the establishment if it was a business. So A to F were on screen one, G to M on screen two and so on. Bart's Corner Shop was on screen one. There'd been no sign of the hooded thugs who had twice robbed and terrorized the shop owner and his wife at knifepoint. Satisfied all was well, Derek checked the other sites on screen one before moving to the next monitor.

His most recent clients, the Williams, were on screen four, and he clicked on their thumbnail image, which brought up the views from all their cameras. Everything appeared to be working and he clicked on the exterior cameras first, enlarging them one at a time to fill the screen. He was pleased with the clarity. Although it was pitch-black outside, the infrared was working well, as he knew it would be, so he could see almost as much as in daylight.

Satisfied that all was well outside their home, Derek now clicked on the image coming from the camera in their living room. It was a comfortable and homely room, welcoming and relaxing. He'd thought so while he'd been there earlier. He assumed the children, Jack and Phoebe, were in bed as there was no sign of them in the living room; just Russ and Julie sitting side by side on their sofa, enjoying a glass of wine on a Friday evening. A cosy scene and one he envied; the snatch of normal family life with the children in bed and the parents spending quality time together. A proper family, not like his.

He clicked on the speaker symbol to engage the microphone in the camera – a little additional touch his clients didn't know they had. Russ and Julie – he felt he knew them well enough now to use their first names – were discussing next year's holiday. They were thinking of taking the children to Disney World in Florida. Very nice, lucky kids. Derek smiled to himself. They were a lovely family and he was pleased he could help them. Reassured all was well in the Williams' home, he clicked the mouse to return their image to a thumbnail, took a sip of water, and then moved the cursor to U. Now to the real business of the night – which might not be so warm and cosy.

Chapter Six

Derek watched as Kevin Brown took his place in the gloomy doorway of U-Beat nightclub. At six foot two inches tall, he was broad chested, with muscles gorged from steroids and weight training. His face was that of a fighter, his nose flattened and misshapen and his skin pockmarked with scars old and new. At twenty-three he was an arrogant bastard who considered himself in peak condition and hoped to enter the world of professional boxing. Before those dreams were realized, to get by he took work where it was offered. Jobs that required a big, bad-looking guy. He was under no illusion about his appearance, and even bragged about it, but it was an asset in the ring and in his other work. If you needed the frighteners putting on someone to warn them off or repay a debt, then it was no good sending along some little prissy. He was the man for the job. And it was surprising just how many who owed money and claimed they had nothing suddenly found a wad of cash when he turned up on their doorstep, even before he'd become 'persuasive'.

Tonight, as with most Friday and Saturday nights, Kevin was working as a bouncer for U-Beat nightclub. There was just him on duty at present but another bouncer would join him at ten o'clock, half an hour before the club opened. They kept the queue in order, sent away those who were already pissed, high, or out to make trouble, then once the club doors opened, allowed the clubbers in one at a time, frisking them as they entered: a quick pat-down, and a search of the girls' handbags, checking for drugs, drinks and weapons. There were already a dozen or so early birds in the queue who wanted to make sure they got in. U-Beat was the only nightclub in Coleshaw town, and there wasn't much else going on so it was popular.

'Hi Kev,' two girls called. Heavily made up and ready for a night out, they tottered over to him on too-high heels.

'Hello, ladies,' he said, straightening. 'How are you?' They were regulars.

Derek shifted in his chair. He had a good idea what was coming next.

'We're good, aren't we?' Chelsea giggled, nudging her friend.

'Yea,' Tracey said. 'We're good.'

'How's the kids?'

'Brats but we love 'em,' Chelsea replied for them both.

'You clubbing tonight then,' Kevin asked, 'or just here to chat me up?'

'That depends, don't it?' Chelsea replied, and they both giggled.

'On what?' he asked, feigning ignorance.

'On whether you let us in, Kev,' Tracey said.

Kevin leant slightly forward, peered out from the doorway at the short queue lining up against the wall to his right. 'If you join the queue now you'll get in no problem,' he said, suppressing a smile.

They giggled again. 'You know we haven't any money, Kev, to pay to get in,' Chelsea said.

'You haven't spent all your benefit money already?' he exclaimed in mock surprise. It was a similar conversation every Friday evening. They were both teenage single mums and didn't have twenty pounds each to get in. Once inside it was easy to get guys to buy them drinks.

'Kev, stop teasing us,' Tracey said. 'You'll let us in, won't you?'

'I'm thinking,' he said, obviously enjoying the banter.

'What you thinking, Kev?' Both girls grinned seductively.

'About what you can do to persuade me,' Kevin said, looking over their heads.

'I can't,' Chelsea said, 'I've got me monthly, but Trace can.'

'Is that right?' he said, bringing his gaze back to Tracey.

'Yea. But you let us both in. Special offer. One for two.' They laughed and his eyes creased into a smile.

He glanced up at the CCTV camera trained on the entrance, at present with him framed in its doorway. There was another camera just inside the door.

'You know where,' he said to Tracey. 'But don't make a song and dance about it or you'll get me fired.'

Tracey took the hint and quickly slipped out of view of the camera and disappeared down the alley that ran alongside the club. Chelsea went to take their place in the queue as Kevin stepped out of the doorway. 'I'm going for a slash, mate,' he told the guy waiting with his girl at the head of the queue. 'I'll be back shortly. Keep an eye on things and I'll let you in for nothing.'

'OK, mate.'

Undoing the button on his black three-quarter-length coat as he went, Kevin turned the corner into the alleyway and out of sight of the camera. He could just make out Tracey waiting for him in their usual place. She and Chelsea were interchangeable and took it in turns to give him his Friday night treat, his bonus to make up for low wages and their ticket into the club. Although they were out of sight of the cameras, he was supposed to be on duty so they needed to be quick. But part of the excitement for him was in the immediacy. The fuck without foreplay.

Flattening her against the wall, he quickly undid his trousers, yanked up her short skirt and pulled aside her thong. She groaned as he thrust into her, from pain or pleasure he didn't know – or care. Hard thrusts, deep inside; he kicked her legs further apart so he could penetrate her fully, animal-like in his taking of her. It could have been anyone he was fucking. But that was probably true for her too as long as it got her into the club. Thrusting faster now, he would come quickly, with no need to hang on in there and wait to satisfy her. She was his for the taking.

Then a sudden movement from behind. Kevin's eyes shot open and Tracey screamed. A flash of silver, the glint of metal. A faceless head with only slits in the balaclava for eyes, the pupils dilated and the whites glowing menacingly in the dark. It was all over in an instant; no time to avoid the knife.

Kevin's face registered shock and surprise before pain. Tracey screamed over and over again as the attacker vanished as quickly as he'd appeared, disappearing out of the alley and into the night.

Blood pumped from the wound in Kevin's neck and spurted down Tracey's front. He staggered back, groaning and clutching his neck. Shaking violently, with her legs barely able to support her, Tracey ran out of the alley and to the front of the club.

'He's been stabbed! Kev's been stabbed!' she shouted hysterically.

He staggered out behind her, both hands clamped to his neck impotently trying to stem the flow of blood, before collapsing onto the pavement in full view of those waiting in the queue, and the camera.

Derek gasped and stared in horror.

The queue quickly dispersed like ants; some fearing

45

that they might be next ran away while others went to Kevin. Chelsea ran to her friend and screamed at the sight of all the blood. Some people were just staring at Kevin on the ground, not knowing what to do. One guy was phoning for an ambulance, another two were actually taking photographs on their phones. Finally, a girl who said she was a trainee nurse knelt beside Kevin and put pressure on the wound to stem the blood while they waited for the ambulance.

'Jesus,' Derek said, unable to take his eyes from the screen. 'He needed to be taught a lesson, but not like that.'

There was then what seemed like an interminable wait before the ambulance and police arrived, but was only seven minutes according to the clock on Derek's computer. The paramedics went to Kevin, one opening a medical bag while the other thanked the trainee nurse and took over the compression on the wound. As they worked to save Kevin's life, the police moved the onlookers away from him, and then began asking them what they'd seen and heard of the incident. They all said similar: that they hadn't seen it happen but the guy was a bouncer at the club and had been stabbed in the alleyway over there.

'He went to have a piss,' the guy who'd been at the head of the queue said. Then Tracey, her clothes stained with Kevin's blood, came forward and told them what had really happened. When the young officer had finished taking their statements, Chelsea asked if the club would still open and if they could get in for nothing.

'Jesus, have you no humility?' Derek exclaimed aloud, appalled.

He watched carefully as the police cordoned off the alleyway, now a crime scene, and the paramedics continued to work on Kevin. Then, with an oxygen mask over his nose and mouth, a drip attached to his arm, and a large dressing covering his neck wound, Kevin was lifted onto a stretcher and into the ambulance, apparently unconscious.

Derek watched the ambulance leave, its blue light bouncing off the buildings and then disappearing out of view. Another police car arrived and a plain-clothed man and a woman got out of the rear. Forensics, he guessed. They exchanged a few words with the officers and then donned their white protective paper Tyvek suits. A spotlight was set up so they could see and they disappeared down the alley while other police officers went inside to speak to the owner. But Derek had seen enough. Powering down the monitors, he feared the worst.

Chapter Seven

'A bit of a naughty boy then, by all accounts,' DC Beth Mayes said, reporting to her senior. 'Literally caught with his trousers down.'

DCI Aileen Peters smiled. 'And no one saw anything, even though it was a Friday night?'

'No. Nothing, ma'am. Once Kevin and Tracey were in the alleyway they were out of sight of the queue. And there's no camera covering the side alley – just one at the front of the nightclub.'

She nodded and glanced at the report in front of her. 'So we're working on the assumption that the attacker was already there.'

'Yes, ma'am. It looks that way. It's a long dark alley, most of which isn't visible from the street. There are plenty of places to hide – behind bins and outbuildings. You wouldn't see someone hiding, especially with what Kevin and Tracey had on their minds. All she's been able to tell us is that the attacker was dressed in black and had a balaclava hood covering his head and face. The CCTV footage from the camera at the front of the club shows a hooded figure going into the alley approximately half an hour before the attack. The same figure can be seen running out after the attack.'

'He left the area on foot?'

'Yes, as far as can be seen on the camera, which is about twenty feet.'

'And no one in the queue saw him fleeing?'

'No. He'd gone before the commotion began and anyone realized something was wrong. The first anyone saw or heard was when Tracey came out of the alley covered in blood and screaming that Kevin had been stabbed. He staggered out after her. That's when their attention was drawn to the alleyway, but the attacker had fled by then.'

'And Kevin didn't see his attacker at all because he came at him from behind?'

'Yes, ma'am.'

'It was definitely a he?'

'From his build, yes.'

'And we've ruled out Tracey or her friend, Chelsea, setting up Kevin? He'd had sex with Chelsea the week before and she wasn't jealous and bent on revenge?'

'According to both girls they were happy with the arrangement. They took it in turns to have sex with him and he let them both into the club for free.'

'It must be a good club,' Aileen Peters remarked dryly.

'And the girls don't see him at any other time? He's not dating one of them?'

'No, ma'am.'

'Are there any other girlfriends on the scene who might not like the arrangement he had with Chelsea and Tracey?'

'Not according to Kevin,' Beth answered. 'We saw him again yesterday in hospital.'

'Did the management know about his arrangement with the girls?'

'No. And they're not happy that they've been drawn into this. It's bad for the club's reputation, especially when their licence is coming up for renewal.'

'Tough. So Kevin can't think of anyone who might have had a grudge against him? Maybe someone he collected money from or an opponent from one of his boxing matches? Someone he'd badly beaten?'

'He says he doesn't keep a record of his debt-collecting duties. It's cash in hand. We're checking out some of the fights he won, but so far nothing. Some of his opponents have form, but for pub brawls etc. None of them has a history of knife crime, GBH or anything premeditated like this. Although Kevin admits he knows some pretty dodgy characters.'

Aileen nodded. 'So no motive and no suspect. At least he's alive. If it was planned, which all the evidence so far is suggesting, then someone was watching him for quite a while to know his movements. That he could be relied upon to be in that alleyway at a particular time on a Friday.'

'Yes, ma'am, it would appear so.'

'Hmm.' She glanced at the file and then up again. 'Perhaps the press release will bring in some leads, but I'm not hopeful. We'll give it our best shot, then put it to bed unless new evidence turns up.'

'Yes, ma'am. Thank you. Just one more thing.'

'Yes?'

'It may be nothing, but there appear to have been some other cases in the area that could be said to be similar. Where it seems that someone has been deliberately targeted and the assailant knew where they'd be at a particular time and day. All motiveless.'

'Really? I wasn't aware of this.'

'No one was, ma'am. It's something I've just turned up.'

'When you say a few, how many are we talking about?'

'I've uncovered five possibles that have happened in the last twelve months. There could be more further back. None of them involved a knife but they appear to be motiveless premeditated crimes against individuals. I know it's a long shot.'

'Go on. I'm interested.' Beth wouldn't be the first DC to find a lead missed by more senior detectives.

'Ron McKenzie's house was broken into last month.'

'Yes, I'm aware of that.'

'He only went out in the evening once a month to attend a Masonic meeting. While he was gone, his house was completely trashed. They didn't take anything but made a real mess, paint everywhere. On one of his bedroom walls they'd sprayed the words: *payback time.* He said he had no idea who was behind it and couldn't think of anyone who would bear him a grudge. There were no leads and no one has been questioned.'

'You said "they"?'

'Forensics said it was possible there were two perpetrators, although they couldn't be certain.'

'It could simply have been an opportunist thief who knew McKenzie's movements, but that doesn't really tally with the words sprayed on the wall and that nothing was taken. Was he having an affair? Is there a jealous husband or jilted lover in the background?'

'Not as far as we know.'

'OK. What else do you have?'

'Tom Murray, a barrister, and a more serious crime. He was knocked down by a motorcyclist four months ago. The bike mounted the pavement and then sped off. There are no cameras in the area but he was adamant that whoever it was had deliberately driven straight at him. A woman who'd just come into the street and saw the attack agreed. She said the rider accelerated towards the victim. Both of them said the rider was all in black, with a black helmet and a tinted visor so neither of them saw his face.'

'I seem to remember we looked into some of the cases he'd worked on to see if anyone could have a grudge big enough to try to kill him. But there was nothing,' Aileen said.

'That's correct. The file's still open.'

'Maybe worth taking another look.'

'Yes, ma'am. Then there was the abduction of Mary

Grey, thirty-six, a single woman living alone,' DC Beth Mayes continued, her voice rising with enthusiasm. 'Whoever took her knew exactly where she'd be at a given time on a given day and that she'd be alone. He also knew her name. She had no idea who he was and didn't recognize his voice. He grabbed her from behind, bundled her into a van and put a blindfold on her. He drove her around for about ten minutes and then stopped the van. Before he threw her out he told her to be more careful in future. She says she doesn't know what he was referring to. There are no suspects and we checked all the vans we knew to be in the area at that time.'

'Is there anything or anyone linking these victims?'

'Not from what we know.'

'Have a look again – acquaintances, place of work, where they socialize.' Her desk phone rang and she picked it up, listened to what the caller said, and then replied, 'I'll be there.' Replacing the receiver, she stood. 'I've got to go. Look back over two years to see if you can find any connection between them. It's possible there's a nutcase out there seeking revenge for some perceived injustice, but I'm more likely to think these are random acts of mindless violence. Worth having another look all the same.'

'Thank you, ma'am.'

Chapter Eight

'You OK, Gov? Paul asked, barely able to hide his smirk.

'Yes, of course,' Derek snapped, coming down from the ladder. 'It's only a small snag. Fetch me the first-aid kit from the van, will you?'

'Not a lot of point in putting it back, was there? Cutting yourself twice in one morning and you always being so safety conscious.'

Derek let the comment go, as he was increasingly having to do with Paul. He knew he wasn't himself today; he had bigger, more worrying issues on his mind than Paul's bad attitude. The incident at U-Beat nightclub kept replaying through his head just as he'd seen it but he needed to try to concentrate before he had any more accidents or let something slip.

Cupping his finger in the palm of his hand to stop the blood dripping onto the floor, he crossed to the small sink in the corner of the room and held it under the cold tap. The room was at the rear of the newsagents and used for storing stock. Cardboard boxes and crates containing bags of sweets, packets of cigarettes, crisps, fizzy drinks and so on were stacked all around him.

He was trying to fit a camera in this room to complement the one in the shop, and then put their system online. Originally Mr and Mrs Osman, the owners of the newsagent, had just wanted one camera in the shop to stop thieving from the displays and for their own protection, but on Sunday evening while the shop had been closed it had been broken into from the rear and stock stolen. They'd phoned him on Monday morning, desperate, and asked if he could fit the extra camera and put the system online. It was a relatively small job but the work wasn't progressing as quickly as it should. He was struggling to concentrate, there was only limited space to move around, and Mr and Mrs Osman kept interrupting him – coming in for stock or to ask him questions when all he needed was to be left in peace to finish the job.

Paul eventually returned, carrying the first-aid box, with his phone still in his hand; taking advantage of him, Derek thought.

'I'll be nurse then,' Paul said.

Derek turned off the cold water tap as Paul set the first-aid box on the work surface beside the sink and took out a plaster. Away from the cold water the cut immediately opened and started bleeding again. 'It's deeper than I thought,' Derek said, holding it over the sink.

'Is there a bigger plaster in here?' Paul asked, rummaging in the first-aid box.

'Should be.'

He found a larger plaster and a sterile pad. 'Give us your finger then, and we'll use this to stop the bleeding.'

Derek held out his hand and Paul steadied it as he pressed the sterile pad on the wound. Gentler than he would have imagined, Derek felt the cool tips of Paul's fingers, the touch of his clammy palm, and the warmth of his body nearby. He was standing close, far too close. Soothed and excited, Derek breathed in the bittersweet seductive mustiness of the teenage boy, a heady mixture of testosterone, perspiration and deodorant. How long since he'd been this close to a young man? He knew exactly, and knew he mustn't go there again.

He took a step back. Paul removed the sterile pad from the wound and then expertly peeled the plaster from its packet and pressed it gently into place.

'Very professional,' Derek said, his voice unsteady.

'Should be; Mum's a nurse. We're all up to speed on first aid.'

'Are you?' Derek asked, feigning ignorance of Paul's home life. 'That's good. Well done. You said "we"?'

'Yes, Mum, Dad, my brother, sister and me,' Paul clarified, closing the first-aid box. 'Although they're my parents' favourites. I'm the runt of the litter.' He threw the discarded packets and soiled dressing into the bin and then looked at Derek, waiting for his instructions. 'What next?'

'Oh, yes. Perhaps you could finish connecting that

camera for me? You know what to do.' His usual instructive manner had gone. The intimacy of a minute ago lingered and Derek was reluctant to let it go. He could identify with not fitting in. Although he didn't have any siblings he was sure if he had he would have been his mother's least favourite: the runt.

'So you're happy with the way your apprenticeship is going?' he asked awkwardly as Paul climbed the ladder.

'Yes. Why?' He glanced down at him.

'Well, I haven't asked you before and it's important you're happy. The apprenticeship scheme will ask you for feedback.'

He shrugged. 'Yes, I'm fine.'

'So no complaints?'

'Apart from the abysmal pay, you mean?'

'You're on apprenticeship rates.' He waited until Paul had finished clipping the wire he was working on. 'And your home life? No worries there?'

'None that you need to be concerned about,' Paul returned.

'And all's going well with your girlfriend?' Derek persisted. He knew Paul had a steady girlfriend because he disappeared most lunchtimes saying he was going to phone her.

'I guess. Although last Saturday was a bit of a bummer after the stabbing at the club the Friday before.'

'You go to U-Beat nightclub?' Derek asked, taken aback.

'Sometimes. The police were inside asking about the stabbing. It seems there might be a connection with some other crimes.'

'They said that?' He struggled to hide his shock. Thank goodness Paul was up the ladder and concentrating on wiring the camera.

'Yes. They were trying to find out more about Kev, the bouncer who was stabbed. We didn't know him.'

'And the person who did it? Do they have any leads?'

'Don't think so. It seems he might have got away on a motorbike. Hey, you've got a bike, haven't you?'

'Yes, but I only take it out on Sundays,' Derek said, a little too quickly.

Paul glanced at him, tightened the last screw, then came down the ladder and waited. 'What next?'

Derek shook his head. 'Nothing. Clear up and go home.'

'You sure? It's only one-thirty.'

'Yes. I'll be here a while talking Mr and Mrs Osman through accessing their system online; they don't appear very computer savvy. Then I'm going home to catch up on some paperwork. I'll see you at eight-thirty sharp in the morning.'

'OK. Thanks.' Paul quickly swept up the last of their mess and left.

Because Mr and Mrs Osman couldn't leave the shop unattended, they came through to the stockroom separately to learn how to access their CCTV online, so it was three o'clock before Derek arrived home. His mother was exactly where he expected to find her – in the living room, watching television. She wasn't surprised to hear him come in early, for his wasn't a nine-to-five job.

'I've put your clean laundry on your bed,' she called. 'Your room could do with a clean, but that's your job.'

'I know, I will,' he said, bristling. She treated him like a little boy.

In the kitchen Derek put his lunchbox in the sink for washing later, poured himself a glass of water and went upstairs to his room where he would stay until she called him for dinner. It niggled him that she went into his room at all. At his age – forty-one – it should have been his domain, and she could have left his laundry in the airing cupboard, but he didn't complain. He always turned the monitors off when he was out and even if she switched them on, which he doubted she would, she wouldn't get any further than the screen savers, as the system was heavily password protected. It was the fact she had entered his territory at all that he bitterly resented, but he felt powerless to say anything.

With his bedroom door bolted, Derek sat in his office chair at his workstation, took a sip of water and powered up the monitors. As soon as they sprang into life he began searching local newspapers for updates on the stabbing at U-Beat nightclub. What Paul had said was worrying him.

The police were appealing for witnesses, the articles said, and anyone with any information should contact the number shown below. They were especially interested in talking to a motorbike rider seen leaving the area shortly after the incident, but there were no more details.

Derek opened the folder where he'd downloaded the

footage from the CCTV camera at the front of the night-club. When he'd watched in real time – as the attack had happened – he'd been concentrating on the actual action; now he scanned it for anything he might have missed. On the very edge of the screen he spotted a figure in black running from the alleyway just after the attack, but there was no motorbike in view.

He rewound to an hour before the incident and trawled through the footage, again concentrating on what was going on at the edges of the camera. His patience was eventually rewarded and he now saw what the police had presumably seen – what looked like the same figure entering the alley thirty minutes before the attack, but not detailed enough to make an identification, and no sign of a motorbike. He watched the footage for a few minutes more, then satisfied he had the same information as the police, closed the file.

Moving his chair to the centre of the workstation, Derek made a brief scan of all the live streams on all four screens, making sure nothing untoward was going on that might require his attention in the families he monitored. He zoomed in on a couple of images, then stopped at the Williams' house, zoomed in and engaged the microphone on the camera in their living room. Mrs Williams was on the telephone, talking to her babysitter whom he recalled was their goddaughter. She was asking if she was free to babysit that evening for a few hours, and apparently she was.

'That's great. Thanks, Sophie, sorry it's short notice,' Mrs Williams said. 'We won't be late. Yes, come here for seven o'clock and Russ will take you home after.' Derek had missed why she and Mr Williams were going out at short notice but he now knew their goddaughter was called Sophie. He liked to know all their names; it made him feel part of the family life he so yearned for.

His mother called from downstairs to say that dinner was ready and he clicked the mouse to put the system into sleep mode before going down. At least this meal would be freshly cooked and not dried or congealed from being kept warm in the oven for hours. She was already sitting at the table in the kitchen, waiting for him before beginning. The table as usual was covered with the faded flowered tablecloth and laid with the correct cutlery and the condiments set in the centre. They ate like this, even though there was just the two of them and even though he was sure she'd have been happier with her meal on a tray in front of the television. It was sad seeing her sitting there waiting for him, touchingly pathetic.

'They're putting CCTV in the flats where my sister lives,' she said, picking up her knife and fork as he took his seat.

'Oh yes?'

'She was surprised we didn't have it here. Why don't we, Derek?'

'Mum, when I asked you, you said you didn't want it. That it would make you feel self-conscious.'

'Yes, it would.'

He looked at her, not sure what to say for the best. 'Don't worry. This place won't be burgled. You're in most of the time and there's little of value here for them to take.'

'Whose fault is that?' she snapped.

Derek didn't reply. He knew the answer only too well. After his father had walked out, his mother had discovered he'd been borrowing heavily against the house and there was nothing left. It had taken Derek years to repay the debts, and the mortgage was still sixty per cent of the value of the house. He resented it too but he wished she wouldn't keep harping on about it. It just made her more bitter.

'Nice bit of braising steak,' he said.

They ate the rest of the meal in silence, then she returned to her chair in the living room while he washed up. It was part of their routine, their almost-harmony. Thank goodness he had his work.

He poured himself a glass of water and went upstairs as the theme tune of the first soap of the evening began in the living room. Dinner was timed around the soaps. She occasionally watched the news but not often. She said there was too much suffering in the world. She preferred the fictional world of the soaps.

What was it the poet TS Eliot said? Derek thought as he entered his room: 'Human kind cannot bear very much reality.' How true. He had liked poetry at school and would have liked to have studied it in higher education, but going to university had vanished along with his father and the debts he'd left behind.

Rolling his chair to the centre of the workstation, he

brought the monitors out of sleep mode and the screens filled with the thumbnail images of the live streams. It was just starting to get dark outside and Derek liked this time of evening most of all. As the natural light faded and the infrared sensors took over, the pictures were tingled with a light pink hue, creating the impression of a magical fairy-tale land. Day and night images were harsh and uncompromising compared to this. He sat back in his chair and savoured the scenes for a moment. Then it was time to get to work.

Leaning forward with his arms resting lightly on the desk, Derek began scanning the thumbnail images and was immediately alerted to the living room of the Williams' home again.

'Sophie!' he said aloud, shocked. She was lying on the sofa with her legs and arms wrapped around a lad Derek hadn't seen before and assumed to be her boyfriend. 'I bet Mr and Mrs Williams don't know he's there.'

He zoomed in so their image filled the screen and clicked on the speaker icon to engage the microphone on the camera. Grunts and groans, heavy breathing, sighs of pleasure accompanied the writhing bodies, as they kissed and groped each other. Disgusting, Derek thought. How old was she? He didn't know but would guess fourteen, and the lad looked a couple of years older. They paused for a moment to drain the last of their drinks, ice cubes melting in the bottom of the cut-glass crystal tumblers.

'Another G and T darling?' the lad said in a voice that presumably was supposed to be an imitation of Russ's.

Sophie giggled. 'Oh, darling, I daren't take any more of their gin; they're sure to know it's been watered down.' She giggled some more.

Infuriated, Derek watched as they set their empty glasses on the floor and continued groping each other. The lad ran his hand under Sophie's top and began fondling her breasts. She closed her eyes and moaned with delight. A few moments later the sound was interrupted by a child calling from upstairs.

'Ignore it,' Sophie sighed from underneath him.

You little cow, Derek thought. Mr and Mrs Williams trusted you to babysit and you've betrayed their trust, big time. But of course it was for reasons just like this that people fitted cameras inside their homes: stealing, underage drinking, and neglecting or maltreating the children or the elderly they were supposed to be in charge of.

As the couple's passion grew, so did Derek's anger and indignation. He loathed it when decent people were taken advantage of. It upset him and made him angry which was why he'd set up his online surveillance in the first place. Deceit and betrayal were near the top of his list of sins and part of his mission was to help those he found being taken advantage of. He hadn't been able to help his mother all those years ago when his father had been deceiving her, so he was making up for it now. It empowered and emboldened him and made him feel more of a man.

The groping resumed and the lad pulled up Sophie's top and lacy bra, exposing her pert tits. He started sucking her nipples. Ignoring his own arousal, Derek concentrated on the screen. The child had stopped calling out now, presumably having given up or gone back to sleep.

'Let's use their bed, it's more comfortable,' Sophie murmured.

The lad raised his head with a stupid grin on his face and climbing off Sophie pulled her to her feet. Giggling conspiratorially, they ran out of the living room and disappeared from the camera's view, presumably upstairs. Time to act.

Derek minimized the image of the now-empty living room and launched the system's email account. He couldn't rely on Mr and Mrs Williams viewing their CCTV recording of the time they'd been out and discovering the betrayal for themselves. Busy people rarely viewed their CCTV footage unless they had reason to – and Derek was about to give them a very good reason.

The third standard email on his list of templates was entitled *camera warning*. Derek clicked on it, inserted the email addresses of both Mr and Mrs Williams and pressed send. He prided himself on monitoring his systems personally. He liked to be in control. With the satisfaction that comes from knowing justice is likely to be swift and sweet, he sat back and waited.

Chapter Nine

In the restaurant the waiter had just asked if they'd like to see the dessert menu.

'I couldn't possibly,' Julie Williams said with a small sigh of satisfaction from having eaten a delicious meal.

'I will,' Russ said.

Julie raised her eyebrows. Russ was supposed to be trying to lose a few pounds that had built up around his middle from too many business lunches.

'There's no harm in looking,' he said with a smile. The waiter went to fetch the menu.

'Have whatever you fancy,' Julie said. 'We don't do this often. It was a lovely suggestion, coming here. Thank you. I've thoroughly enjoyed it.'

'Good, I'm pleased.' He reached across the table and took her hand. 'I know I don't say it often, but you do know I love you, don't you?'

'Yes, of course,' she said, returning his smile, 'although it's nice to hear it. I love you too.'

The waiter returned with the large leather-bound menu and set it in front of Russ, open at the dessert page.

'I'll give you a minute to decide,' he said, leaving them to study it.

Russ began reading out the list of delicious desserts: 'Chocolate fudge cake, banoffee pie, raspberry trifle, apple pie, cheesecake. Hmm.' Julie smiled. 'And all served with whipped cream. Are you sure I can't tempt you?'

'No, I couldn't possibly. You have one though.'

Russ felt his phone in the top pocket of his shirt vibrate with an incoming text message, and took it out without taking his eyes from the menu. Then Julie's phone in her handbag beside her chair also bleeped. He glanced up and putting the menu on the table swiped the screen on his phone. Julie took her phone from her bag. They always checked messages straightaway when they were out in case it was their babysitter with a concern about the children.

'It's an email from Home Security,' Russ said. 'Subject, *camera warning.*'

'So is mine,' Julie said, immediately concerned.

He read out the message as Julie saw the same words on her phone: '*This is an automated message to alert you to a possible breach of security in your surveillance system. Please log in and check your cameras now. If you have forgotten your password, click on the link below.*'

'Do you think there's something wrong?' she asked anxiously.

'It could be a camera malfunctioning but we should check as the message says. You know our password?'

She nodded and with mounting concern logged in.

Silence as they both viewed the images coming from the cameras in their house, less defined on the small screens of their mobiles compared to the monitor on the wall at home.

'Everything looks all right,' Russ said enlarging the images one at a time as much as the screen size would allow.

'But where's Sophie?' Julie said. 'I can't see her in the living room.'

'Making a cup of tea?' Russ offered. 'Or in the bath-room, or checking on the children. Don't worry. I'm sure everything is fine but we'll phone her to make sure.'

'I'll phone her mobile,' Julie said, bringing up her list of contacts. 'The landline will wake Jack and Phoebe.'

She pressed for Sophie's number as Russ continued viewing the images being sent live from their cameras.

'Come on, Sophie, pick up. Where are you?' Julie said agitatedly as her mobile rang and rang.

'I've just spotted her phone on the table in the living room,' Russ said. 'It's probably on silent. Try the landline.'

Julie cut the call to Sophie's mobile and pressed their home number. It rang and rang. Panic kicked in. 'Where the hell is she?' Then finally it was answered with a quiet, 'Hello?'

'Sophie. It's Julie. Is everything all right?'

'Yes. Why?'

'We had a message from the security firm saying there might be something wrong.'

'No, everything is fine here, honestly.'

'You took a long time to answer the phone.'

'I've been upstairs checking on the children.'

'Oh, OK. Thanks,' she said, relieved. 'And no one has called at the house?'

'No.'

Julie didn't want to panic the girl by saying the email had mentioned a possible breach in security. She'd said everything was fine so it was very likely an insect had tripped the system as had happened in the past, but this time the CCTV had triggered an automated email. 'We won't be long. We're just finishing off,' Julie said.

'OK. No worries. See you later.'

She said goodbye and returned her phone to her bag. 'She says everything is all right and she was checking on Jack and Phoebe. I guess it was an error?'

'Maybe,' Russ said hesitantly, still studying his phone and the image from the camera in their living room. On the floor beside their sofa he'd noticed two empty whisky glasses. Suddenly Sophie and a young man appeared in the living room, dishevelled and tucking in their clothes. He turned the phone to show Julie the screen.

'Who's that?' she cried, her hand shooting to her mouth.

'Boyfriend, I guess. She didn't tell you he was coming?'

'No, of course not!'

Russ summoned the waiter for the bill as Julie threw on her jacket.

'No dessert or coffee, Sir?'

'No, thank you; just the bill.'

Russ settled it quickly and they left, with him trying to reassure Julie that the children were safe, but that it made sense to go home straightaway. She didn't need telling twice.

Outside, the chill in the autumn air seemed even sharper now and Julie pulled her jacket closer. 'You're taking it very well, Russ, but I'm furious with her. I trusted her implicitly. Just wait till I see her!'

'I'm sure Sophie wouldn't have neglected the children,' he said, unlocking the car. 'She's done what many teenagers do – acted irresponsibly.' They got in. 'And to be honest, Jules, if she'd asked us if she could have her boyfriend round we would probably have said yes.'

'Would we?' Julie snapped the buckle on her seatbelt into place. 'You might have but I certainly wouldn't. She's fourteen, Russ. A minor. I dread to think what her parents will say. They'll need to know.'

'Let's see what Sophie has to say first, shall we?' He started the engine and pulled away. 'Perhaps they've just been sitting there playing Scrabble.'

'It didn't look like Scrabble to me.'

In contrast to the atmosphere and conversation during their journey to the restaurant – which had been light and convivial with the promise of a romantic meal for two at their favourite restaurant – it was now loaded with anxiety and recrimination. The silence was only broken by Julie's morbid conjectures: 'I can't see how she's been looking after the children properly if she's been cavorting with her boyfriend . . . Supposing one of the children

70

woke and saw or heard them? I bet she tried to switch off the camera in the living room so we couldn't see them. That would have triggered the email, wouldn't it?'

'Yes, good point,' Russ agreed. 'But try to calm down, Jules, there's no real harm been done. She said the kids are fine and we don't want a big fall out between our families.'

Julie stiffened. When it came to the children's safety and wellbeing she couldn't accept Russ's platitudes. In other circumstances two teenagers canoodling on her sofa wouldn't have caused her the same upset and indignation, but anything to do with the children was an entirely different matter. She'd have fought off a pack of hungry wolves to protect Jack and Phoebe, so strong was her in-built maternal instinct. And of course she also felt some responsibility for Sophie, who was only fourteen and her goddaughter.

Five minutes later they pulled onto their driveway and Russ cut the engine. Julie immediately threw open her car door. 'Let me handle it,' Russ said, touching her arm.

With her face set in reluctant compliance, she followed him to their front door and waited as he unlocked it, glancing up at the camera. If Sophie was looking at the monitor in the hall she'd be able to see them now. Russ opened the front door and she followed him in. The house was quiet as it should be. Sophie was in the living room sitting on the sofa with the television on low.

'Hello,' she said sweetly, standing as they entered. 'Did you have a nice time?'

'Yes, thank you,' Russ said, looking around the room. There was no sign of the glass tumblers. Presumably she'd washed and dried them and returned them to the cupboard. 'Was everything all right here?'

'Yes. Perfectly.' She picked up her phone ready to leave, apparently eager to go. 'Will you be giving me a lift home or shall I call a cab?'

'I'll take you,' Russ said.

Julie couldn't contain her anger any longer. 'Who was that lad you had here while we were out?' she demanded.

'Pardon?' Sophie said indignantly. 'I don't know what you're talking about.' But her cheeks were already flushing red.

'Don't play the innocent with me,' Julie flared. 'You had your boyfriend here.'

'No, I didn't.'

'Well, who was he then?'

'Who?'

Sensing that Sophie was about to dig herself further into a hole with more lies, Russ stepped in. 'Sophie, you're not in any trouble but—'

'Yes, she is,' Julie put in.

'Why? What are you accusing me of?' Sophie hissed.

Julie pointed to the camera in the far corner of the room. 'We saw you with your boyfriend in here.'

Sophie looked at the camera and then at them. 'You've been watching me through that?' she said astounded. 'Spying on me!'

'There! So we know you're lying,' Julie snapped.

'No,' Russ said touching his wife's arm for her to calm down. 'Not spying.' It made them sound like voyeuristic perverts. 'Sophie, we received an email alert saying there could be a problem with the security system so we viewed the images coming from the cameras on our phones. Not only the outside ones but the one in here too. Only for a couple of minutes.'

'You can see all of this room?' Sophie asked.

Russ nodded.

'What about upstairs?'

'There aren't any cameras upstairs.'

'Why do you want to know that?' Julie demanded, but she'd already guessed. 'You took him to our bedroom, didn't you? You little cow. Wait till I tell your parents.'

'No, don't do that!' Sophie cried, her eyes filling. 'They'll be furious with me.'

'For good reason,' Julie said. 'Not only have you betrayed our trust but theirs too.'

'I didn't mean to,' she cried. 'I promise it won't happen again.'

'Too right it won't!' Julie fumed. 'You won't be babysitting for us again.'

Sophie's tears fell.

'All right, enough,' Russ said stepping in. 'I'll take you home now.'

'You won't tell my parents, will you?' Sophie asked Russ in a small, plaintive voice.

'No, not tonight,' he said. 'But I think you need to talk to them.' Then to Julie, 'We'll discuss this later when I get back. OK?' He could see how wound up she was and knew she could easily phone Sophie's parents – their long-time friends – and say something she might later regret.

Julie gave a curt nod and then, taking a twenty-pound note from her purse, thrust it at Sophie. 'Here's the money I owe you for tonight. Count yourself lucky I'm paying you after the way you've behaved.' She turned and began towards the hall. 'I'm going to check on the children.'

'I'll see you shortly then,' Russ called after her, and led the way out to the car.

'I'm sorry,' Sophie said as they got in. 'I really didn't mean to upset you both, but please don't tell Mum and Dad.'

'I won't. We all make mistakes. Jules was very worried about the children. You feel differently when you're a parent.'

'Thank you. Will you tell her how sorry I am?'

'Yes, of course.' Russ started the engine and pulled away. 'Sophie, one thing I don't understand is why we were sent the email alert in the first place. Do you have any idea?' She shook her head. 'We weren't broken into and all the cameras are working so the only other reason I can think of is that the system was tampered with. Did you or your boyfriend touch the monitor or any of the cameras in any way? Please be honest, I'm not angry.'

'No. Honestly. I didn't even realize that camera in the living room was working. It wasn't showing a picture on the screen in the hall.'

'We only have the outside cameras showing on the monitor. So neither of you tried to switch if off?'

'No.'

★ ★ ★

74

At home Julie had checked on the children – they were both sleeping peacefully – and was now downstairs viewing the recording on the monitor in the hall. She had all the camera images showing and the digital display at the bottom of the screen showed the date and time. She had rewound the tape to where Sophie had arrived to babysit at 6.50pm, and had watched her on the camera trained on their front door as she'd rung the bell and Julie had let her in. Then the camera in the living room showed the three of them talking although she couldn't hear what they were saying as there was no sound, before she and Russ said goodbye and left. Outside, the camera covering the drive showed them getting into their car and pulling away. Julie then saw Sophie sitting on the sofa texting, presumably to tell her boyfriend they'd gone. Within five minutes he was at their front door, so either he lived in the neighbourhood or he'd been waiting out of sight close by. He didn't press the bell so Julie guessed Sophie must have told him to text her when he arrived as the doorbell might wake the children. They kissed on the doorstep and then the camera in the living room showed the lad making himself comfortable on the sofa and Sophie leaving the room, grinning. She returned with two glasses containing what looked like gin or vodka and ice.

Ten minutes passed when they sipped their drinks, laughed, snogged and groped each other. Julie fast-forwarded the tape and then stopped as Sophie stood, picked up their empty glasses, left the living room and returned with refills. Cheeky little cow! Then sprawled on the sofa with their drinks on the table, they continued their heavy petting. At one point they stopped and cocked their heads as though they might have heard something and Julie hoped it wasn't one of the children calling out and being ignored. Another five minutes or so and Sophie had her hand down his trousers and his mouth was on her breasts. It was getting close to the time the email had been sent. Julie looked at the footage sent from the outside cameras but nothing untoward was showing there. More heavy petting; she fast-forwarded again and then slowed the tape to 'play' mode again as the lad stood. Clearly aroused, he pulled Sophie up and they disappeared from view, presumably going upstairs to her bedroom to have sex.

The living room stayed empty, and the outside cameras showed no sign of any disturbance that could have tripped the alert. She continued to watch, her anger growing. Russ had been studying the dessert menu now and the emails would shortly arrive on their phones. Another few minutes and she guessed it was the time she'd phoned Sophie's mobile, but she could see it now lying on the table in the living room. She'd then called the house phone but the living room remained empty so the little minx must have answered the extension in their bedroom. She inwardly fumed as she pictured Sophie untangling herself from her boyfriend to reach out of bed and pick up the handset, just as she and Russ did sometimes. No wonder it had taken her time to answer. She'd been having sex in their bed when she'd phoned!

A minute later she saw them rush into the living room

tucking in their clothes, now aware that she and Russ were returning. The boy grabbed his jacket and went out the front door while Sophie tidied up the living room, smoothing the sofa cushions, taking out the glasses. She reappeared in the living room, sat on the sofa and switched on the television. Then to her horror Julie saw her daughter appear in the doorway of the living room, possibly woken by the home phone ringing. She watched as Sophie went over to her and disappeared from view, she assumed taking Phoebe back upstairs to bed. She must have only just dropped off to sleep again when they'd arrived home.

Julie watched as she and Russ came in, her face set in anger and shouting at Sophie while Russ tried to keep the peace. She saw herself thrust the twenty-pound note into Sophie's hand, then leave to check on the children while Russ took Sophie home. Thank goodness nothing worse had happened, she thought, and thank goodness they'd taken the engineer's advice and had a camera installed in the living room or they'd never have known. What was it he'd said? *Many of my clients who take this option are surprised by what they find goes on in their absence.* He'd certainly been right there! Returning the screen to the real time images, Julie left the monitor and went upstairs to change the linen on their bed.

Chapter Ten

'It is a sad fact that stabbings and break-ins are very good for business,' Derek said to Paul as he drew the van to a halt outside U-Beat nightclub. It felt strange coming back here after what had happened but there was a job to be done. 'If everyone was kind to each other and obeyed the law I'd be out of work and there'd be no apprenticeship for you.' Derek threw him a wry smile. 'As it is people behave like animals with callous disregard for their fellow human beings, so business is flourishing.'

Paul nodded disinterestedly as he checked his phone. He'd heard similar before from Derek. Derek turned slightly towards him in his seat and Paul knew what was coming next: a description of the job they were about to do. Derek often repeated himself as if no one else grasped anything first time, which Paul supposed came from living with his mother who was old.

'So we're going to install two cameras today – one at the end of that alley over there that runs alongside the nightclub.' He pointed.

'Where Kev was stabbed,' Paul said.

'Yes. And the second camera at the rear of the premises. It's straightforward. They've also asked me to check if any additional cameras are needed inside, but I think they're well covered. Ready then, lad? Phone off or on silent. I know it's not a private home but the same rules apply.'

'Of course,' Paul said amicably, switching his phone to silent and sliding it into the pocket of his jeans. 'Are you leaving the van here? It's on a yellow line.'

'I know,' Derek said, irritated, 'but there aren't any parking bays free and we're trade so I can leave it here while we unload.'

'The last time you did that you got ticketed,' Paul reminded him with a smirk.

'And if you remember it was rescinded on appeal. They need to train their traffic wardens better.' His hand was on the door ready to get out when his phone vibrated with an incoming call. He checked to see who the caller was and pressed to accept the call. 'I won't be a minute, lad,' he said to Paul. Then, 'Good morning, Mr Williams.'

'Is that Derek Flint?'

'Yes. How are you and Mrs Williams?'

'Well, thank you. I'm sorry to trouble you but my wife and I both received email alerts to our phones yesterday evening about a breach of security.'

'Yes, I know.'

'You do?'

'A copy of any alert comes to me. I saw it this morning.'

'OK. So do you know why it was sent? We've been through the tape twice but can't see any reason. We were out at the time and the message gave us quite a shock. We went straight home.'

'There was no need to do that,' Derek said. 'The advantage of being able to access your cameras online is that you can check all is well from a distance without the need to dash home. I'm sorry, I should have made that clear.'

There was a short silence. 'Our babysitter was here looking after the children so we thought it best to return. But we're puzzled as to what could have tripped the system.'

'I see.' Derek pondered. So he wasn't going to share what he'd seen when he'd logged in. 'Mr Williams, I remember you said you trusted your babysitter implicitly but to be honest the most likely cause for the email alert was that the system was interfered with, assuming your house wasn't broken into. Do you think your sitter might have tried to turn off one of the cameras without the correct password?'

'She says she didn't touch anything.'

'In that case the internal camera could have been triggered. It has an in-built motion detector. If there was a lot of movement in the living room, for example, by someone dancing or jumping maybe, it could have triggered the alert.'

'Oh. Yes, that could have been it.'

'These cameras are very sensitive; they're meant to be. But if it happens again give me a call and I'll come and check. I can adjust it if necessary, although given what happened to you before you had the cameras I would think you want everything working as it should be.'

'Yes, of course. Well, thank you. I'll tell my wife.'

'You're welcome. Was there anything else?'

'No, that's it. Goodbye then.'

'Goodbye, Mr Williams.' Derek returned the phone to his jacket pocket as Paul looked at him questioningly. 'Nothing for you to worry about, lad. Now come on, out you get, there's work to be done.'

'They haven't caught the geezer who stabbed Kev the bouncer,' Paul said half an hour later as Derek came down from the ladder they'd propped against the side of the club.

'Apparently not.'

'I read in the paper they are still appealing for witnesses which means they haven't a clue,' Paul said.

'It would have been a different matter if they'd had one of these installed in the alley,' Derek said, taking the new camera from its box. He'd marked the position where the camera had to be and now passed it to Paul. 'You know what to do. So no more talking. Concentrate on the job and remember you're at the top of a ladder so don't step back.'

Paul didn't laugh. It wasn't as ludicrous as it sounded. It was easy to forget you were at the top of a ladder when you were concentrating hard. He'd forgotten once and had taken his foot off the ladder and been about to step back when Derek had shouted. The ladder would have toppled for sure had Derek not been holding it. A lesson well learnt and not the only one, although Derek didn't know about those.

With the drill in one hand and everything else he needed in the tool belt around his waist, Paul went up the ladder. All that could be heard for some moments was the sound of the powerful cordless electric drill boring into the brick; red brick dust plumed out before dispersing into the air. Holes drilled, Paul screwed the mount into place and then returned down the ladder for the camera.

'Don't drop it,' Derek said passing it to him, 'or you'll owe me for sure.'

Paul gave a tight smile at his not-funny joke and carefully carried the camera up the ladder. As he worked overhead Derek allowed his gaze to wander down the alleyway. It was light enough now to see to the end but come night it would be pitch-black, and there were plenty of places for a would-be attacker to hide in wait for their victim. He doubted the attacker would ever be caught unless he was known to the victim.

The new camera in place, Paul came down the ladder.

'Now round the back of the club,' Derek said.

A very basic six-foot wooden gate secured by a single bolt was all that separated the alleyway from the rear of the club. It was possible Kevin's attacker had come through here and been hiding behind the club and not in the alleyway at all, Derek thought, and wondered if the police had considered it. Not that it was likely to add much to their enquiry as there hadn't been a camera here either. The club owner's original reason for installing CCTV had been to identify clubbers causing trouble inside and on their way out.

By three o'clock the two new cameras had been wired into the system and Derek and Paul were in the club's office with the manager as he viewed them on his desktop monitor. Satisfied all was well and the manager was happy, Derek thanked him for his custom and, leaving his business card, said goodbye.

Once in the van they both spent a few moments checking their phones.

'Three missed calls from Mr Osman and a voicemail message,' Derek said out loud, concerned. 'I wonder what he wants?' He pressed to retrieve the voicemail message. As he listened his face paled. 'Their shop's been broken into again.'

'The newsagents?' Paul asked. Derek nodded. 'But we've only just fitted the new camera.'

'I know that, lad,' Derek said tersely.

'How did they get in?'

'He didn't say, but he's upset and blaming me. We're going there now.'

Unsettled, Derek returned his phone to his jacket pocket and pulled away from the club. Remembering the location of the Osman's shop from his previous visit he made a series of left and right turns, using the back roads; his

83

expression one of grim determination as he concentrated on the road ahead.

'You know the area well,' Paul remarked. 'All these shortcuts.'

'I should do, I've lived here all my life,' Derek replied brusquely, his mind on other things.

'So have I but I didn't know some of these roads existed.' Paul paused as if considering something. 'I suppose the guy who knifed Kev must have had a good knowledge of the area to avoid the cameras, or the police would have caught him by now.'

Derek glanced at him, the beginnings of a small tic agitating at the corner of his eye. It happened sometimes when he was stressed. 'Possibly,' he said.

'Why's the shop owner blaming you?'

'I don't know. Something to do with the insurance company. He wasn't making much sense.'

Paul fell silent for a while, then keeping his gaze ahead, asked, 'How come you didn't know?'

'Know what?'

'About the break-in at the newsagents?'

'I'm not clairvoyant, boy, am I?' Derek barked, the tic flickering.

'But this morning you told Mr Williams you always got a copy of any email alert sent when there's been a breach of security. Why didn't that happen with the news-agents?'

Derek's hands imperceptibly tightened on the wheel but there was only a heartbeat before he replied. 'Good point, lad. I'll need to check when I get back to the office. Not just a pretty face, are you?' His tense expression undermined his stab at humour.

Ten minutes later he drew up outside the newsagents and they got out. The shop appeared to be open for business as usual and there was no sign of a break-in or of the police, which was a relief. Their presence always complicated matters in Derek's experience and they made him feel uncomfortable.

The old-fashioned doorbell clanged as they went in. Mrs Osman was at the counter serving a customer while another two customers were browsing the displays of magazines and greeting cards.

'He's out the back,' Mrs Osman said to Derek, looking past the customer, 'and he's not happy. You'd better go through.'

She raised the counter to allow them access and then opened the door behind her that led to the stockroom. Derek went in first. Mr Osman was sitting at the small table surrounded by boxes of stock and jabbing two fingers at the keypad of his laptop. Derek's gaze swept the room; there was no sign of a break-in here either.

'So you've come at last,' he said, obviously annoyed.

'I'm sorry, Mr Osman, we came as soon as we could. I've only just listened to your message. We've been tied up on a job all day. What happened?'

'He got in through that door,' Mr Osman said, nodding to the back door. 'I'll show you if I can find the place on this bloody thing.' He stabbed a finger at the laptop again.

'My wife downloaded a copy for the police but now I can't find it.'

Derek watched for a few moments as Mr Osman tried in vain to locate the correct link.

'Shall I try to find it for you?' he asked at last.

'Yes, go on then! Stupid thing.' He pushed the laptop roughly across the table to face Derek. Two taps and the website was up.

'What's your password?'

Mr Osman looked at him blankly.

'Your initials plus ten,' Derek prompted.

'I know,' he said, irritated.

The cameras were now on-screen and Derek tilted the laptop so Mr Osman could see it. 'When was the break-in approximately?' he asked. Paul stood behind them peering over their shoulders at the screen.

'It was 1.45am. It will be seared on my mind forever.'

Derek pressed fast rewind until the clock showed 1.30 am.

'It's the back camera you need, not the front,' Mr Osman snapped impatiently as Derek enlarged the image for the camera in the shop. 'They didn't come in through the front door, for heaven's sake!'

'I appreciate that, but I want to see if the camera in the shop picked up anything. It looks out towards the front shop window and door so it might have picked up anyone loitering outside.'

At 1.42am a lone figure wearing a hoodie could be seen passing in front of the shop.

'There he is!' Mr Osman said, his finger flying to the

screen. 'I missed that. I wonder if the police saw it?' But Derek knew that, even if they had spotted this image, it was worthless for identification purposes. The intruder had kept his head down and tucked well inside his hoodie, as if he was aware the camera inside could pick him up.

Concentrating hard, Derek tapped the keypad to bring up the camera in the stockroom. The same figure appeared at the back door and walked straight in. Derek paused the tape and looked at his client. 'The door appears to have been unlocked, Mr Osman?'

'I know, I know!' he replied agitatedly. 'It seems I might have forgotten to lock it. I told the police I'd locked it but then your bloody camera shows otherwise. The insurance company won't pay. I'd have been better off without your damn camera. I always check I've locked the doors before we leave the shop but on this one occasion I didn't!'

It wasn't the first time Derek had come across someone becoming careless after having a security system fitted, lulled into a false sense of safety by the installation of CCTV. There wasn't much he could say. Of course the insurance company wouldn't pay if the owner had left the door unlocked, but it was hardly his fault so there was no need for Mr Osman to take it out on him. He pressed play again to continue the tape and they watched as the hooded figure began emptying the boxes in the stockroom, tipping them out and trampling on their contents: crisps, sweets, cigarettes and so on, then jumping all over them for maximum damage.

'You see, your camera is useless,' Mr Osman said, giving

the screen another hard poke with his finger. 'You can't see his face. That cretin knows that if he keeps his hood up and his face down he can't be identified. The police said that criminals know this and that no one responds to an alarm. What fucking use is security? I had to clear up that lot. I can't sell it; my stock is ruined and the insurance company won't pay.'

Derek sighed. 'I'm sorry this has happened, but I'm not to blame. No system is a hundred per cent effective. I did my best with the budget you had in mind.'

There was a moment's silence before Paul said quietly, 'It's a hell of a coincidence.'

'That's what I thought,' Mr Osman agreed vehemently. 'One hell of a coincidence!'

Derek remained very quiet.

'Did he receive the email alert like the Williams' did?' Paul asked Derek.

'What email?' Mr Osman demanded.

Paul looked to Derek to explain and when he didn't he took the initiative. 'Home Security send an automated email alert to the client if there is a breach of security or the monitor or cameras malfunction. It advises you to log in straightaway. You and your wife should have received an email.'

'No. We certainly did not.'

'That would explain it then,' Paul said to Derek in a flurry of satisfaction. 'The system must have developed an error so the automated email wasn't sent.'

'What error? What email?' Mr Osman demanded, growing increasingly frustrated.

'You were supposed to receive an email alerting you to a possible breach of security,' Paul continued, feeling he was been very helpful. 'But due to an error with the system the email wasn't sent.' He looked at Derek, waited for some words of praise as he'd help solve the problem, but Derek was staring blindly at the laptop.

'I see, well, thank you, young man.' Mr Osman's face lost some of its anguish. He turned to Derek. 'If your system was malfunctioning then I should be in with a chance of claiming from my insurance. I mean, if I'd received that email as I should have done, I could have alerted the police at the time of the break-in, and there would have been a good chance the culprit was caught in the act. So it seems your system is at fault, not me.' He glared at Derek. 'Even if I only get a proportion of my claim it will be better than nothing. Failing that I could probably sue you for my lost stock as your system didn't do what it should. I assume you are well insured?'

Chapter Eleven

'I don't want to piss on your parade,' Matt Davis said, leaning forward so he could see Beth Mayes over the top of their computer screens. 'But you really are wasting your time pursuing that line of enquiry.'

'Thanks for your vote of confidence, arsehole,' she returned.

'Charming!' Matt said with feigned indignation. 'All I'm trying to do is save you the embarrassment of having to go back to boss lady with nothing but hours of wasted police time. Burglaries, muggings and assaults happen everywhere all the time. They aren't all connected by some giant conspiracy theory or six degrees of separation.' He grinned provocatively.

'Sit down, shut up and get on with your own work,' Beth said lightly. 'You'll eat your words when I find the connection, and then I'll be first in line for promotion.'

They'd started together as DCs and often teased each other about who would get promoted first. Beth enjoyed their banter, although even she was close to admitting defeat in this investigation. There'd been no fresh leads for the nightclub stabbing despite the press release. And the five other cases she'd told the boss about, plus the twelve possibles she'd unearthed from the year before, all remained without any common linking factor other than they were premeditated, motiveless and unsolved. If she could find a motive then she'd be halfway to solving the crimes, but without one it was whistling in the wind. Yet despite trawling through megabytes of data including whether the victims had served time in prison, accrued any large debts, their work history, sexual orientation, any unusual hobbies, and so forth, there was nothing else linking them apart from the premeditated nature of the attacks. Yet she still felt there was something staring her in the face that she was missing.

'Here's one for you,' Matt said a few minutes later, smiling as he dropped the printout over the top of her monitor. The paper floated to her desk and she picked it up.

'It's a routine break-in,' she said. 'This is a joke, right?'

'Not at all. It's the second time the shop has been broken into in under a month. The owners are claiming it's racially motivated and that we haven't bothered to investigate properly. Boss lady wants us to be seen to be doing the right thing. I would offer to go but you're so good at PR and I've more important things to do – like solving crimes.'

Beth poked her tongue out at him and taking the printout,

unhooked her jacket from the chair and left the office. She needed a break, a breath of fresh air; staring too long at the computer screen was fogging her brain so she couldn't see the wood from the trees. Fifteen minutes to the newsagents, fifteen minutes pacifying Mr and Mrs Osman and she'd be back at her desk again in an hour. Sometimes just a change of scenery sparked the mind into making a connection, solving a puzzle that had otherwise eluded her.

Beth parked the unmarked police car in the layby outside the parade of shops. There were five shops in all, with the newsagents at the end. These small shops were easy targets for thieves and vandals. Usually family-owned, they ran on tight budgets and didn't have the funds for decent security like the bigger shops did. Possibly it was the same lad who'd broken into the infant school down the road the weekend before. He hadn't taken anything of value but had made a mess: spraying the floors, walls and windows with black gloss paint, destroying the children's artwork, upending the tables and desks. It had been too easy for him to remove the slats from the old louvre window in the children's toilets and get in that way. Like the shop owner leaving his door unlocked, it was an open invitation to an opportunist. Even so, she'd do her job to the best of her ability as she always did.

Inside the shop she went up to the counter. 'DC Beth Mayes,' she said, flashing her ID card. 'Mr and Mrs Osman?' They were both behind the counter although there was no one in the shop to be served.

'Come through, would you like a drink?' He seemed very pleased to see her.

'That's kind, but no thank you.'

She followed him into the back of the shop that was used as a stockroom and looked around. 'You don't live in the flat above the shop then?' she asked. Each of the shops in the parade had a flat above it.

'No. My cousin and his family live there. My wife and I have our own house a few miles away.'

'And no one in your cousin's family heard anything on the night of the break-in? I'm assuming one of our officers asked but I thought I'd check.'

He shook his head. 'Nothing. But it's break-ins. Plural. Twice in under a month. And the insurance company are wriggling.'

'As they do,' she said.

'So I need a copy of your police report to give them.'

'Certainly.' She could have sent it in the post; it didn't need a personal visit.

'But you must mention in your report that after the first break-in I took extra precautions by having another camera fitted. It will help with my claim.' She nodded. 'Also, I've now found out that the security system was malfunctioning at the time of the break-in, which will help my case.'

She looked at him, puzzled. 'What sort of malfunction? The tape was downloaded successfully. We have a copy of the relevant footage on file at the station.'

'The company should have sent me an email alert at

the time of the break-in so I could phone you and then you could catch him, but that didn't happen.'

If only it were that simple, she thought. 'And the problem with the security has been fixed now?' she asked, glancing up at the camera bearing a Home Security logo.

'I would think it has. So you will send the report I need for the insurance company?'

'Yes. And rest assured we are doing all we can to catch the culprit.'

'Culprits,' he corrected.

She frowned. 'Why do you say that? The CCTV footage shows one person.'

'But a different one from the first time.'

She frowned again, puzzled.

'Come on, DC Mayes, I haven't got to do your job for you, have I? In the first break-in they stole my stock; in the second he just trashed the place. Different motives, so surely different intruders?'

She thought for a moment. 'It's possible,' she conceded. Although she knew the investigation was working on the theory that it was the same intruder, which statistically was most likely: burgled once and they were likely to come back and burgle again unless good security was installed.

'Either way it's a big coincidence that the one night I forget to lock the back door, in he comes.'

Or perhaps it wasn't just once you forgot to lock it, she thought but didn't say.

★ ★ ★

An hour later Beth was back at her desk. 'If it was the same intruder, why would he steal the first time and then just trash when he goes back?' she said to Matt.

'Pass. What's the correct answer?'

'No. I'm asking you. It's not a trick question. It doesn't make sense.'

He looked up from his screen. 'You're talking about the newsagent, right?' She nodded. 'Perhaps he didn't like the crisps and sweets he sold?'

'You are a dope. I'm serious. It's been assumed it was the same person but why did he just trash the place second time around? Trashing is a different crime with a different motive and a different offender profile. And if it wasn't the same guy then it's even more of a coincidence if Mr Osman is right and he did usually lock up.'

'*Que?*' Matt asked puzzled.

'Mr Osman is adamant that he always checks all the doors are locked before leaving the shop to go home, and the one night he didn't, he was broken into. It seems there was a problem with the security system – it didn't alert him to the break-in – but that's neither here nor there. What I'm saying is that if it was the same intruder then it's reasonable to suppose he went back, aware of the layout this time, and it was easy to get in. But if it was someone else then he was very lucky that he happened to go there on the night the door was unlocked.'

'Or Mr Osman often forgets to lock up.'

'Yes, I know. But I think I'll spend a few minutes looking at the CCTV footage for the weeks before the break-in to see if it shows anyone loitering around the shop. The camera at the rear was only installed two weeks ago so it won't take long to have a quick whizz through.'

Matt grinned broadly. 'And who knows, you might be able to add yet another case to your conspiracy list so that before long every crime in the world will be linked by a giant string theory.'

She took a sheet of paper from her desk, rolled it into a ball and lobbed it over the top of her monitor.

'Missed again!'

Chapter Twelve

'You spend too much time locked in your room with all those computers,' Elsie Flint said as she and Derek sat down to eat. 'That's what puts you in a bad mood. It's not healthy. Why don't you go down the pub like normal men? That's what your father did.'

He glanced at her, saw her jaw set in a grim expression and hated her when she was like this.

'And look where that got you,' he returned, and immediately regretted it. She looked crest-fallen, her usual hard-bitten determination replaced by vulnerability. She could change in a second and it stung now as it always did. 'I'm fine, Mum. I've just had a few difficult days.'

'Doing what?' she asked, an edge of criticism creeping back into her voice.

'There have been some incidents on premises where

I've fitted CCTV. It's nothing for you to worry about but Paul was no help.'

'Paul?' she asked, eyeing him carefully.

'Yes, my apprentice. I had to let him go.'

'Oh. They change so often I can't keep up. What did that one do or not do?'

'It's a long story, I've dealt with it,' he said, and changed the subject. 'Nice bit of lamb. Not too well done.'

'Good. At least I've done something right.'

Half an hour later, Derek sat at his workstation with his bedroom door bolted, continuing where he'd left off before dinner. Beads of perspiration had gathered on his forehead and his mouth was dry, not from anything his mother had said but because of the crisis that seemed to be unfolding in his business. Three break-ins in as many weeks to properties where he'd fitted the CCTV and where the footage from the cameras was of no help in solving the crimes. It was unprecedented and the clients were furious. He relied on word of mouth recommendation and business was dropping off. The stress of it was taking its toll.

The incidents had all happened when he'd been away from his monitors – at work or asleep – so, unlike the Williams (and others he'd helped), he hadn't been there to send a warning email alerting them to what was happening. While these break-ins weren't the most serious of crimes – no one had been physically hurt – to have your property broken into was disturbing and traumatic for the owners. Surely there must be something – a shadow, someone or something out of place, an irregularity that could give a clue to what had happened or even help catch those responsible? That was, after all, why these people had fitted CCTV in the first place.

Sandra was already at work in The Mermaid but he didn't linger there now. Much as he liked her, he wasn't in the mood; his thoughts were full of more pressing matters. As satisfied as he could be that all was well with the other clients he monitored, he returned to the footage of the premises that had been broken into, going through them again sometimes for the fourth or fifth time. Exactly what he was looking for, he couldn't say, but he was now concentrating on the edges of the images, searching the peripheries for anything he might have previously missed as he had done with the nightclub stabbing. But as he continued examining the footage – peering down side passages, into hedges and shrubberies, through people's windows where the camera angle allowed and enlarging the images until he could even see the food on their plates – nothing new appeared.

Suddenly he started as a large eye appeared on the screen, a pop-up advertisement with a camera lens at the centre of the eye in place of the pupil. Beneath the image were the words 'Watching You'.

'Bloody advertisements!' he cursed.

He clicked on the small white cross in the corner of the box to close it but the image perversely remained, obliterating most of the screen and making further work impossible.

'How the fuck did that get in!' He ran the most advanced security software, which updated automatically and was supposed to keep out this sort of thing: malicious spyware, viruses, hackers and pop-up adverts. He knew search engines were often to blame for pop-ups; they were becoming increasingly clever at placing tracking 'cookies' on computers, which not even advanced spyware immediately recognized. A cookie had probably identified his business from the surveillance equipment he'd viewed online and now he was being targeted as part of the company's advertising campaign.

There was no company name showing on the advert yet but doubtless that would follow soon. He clicked again on the corner of the box but the eye remained staring out at him. *Watching You*.

'Fuck. Watching you too, mate!' he said aloud. Did firms really believe this type of aggressive advertising would win them new business? He certainly wouldn't be buying from them ever – when he found out who they were.

Unable to remove the pop-up by clicking on its close box, he now clicked on the cross in the corner of the screen to close the whole page, but that was frozen too. 'Damn!' he said, stamping his foot, and tried again. A standard software message appeared – *End task: this programme is not responding*.

'I bloody know that!' he cried.

He clicked to end the task and waited but again nothing happened. The whole computer was deadlocked! Anger spilled over as he pressed the caps lock key to see if its light came on. The bloody pop-up had snarled up the whole system. He pressed control–alt–delete to open the windows task manager to try to end the program, but that didn't work either. Red in the face and furious that he was wasting so much time on this, there was no alternative but to switch off the computer at the plug. It wouldn't do the machine any good but there was no other choice. He flicked the power switch and watched the advert disappear as all four screens went blank.

Derek waited thirty seconds to make sure all the electricity had gone so the connection with the Internet had been severed, and then rebooted. The screens came back to life with various standard warning messages telling him that the computer hadn't been shut down properly – which he knew – and did he want to start it in safe mode? No, he didn't.

More technical information followed as the system configured and finally it was up and running again, the screen savers drifting leisurely across the monitors. Thank goodness. Before logging into his surveillance website, he checked his spyware settings but nothing seemed to have changed, and the last update had only been an hour before so he should have the latest protection. But to be on the safe side – and Derek was always cautious and played safe when it came to surveillance – he went into the computer's control panel and cleared out all the cookies, temporary Internet files, browsing history, saved passwords and web form information. Only then did he log in to his website and as he expected there was no sign of the pop-up.

He returned to where he'd been checking the footage from the break-ins and continued but still couldn't find anything of significance. There was no indication in the days leading up to any of the break-ins that anything untoward had happened or was about to happen. Sometimes you could see someone loitering or a new untrustworthy cleaner or shop assistant had been appointed, but that didn't apply here. He had nothing to work on, no leads, and, with the number of cases growing, he felt he was losing control over his empire. He pressed rewind and began going through the footage again.

A little after 10.30pm Derek heard footsteps on the stairs and then the floorboards on the landing creak as his mother came up to bed. She always switched off the television at half past ten and went to bed straight after, although she never slept well. He often heard her moving around in her room at night and sometimes she went downstairs for a drink. Now, following her usual routine she went first to her bedroom to fetch her nightwear and then took it to the bathroom where she washed and changed. Exactly fifteen minutes later she returned to her room calling 'goodnight' as she went.

'Goodnight, Mum,' he returned, keeping the irritation from his voice.

His eyes were sore from staring too long at the footage of the break-ins. He admitted defeat for now and closing the file returned all four screens to the images of his clients. He loved spending time with them, which he did as much as possible. They reached out to him with friendship and support in a way real life didn't. In return for keeping them safe and on track, they gave him (although, apart from the girls at The Mermaid, they didn't know it) their unfailing company.

As he watched and shared in their daily lives, he felt a warm frisson of belonging to a family in a way he never had with his own family. Even when his parents had been together he couldn't remember feeling their warmth and being cherished. He particularly enjoyed it when his clients had friends or relatives visit; he felt included in their social circle – a unique feeling, for he and his mother rarely had visitors. Sunday lunches were his favourite; they often stretched for hours, the adults remaining at the table, talking and sipping their wine as the children played nearby. These people loved and cared for each other in a way that was foreign to him and moved him deeply. If they did fall out – which he'd discovered even the closest of families and friends did sometimes – then they always made up. Being with them, embraced by their families, calmed and soothed him so much that he often left the images running while he did other things in his room, reassured that his extended family were just a few steps away.

By midnight, most of the downstairs rooms in his clients' homes were empty, the occupants having gone to bed. Only the night owls remained up and the few on shift work – doctors, nurses and other healthcare workers who were either about to leave for work or had just returned and were winding down. Mostly the houses were in darkness, the alarms set for night-time and the occasional security light flashing on when a cat or fox walked by. A crescent moon shone between passing clouds. Derek yawned. He needed to get some sleep too. He had to be up early in the morning. He was meeting prospective clients at 8am, a professional couple who had asked him to give them an estimate before they went to work.

Stifling another yawn, he prepared to shut down the system, calmer now from spending quality time with his families. He gave the screens one last glance ready to say goodnight, but then stopped dead.

What the hell! Screen two: he enlarged the image to full size. It was the house where Mr and Mrs Khumalo and their three children lived, one of his larger properties. Oh no! Please no. Someone was in their back garden. He could make out the outline of a figure in the shrubbery, moving low and cat-like, keeping close to the fence, going from bush to bush. Derek stared in horror, his breath coming fast and shallow. The figure crept along the right-hand side of the lawn, then, breaking cover, ran from the shrubbery and quickly across the patio to the conservatory. Dressed all in black and with a three-holed balaclava covering his head, he appeared to know how to avoid the light sensors. The floodlights concentrated on the conservatory and patio doors didn't come on.

'Shit!' Derek cursed under his breath.

He watched helplessly as the intruder moved one of the wrought iron chairs from the garden table and, placing it at the foot of the drainpipe, shimmied up like a leopard climbing a tree. His stomach churned. Dear God, this couldn't be happening. Not another one! The bedroom window directly over the conservatory was slightly open. The figure knelt on the toughened glass of the conservatory roof and, sliding his hand into the gap, eased open the window. A second later he was in the bedroom and out of view, the window left open behind him.

Sick with fear, Derek grappled with the keyboard, hands trembling as he pulled it towards him and began to type. He glanced between the images of the house on screen two as on screen three he brought up the Khumalos' file. He needed to know how they wanted to be notified – phone, email or text. They'd opted for phone message – to Mr Khumalo's phone. Sweating profusely, Derek moved the cursor to the phone icon, entered Mr Khumalo's number and clicked send. It was his red alert message, the highest of all his warning messages, and only used when there was imminent danger.

The sound of Mr Khumalo's mobile phone ringing came through the computer, but the call was redirected to voicemail. Oh no! Derek's message played – his voice disguised with a digital recording: 'This is a security alert from your surveillance company. Check your monitor, windows and doors immediately. There may be an intruder on the premises. If you see anything suspicious call the police. Do not ignore this message.'

The messaged ended and the phone reset. Hopefully Mr Khumalo had heard his phone ring and was now checking the message.

Derek stared again at screen two, his heart drumming loudly, his palms sweating. What was happening inside their house? What was the intruder doing? He couldn't see into the bedrooms. Take what you want but don't harm them, please, he begged. They're my friends.

Suddenly the figure reappeared at the open window and climbed out. He'd only been inside for a couple of minutes and didn't seem to be carrying any stolen goods. No bag or rucksack, which might have contained stolen items. Perhaps he'd stuffed smaller items like jewellery into his pockets, Derek hoped, as the alternative – that he'd done them harm – was too awful to contemplate. Or maybe – and please let this be so – he'd been disturbed.

Derek watched, his heart racing, as the figure slid effortlessly down the drainpipe and dropped to the patio. As he landed he must have been caught in the range of one of the light sensors for a floodlight flashed on, but the figure was already away, running back along the edge of the garden and then out through the gate at the rear, presumably as he'd entered. Derek knew that a small paddock lay behind the house where the Khumalos' daughter kept her pony. At the time Derek had surveyed the property to estimate for the security system he'd pointed out the gate was an easy access point for any would-be intruder, but Mr Khumalo had said his daughter needed to get in and out to tend to her pony, and anyway you couldn't secure all the grassland beyond, which was true. So Derek had been instructed to fit an additional security light in the paddock, which came on now as the intruder completed his escape.

He remained very still, staring at the image of the back of the house. Had Mr Khumalo listened to his phone message now? Had he, his wife or any of his children been woken by the intruder or the security light flashing on? Or – heaven forbid – was the crime so heinous they would never wake at all?

From memory Derek knew that the main bedroom was at the rear, and he thought the bedroom over the conservatory might be that of the Khumalos' youngest son, but he couldn't be sure. If they'd raised the alarm then the police should arrive shortly, but as he watched and waited and the minutes ticked by, no lights came on in the house and the bedroom curtains remained closed. Half an hour later, Derek conceded his message had remained unheard and feared the worst.

Chapter Thirteen

'There he is,' Mr Khumalo said, pointing to the monitor on the wall in their hall. 'So much for the additional security cameras!'

DC Beth Mayes and her colleague Matt Davis watched as the figure in black moved effortlessly down the garden, across the patio, then up the drainpipe and in through the back bedroom window. 'No hesitation or looking around,' Matt said. 'He seems to know the layout very well.' They fell silent as a minute later the figure re-emerged from the window and fled.

'And you've no idea who it could be from his build?' Beth asked Mr Khumalo. 'He's caught in the floodlight for a few seconds.'

'None at all,' he replied.

'And you're sure he didn't take anything?' Matt asked. 'Not that he was in the house very long.'

'We're sure. We've had a good look around. It seems he placed the voodoo doll on my son's bed and left.' The macabre doll had been bagged by forensics. It was about eight inches tall and crudely made out of rough fabric, with buttons for its eyes and a large hatpin stuck through its chest.

'We'll need a copy of the footage from the cameras,' Beth said. 'The security firm can advise you how to download it if you're not sure.'

'I'll see to it later,' Mr Khumalo said with a slightly dismissive nod. He returned the monitor to real time and led the way into the living room where he waved for them to sit down.

'Given the intruder appears to be very familiar with the layout of your property,' Beth said, 'I'd also like a list of all the trades people who have worked here over the last six months. Including window cleaners, electricians, gardeners and so on. Anyone who has had access to the property.'

'Yes of course, I'll ask my wife to make a list when she returns from taking the children to school. She will have a better idea of who has been here during the day as she takes care of the running of the house.'

'Thank you,' Beth said. She and Matt had spoken to Mrs Khumalo and the children before they'd left for school, but none of them had seen or heard anything beyond what had already been reported: that their six-year-old son had woken in the morning to find the sinister voodoo doll on his bed.

'What about business associates?' Matt asked. 'You said you feel this was aimed at you rather than your son, so who could have a grudge against you strong enough to do this?'

'I've no idea.' He shrugged. 'Most of my business is in Africa but the type of people I deal with wouldn't engage in a silly prank like this. If they were upset with me they'd tell me to my face or if they were very upset I would just disappear.' He gave a wry smile. 'I doubt they'd go to the trouble of playing with dolls.'

'You're taking this very well,' Beth said. 'It was a grizzly discovery for a child to make. It spooked me when I saw the doll, and the fact someone had been in his room while he slept.'

'My wife was more upset than my son,' he said. 'She can be a bit superstitious but we're Christians and we're educated people. The power of the voodoo doll cannot touch us here. Such nonsense belongs to ancient tribal Africa, although there are still plenty in the villages who believe in its power today. I am more concerned that someone managed to infiltrate my home so easily. I want that person caught and punished – whatever his motive.'

'As do we,' Matt said.

'The phone message you were sent alerting you to the break-in,' Beth asked. 'Could we listen to it, please?'

'Certainly.' Through the massive sliding patio doors of the living room, forensics in their white disposable Tyvek suits could be seen working beside the conservatory, having finished upstairs. Mr Khumalo retrieved his phone from the coffee table and put the phone on speaker. A digital voice came through: 'This is a security alert from your surveillance company. Check your monitor, windows and doors immediately. There may be an intruder on the premises. If you see anything suspicious call the police. Do not ignore this message.'

'And you didn't listen to the message until this morning?' Beth confirmed.

'That's correct. I always put my phone on silent at night. I was just checking it this morning when my son ran into our bedroom carrying the doll. I rushed into his room and saw the open bedroom window. I checked my other children were all right and dialled 999. I am just pleased that my family is safe. We could have been murdered in our beds. I'm very angry that the security firm did not properly protect us. I shall be speaking to them later in no uncertain terms.'

'And the message was sent because?' Beth asked, continuing her train of thought.

'Because we were broken into,' Mr Khumalo said a little disparagingly.

'I mean what triggered it?' she said. 'It's an automated message from the sound of it so what alerted the system that something was wrong here?'

Mr Khumalo paused to consider this. 'I've no idea. You'd have to ask the firm how it works.'

'And they are?' Beth asked.

'Home Security. A man called Derek Flint runs the outfit.'

'So you don't have any pressure-activated pads under

the windows that could have alerted the system?' Matt asked.

'No,' Mr Khumalo replied. 'It wasn't mentioned when I discussed with the firm what was needed, and to be honest I doubt I would have thought it necessary upstairs anyway. We have the cameras running the whole time downstairs, and the intruder alarm is on throughout the house when we're all out, but on just downstairs at night. Otherwise every time one of us used the bathroom the alarm would go off.'

Matt nodded. 'I understand.'

Mr Khumalo glanced at the clock on the mantelpiece. 'I'm sorry, but I have a telephone conference call booked in ten minutes.'

'We've finished,' Beth said. 'But forensics will be here for a while yet.'

'That's not a problem. My wife will be back soon.'

'Here's my business card,' Beth said, handing it to him. 'We'll be in touch, but if you think of anything in the meantime then please phone us. I know you said you're certain it's not someone you know but please give it some more thought. It's the most likely outcome. Be assured we will do everything we can to catch the person, and I would recommend reviewing your security.'

'I intend doing so,' he said bluntly. 'But it won't be with the same firm. Not after this.'

'No, quite,' Matt agreed. They stood and Mr Khumalo saw them out.

★ ★ ★

'Of course it's someone he knows,' Matt said as they returned to their unmarked police car. 'How many criminals do you know who specialize in breaking and entering to leave a voodoo doll on a child's bed and the jewellery untouched? It's ridiculous.'

Beth nodded. 'Do you think he already knows who it could be?'

'I'm sure he's got his suspicions. And I wouldn't mind betting he gets to them before we do. I just hope it's not on our shift.'

They were in the car now; Beth was in the driver's seat but she'd made no attempt to start the engine. 'Perhaps forensics will come up with something. The doll was obviously handmade so hopefully it will contain the offender's DNA, which, with a bit of luck, will match someone on our database.'

'And the tooth fairy and Santa Claus are real,' Matt said cynically, fastening his seatbelt.

Beth laughed. She liked working with Matt, liked his sense of humour and ready wit. He could be serious when he wanted to be, and they made a good team, bouncing ideas off each other, although he'd be the first to admit that she was better at PR. *It's because you're a woman*, he joked. *It's because you open your mouth before your brain is engaged*, she'd retaliated. Matt had a tendency to say the first thing that came into his head, which often made him sound tactless and uncaring, which he wasn't.

Beth still hadn't started the engine but was gazing past him to the Khumalos' splendid house and the alarm box mounted high on the front wall, just below the eaves.

'Matt, you remember that newsagents I went to that had been broken into a second time?'

'Yes, you mean the one you spent hours looking at the CCTV footage to see if you could add it to your string theory, then had to admit there wasn't a link at all?'

'I was trying to establish if it was the same intruder,' she corrected, aware he was joking. 'Probably just coincidence but the newsagents and the Khumalos use the same security firm – Home Security. I know it's a long shot but I wonder if it might be worth seeing if it was the same engineer who fitted the cameras on both premises?'

'Long shot! More like a flight of fantasy!' Matt laughed. 'What about the more obvious explanation that the security firm is crap. Mr Khumalo didn't seem too impressed. But I'm game if you want to go. It'll be a bit of light relief before I go back to my desk and follow up some real leads.'

She smiled and started the engine. 'So make yourself useful and find out where Home Security is based, and we'll pay them a surprise visit.'

Chapter Fourteen

Derek's hand trembled and he felt hot and sick as he sat in his van and listened to the voicemail message. He'd heard his phone vibrate with an incoming call while he'd been talking to the prospective clients, but had waited until he'd finished and was in his van before playing the message. Mr Khumalo was so angry it was frightening. Derek didn't like anger and people shouting at him. It upset him, made him scared and reminded him of his father.

Painful memories came flooding back of when he'd lain in bed as a child, listening to his father shouting at his mother, pushing her around and sometimes hitting her when he'd returned home drunk from the pub. Derek had spent the rest of his life avoiding anger and confrontation, and always tried to be nice to people. Yet now Mr Khumalo – one of his most prodigious clients whom he respected – was shouting at him: criticizing him and his work practice, saying that sending a recorded message was useless and that he'd sue him for negligence, despite the system doing its job. It was of no consolation that it wasn't really his fault. Mr Khumalo was angry with him and that was enough.

The message ended with Mr Khumalo saying that he was terminating his contract as of now and would be using another security firm in future – one who knew what they were doing. And he'd let it be known Home Security was rubbish and couldn't be trusted. Derek lowered his phone, his eyes brimming. He supposed he should really return Mr Khumalo's call and apologize for what had happened, then try to make amends by offering to upgrade his surveillance system at cost price only. That would have been the adult, manly, thing to do, but Derek knew he wasn't brave enough and Mr Khumalo had sounded far too angry and intimidating to approach even over the phone. He reminded Derek too much of his father, who he would never have approached when he was angry. Spineless, his father had called him and he supposed it was still true today.

A spineless coward. He had failed to protect his mother and now lived with the consequences that she was a bitter, dispirited woman. The only place Derek hadn't felt weak and ineffectual was at work: seated in front of his monitors and in charge of his empire. Yet even there he seemed to be losing his grasp.

He was about to return his phone to his jacket when

it rang again, making him start. Not Mr Khumalo, please no. He checked the caller display. A new number; the phone hadn't recognized it. A new client maybe? How wonderful. It was just what he needed. When one door closes, another opens, he thought, brightening at the prospect, and accepted the call.

'Is that Mr Flint of Home Security?' the male voice asked.

'Speaking,' he said in his most professional voice. Fantastic. It was new business.

'Good morning, Mr Flint, I'm DC Matt Davis from Coleshaw CID. Would it be possible to meet with you today? I have a few questions I'd like to ask you as part of a routine enquiry.'

The colour drained from Derek's face, a knot formed in his stomach and it was a moment before he could reply. Struggling to keep his voice even, he said, 'What is this about? I'm very busy.'

'It's in connection with a break-in on premises where your surveillance has been installed. If you're free now that would be perfect, otherwise a time to suit you. My colleague and I are parked outside your office but clearly you're not here.'

'You're outside my office?' he repeated, horrified.

'Yes. We thought there might be some clerical staff here who could help us, but the door to your office is locked. The receptionist in the electronics firm next door said you rarely use it.'

Derek fought to control his breathing. His chest felt

tight and his palms sweaty. 'It's just a base,' he stammered. 'She's right, I'm not there much.'

'If it's more convenient we could visit you at home?'

'No,' he said, far too quickly. He forced air into his lungs to try to calm himself. 'I'll come there now, but it will take me a good fifteen minutes.'

'No problem. We'll wait outside in the car.'

Heart drumming loudly and sick with fear, Derek started his van, swung out from the kerb and quickly completed a U-turn. Hell! What did they want? What break-in? Where? He hadn't thought to ask. The police knew where his office was and where he lived. They were parked outside his 'office' now and had been asking questions about him in the firm next door. Shit! It had never happened before. He'd met the police by chance sometimes on premises that had been burgled but they never sought him out. Perhaps it was nothing to do with a break-in after all – perhaps his past was catching up with him. His mother had said it was bound to happen sooner or later – that such an evil act would come back to haunt him. Now it had.

His hands clenched the steering wheel as he drove as fast as the speed limit allowed, going through amber lights and taking corners in third gear. He needed to get there quickly to avoid the police spending more time talking to the receptionist of the electronics firm next door again. She was a nosy cow who never seemed to have enough work to do and spent most of her time filing her nails and gazing out through the office window. He would have sacked her if she'd worked for him but he supposed she was kept on because of her long blonde hair and big tits. She'd watched him come and go over the years, and he knew she didn't like him. He'd overheard her refer to him as 'that creep next door' when she'd been talking to a colleague on their way in. He wondered how much she'd already told the police and his stomach contracted.

He took another corner too fast. The van rocked and he touched the brake. The officer had said it was routine, Derek reminded himself, and tried to calm down. The officer – what was his name? Davis? Yes – had said it was part of a routine enquiry into a break-in, but if it really was then what did they want him for and which break-in had he meant?

The Khumalo break-in seemed a strong possibility although there were others to choose from, he acknowledged bitterly. But why speak to him? Not because they wanted the footage from the cameras; that was for the clients to download, and if they needed help, the client contacted him. It wasn't a police job, or it hadn't been in the past. They'd only crossed paths if they were still at the crime scene when he helped the occupants download camera footage, or he had to repair a broken alarm or reconnect a camera disconnected in an attempted burglary. But the police had never asked to speak to him personally before, not since . . . No. He gave himself a shake. He wouldn't think about that now.

And now they were waiting for him outside his office. He entered the industrial estate, his mouth dry and the tic at the corner of his eye agitating furiously. His office was at the far side in a two-storey block in the oldest, cheapest, and most neglected part of the estate. As he approached, he saw a black Volvo parked right outside and guessed it was the police. Slowing further, he pulled over and drew to a halt, parking a few feet in front of the car. The car doors opened and two officers got out, a male officer from the passenger side and a female who'd been driving. Derek wiped his sweaty hands down his trousers and got out, leaving his phone in the van.

'Good afternoon, DC Matt Davis,' the male officer said as he approached. 'We spoke on the phone. This is my colleague, DC Beth Mayes.'

Derek nodded. 'I got here as soon as I could.'

'It's appreciated. Shall we go inside?' Davis asked.

'We can, but there's nothing much to see. I haven't used it for years. I just keep it as my business address.' He knew his reluctance made him sound guilty, as if he was trying to cover something up, so he immediately turned and led the way in.

They walked past the large plate-glass window of the firm next door, Eastbury Electronics, where the cow of the receptionist was standing up for a better view, clearly unable to contain her delight. As they entered the building he saw Davis throw her a smile and she fluttered her long fake eyelashes ridiculously and pursed her lips.

'This is the office,' he said, stopping outside the second door on the left. Unlike the smart glass door opposite, the door to Derek's office was the original, now chipped and in dire need of a coat of paint. It bore no company name but simply announced Unit 3.

'So there are twelve offices in this building?' Beth remarked as they waited for him to unlock, referring to the signage board on the wall listing the companies.

'I suppose so,' Derek said, struggling to turn the key. 'This is the smallest and cheapest. I use it for storage sometimes.'

Finally managing to open the door, he flicked on the light and they followed him in.

'Smallest and cheapest isn't wrong,' Matt quipped under his breath.

Beth threw him a warning look, although he was right. She'd seen bigger and better equipped cupboards. An old wooden table had been pushed against one wall with a single grimy chair beneath it. A metal filing cabinet circa 1950s was against another wall and a couple of large empty cardboard boxes were beside it collecting spiders. The only natural light came from a single small window covered with wire mesh at the very top of one wall. A bare light bulb hung from the centre of the ceiling, highlighting the starkness of the room. It smelt musty and shut up.

'I see what you mean about not using it much,' Matt said, taking a turn of the room.

'Is this your main office then?' Beth asked, as surprised as Matt was to see inside.

'It's my only office,' Derek replied, his tic agitating. 'As I said, I hardly use it now.'

'The photographs on your website show something a

little more upmarket,' Matt remarked, unable to suppress the sarcasm in his voice.

'That was a standard picture taken from the Internet,' Derek said defensively. 'Lots of small businesses use them. We can't all afford grand offices but you have to create a good impression online now. Word of mouth recommendation is no longer good enough.'

'So clearly no one actually works here,' Beth said, stating the obvious but needing it confirmed.

'No. Installing surveillance takes place in homes and businesses, not in an office. There's no point wasting money on grand premises.'

'Business isn't good then?' Matt asked, coming to a standstill a few feet from him.

'It's a quiet time.'

'Really? I am surprised. It isn't for us. Crime is up in the area. I'd have thought that was good for your business?'

Derek said nothing but absently touched his eye to silence the tic.

'So where do you keep your stock if it's not here?' Beth asked.

'On the van mainly. All the tools and wiring are kept there. Then I order in the bigger stuff, the cameras, monitors and so on as they are needed. Each client's order is different and specific to their requirements.'

'And that stuff is delivered where?' Matt asked.

'Here or to my home.'

'So presumably your computer and paperwork for the business are at your home too?' Beth asked.

Derek nodded and wiped his sweating palms down his trousers again. 'Yes. I do all my admin work there in the evenings and weekends. There's no other time.'

'So you don't have any clerical staff at all?' Matt asked, struggling to suppress his dislike of the man.

'No, there's no need. But why are you asking me all these questions? You said on the phone you wanted to talk about a break-in.'

'Yes. I'm getting to that,' Matt said tightly.

'We're just trying to establish the extent of your business,' Beth said. 'The business card you give your clients, and your website, suggest a large, well-established organization.'

'My company *is* well established,' Derek snapped, finally losing his patience. 'I've been in this line of work for over fifteen years. I have built up a good reputation.'

'Yes, I'm sure,' Beth said conciliatorily. There was nowhere to sit so they'd have to continue this interview standing. 'We're investigating two break-ins in the area where your CCTV had been installed.'

Derek regained his composure. 'I'm always very concerned to hear of a break-in where my company has fitted the surveillance.' He felt on safer ground now. 'Where are they?'

She caught Matt's look. 'I think you may know. One was at a newsagents owned by Mr and Mrs Osman and the other at the home of Mr Khumalo. We were there this morning. In both cases we're a bit short of evidence and we were wondering if you kept a copy of their CCTV footage?'

'No, not usually. It's the client's responsibility. Why? Have they wiped it?'

She didn't reply. 'So once the system is up and running your company has nothing more to do with it?'

'Not beyond repairing and maintaining, and giving any help if necessary. These systems are very sophisticated and can confuse the less technically minded.'

'I dare say,' Matt put in.

'Thank you, Mr Flint,' Beth said, again countering Matt's abrasiveness. 'What triggers the automated messages? Mr Khumalo unfortunately didn't listen to his until this morning, and Mr and Mrs Osman say they never received one.'

'I can't be responsible for people not picking up their messages,' Derek said, again irritated. 'I do what I can within their budget and no system is infallible. Some cameras rely on motion so a burglar climbing through a window could trigger it.'

'Mr Khumalo had that type of camera?' Beth asked.

'As far as I can remember.'

'Mr Khumalo said he was going to contact you. Has he?' Matt asked, taking another turn of the room.

'He left a message on my voicemail.'

'Just a couple more questions, Mr Flint,' Beth said. 'How many engineers do you employ?'

'I'm the only full-time qualified engineer and I take on help as I need it.' It would be easy enough to find out that there was only him and an apprentice.

'So who fitted the surveillance in the newsagents and Mr Khumalo's home?' she asked.

Derek looked thoughtful for a moment. 'That would be Paul.'

'Surname?' Matt asked.

'Mellows.'

'We'd like to speak to him,' Beth said.

'I'm afraid he doesn't work for me any more. Like many of the young lads I take on as apprentices they learn the skills and leave to work for a bigger firm with more money. I guess I teach them too well,' he finished with a rueful smile.

'Can we have his contact details please?' Beth asked.

'They'll be on file at home. I'll have to send them to you.'

Matt was about to say something but Beth stepped in. 'Thank you, Mr Flint, you've been very helpful. Here's my card. If you could phone, email or text me Paul's address, I'd be grateful.'

Derek saw his hand tremble as he accepted the card.

'We'll see ourselves out,' Matt said. They turned and left, closing the door behind them.

Derek remained where he was, hot and nauseous. Of course they'd want to speak to Paul. Why the hell had he said that? Panic. Bile rose in his throat and he swallowed hard and took a deep breath. He needed to calm down and try to think what to do for the best . . .

'Smarmy git,' Matt said as soon as they were outside and out of earshot.

'I know, but it doesn't do any harm to be polite,' Beth admonished. 'You really wound him up in there.'

'Sorry.' He threw the receptionist of the firm next door a smile as they got into the car.

'You're incorrigible,' Beth said indulgently.

Matt sat in the passenger seat gazing out of his side window and enjoying the attention coming from the receptionist who'd been joined by a female colleague. 'So what's Derek been up to do we think?' he said, without shifting his gaze.

'Maybe nothing. Perhaps he's doing what a lot of blokes do and making himself appear more important than he is.'

'Point taken,' Matt said, drawing his gaze to the front. 'But wouldn't you have expected him to ask what had been stolen from the Khumalo's house? He didn't seem interested in the details. I think I might have been if it was my company who'd installed the surveillance.'

'I expect Khumalo told him when he phoned. I can't imagine he minced his words.'

'So why didn't Derek mention it? That nothing had been stolen but a voodoo doll had been left on the bed? I mean, it's not an everyday occurrence.'

'Agreed. So while I drive us back to the office, why don't you run a check on Mr Flint?' She started the engine as Matt lifted the lid on the car's laptop but waited before pulling away so that he could enter the Home Security van's registration number into the Police National Computer.

For some minutes as Beth drove, all that could be heard from inside the car was the sound of Matt tapping the keyboard. Then:

'Well! Well!' Matt said with a self-righteous grin. 'I'm not just a pretty face.'

'Not even,' Beth returned.

'I knew our Derek was hiding something. He was caught cottaging – having gay sex in a public toilet – nine years ago and prosecuted for gross indecency. He pleaded guilty and got off with a fine. Uniform caught him in the act after a member of the public reported him with another lad.'

'So he has different sexual preferences to you, but that doesn't help with the present enquiry,' Beth said.

'No, but this might: another break-in where his firm had installed the CCTV.'

Chapter Fifteen

'You're home very early,' Elsie Flint remarked as Derek let himself into the hall.

'I'm not feeling well, and I can come home when I want to, can't I?' She'd made it sound as though he hadn't a right to be there during the day.

'Well, don't go giving me your germs. I hope you've had your lunch. There's nothing in the fridge, I need to go shopping.'

Thanks for your concern, Derek thought but didn't say, and why not go shopping? You've nothing better to do. 'I'm not hungry,' he mumbled.

He poured himself a glass of water and went upstairs, accompanied by the mundane dialogue of early afternoon television. Going into his bedroom, he bolted the door. Thank God. His one safe haven. He still felt sick, although he suspected it wasn't from any illness but the visit he'd

128

just received from the police. It had badly shaken him and he was kicking himself for the way he'd handled it.

He took a sip of water, dumped his jacket on the bed and powered up the computer. Khumalo must have pointed the accusing finger at him. He'd been so angry and out to blame him in the message he'd left on his voicemail and had obviously told the police. Now they were going to speak to Paul. It couldn't get much worse. Why he'd laid the blame on Paul he still didn't know. It was the first thing that had come into his head. He hadn't had time to think it through and consider the consequences. Of course the police would want to talk to Paul now he'd implicated him. He'd have done better admitting he'd installed the surveillance at both properties, but he'd panicked.

He needed to speak to Paul quickly before the police did. But what to say to smooth over what had happened between them and get Paul on his side? Perhaps he should offer to give him his job back but even as he thought it he knew that wouldn't work. The reasons he'd got rid of Paul in the first place – that he knew too much – hadn't gone away; indeed this last development would add to the problem.

Perhaps he shouldn't have let Paul go in the first place? It had been a knee-jerk reaction, but then what alternative had he had? Pointing out to Mr Osman that an email should have been generated! He doubted many of the other lads he'd taken on over the years would have spotted that, but Paul was far more technically minded, computer savvy and on the ball than most. He'd been interested in the business of surveillance from the start – too interested.

Whereas the other lads had been content to hang cameras and check alarm bells, Paul had repeatedly asked about the company's online presence, feeling it could be improved upon. Either Paul was brighter than he'd given him credit for, or Derek was getting careless and becoming complacent. Either way he'd really cocked it up.

He clicked on the file that contained the details of his apprentices, as thorough in collecting information about them as he was on his clients. Eighteen apprentices since he'd signed up for the scheme ten years before, averaging two a year, which was just about acceptable before the administrators of the scheme started to complain. A few – the less astute ones who could be relied upon not to learn too quickly or pry – he'd allowed to stay longer, but not Paul. He'd only been with him five months. Too clever by half for his own good, he thought again, but what he was going to say to him he didn't know.

He could hardly come clean and admit what he was up to and that the reason the email hadn't been sent to the Osmans was because there *was* no automatically generated email. It relied on him sending it if he saw something untoward, which he hadn't done with the break-in at the Osmans because he'd been asleep. Paul knew enough about the laws governing surveillance to know that what he was doing was illegal.

Reading Paul's details, Derek saw that he lived at home with his parents, older brother and younger sister. The landline number was included, as was all their ages. His father was a builder and his mother a nurse. None of his family had criminal records or anything dodgy that Derek knew of, so there was nothing he could use to put pressure on Paul. Paul had been very angry when he'd told him he was terminating his contract and had called him some nasty names like creep, perv, arsehole and so on. Not appropriate or nice. Hopefully he'd had time to calm down now, but, even if he hadn't, Derek still needed to speak to him, or the police would just turn up and start asking questions and no doubt Paul would tell them everything he knew. Why shouldn't he?

Using the VPN – Virtual Private Network – software he'd downloaded that allowed the user to browse and phone anonymously, Derek plugged in the handset and dialled Paul's mobile number. He answered on the third ring. The nausea in Derek's stomach rose and he swallowed hard.

'Paul, it's Derek Flint.'

'What the fuck do you want?' Paul demanded. 'Why are you phoning me and on a private number?'

'Paul, I'm sorry things didn't work out with you working for me, but I need to talk to you, ask you something.'

'About what? You had no right to fire me like that. I could report you to the manager of the apprenticeship scheme.'

'I didn't fire you. I let you go.'

'Same thing. You owe me wages.'

'I paid you up to the end of the month.'

'Yes, but I should have been given compensation in lieu of notice.'

Derek knew there was no legal obligation for him to compensate Paul, that was why he used the apprenticeship scheme: he could take on help and let the lads go as and when he wanted to, although he wasn't going to antagonize Paul by telling him that now.

'I'm sure we can work something out,' Derek said, at his conciliatory best.

A small silence, then, 'Why are you phoning me?'

Derek cleared his throat and concentrated. 'The police want to talk to you about the break-ins at some of the properties where we installed CCTV. I thought you should know so it doesn't come as a complete shock, so you don't blurt out something you might later regret.'

'Are you threatening me?'

'No, of course not. I hadn't meant it to sound like that.'

'I don't mind talking to the police; I've done nothing wrong,' Paul declared adamantly.

'I know you haven't. But if they start asking about my business can you say you don't know anything about how it works and that you made some mistakes? I mean, you might have seen and heard stuff you didn't completely understand.'

'Or understood too well.'

Derek felt his heart step up a few beats. 'What do you mean? Like what?'

'Like something dodgy. I'm not sure what it is yet but I bet I could find out. If you're in trouble with the police then I'm guessing it's your own fault.'

'I'm not,' Derek blurted too quickly. Then, 'You won't

say anything like that to the police if they visit, will you?' A long silence. 'I could make it worth your while.'

'How?'

'I could give you good references for your interviews.'

'Do me a favour!' Paul sneered. 'You'll have to do better than that.'

'What do you want then?'

'Money.'

'That's blackmail.'

'Suit yourself. No skin off my nose. I don't mind talking to the police, I've got nothing to lose.'

'No, all right, stop. I'll give you a month's wages. Two hundred pounds.'

'A thousand,' Paul said.

'What!'

'I'm guessing it must be worth that or you wouldn't have phoned.'

'All right, a thousand then.' He wiped the sweat from his forehead. 'But no more. I'll pay you after the police have spoken to you.'

'Before. You might not give it to me after.'

'Half before and half after.'

'Done. I'll have the first lot tonight.'

'Tonight?'

'Yes. You know where I live. Put the cash in an envelope with my name on it and push it through my letter box.'

'All right, I will,' he stammered.

'At eight o'clock exactly. I'll be waiting on the other side of the door. Make sure no one sees you.'

'You won't tell anyone I've given you the money, will you?' Derek asked pathetically.

'You'll just have to trust me on that. Five hundred quid, at eight o'clock sharp.'

'Yes, I heard.'

Derek cut the call, sat back in his chair and gulped in air. A thousand pounds! It was his own stupid fault for ever implementing Paul in the first place. Hopefully this would put a stop to it once and for all but he'd need to make sure. He now logged the amount in the accounts file on his computer just as he did with all his business transactions.

Eight o'clock, Paul had said. Plenty of time before he had to leave. It had been a shit-awful day and he desperately needed to spend time with his family. He craved their comfort and support. But as he zoomed in on the live streams coming from his clients' cameras, the business with the police and Paul overshadowed any pleasure or comfort. Many of the houses were empty in the afternoon with the parents at work and the children at school.

He looked in at the Khumalos' house but that was empty too, as was the Williams'. Since the night their babysitter had behaved so deplorably they hadn't been out in the evening. He'd heard them discussing the difficulty in finding a trustworthy and reliable babysitter. 'I mean, if you can't trust your goddaughter then who can you trust?' Mrs Williams had declared.

Derek hoped they found a sitter soon so they could go out again together. They were a nice couple and deserved an evening away from their kids. Ironically, Derek had recently taken on a client who was a qualified nursery nurse. She lived a mile away and supplemented her income by occasional babysitting. She'd be ideal. When things settled down again he'd give some thought as to how he could bring them together. He liked to help nice people.

A movement on another screen caught his eye, and he quickly enlarged the images coming from the Hanks' house. Mrs Hanks was opening the front door to her lover again; a sleazy salesman named Tim Riseman.

Derek was furious. The deceit made his blood boil. The affair had been going on for six months after Riseman had called one afternoon selling conservatories. Derek was finding it difficult to contain his anger. Every second Tuesday, while Mr Hanks was at work, his wife had sex with this seedy bastard. Not only was she making a fool of her husband – who was a decent guy – but Derek knew from listening in that Mr Hanks hated his job and would have retrained as a nurse had he not had to maintain the standard of living dictated by his greedy and materialistic wife. Derek had been holding back from intervening, not wanting to raise suspicion while Paul had been with him, but now he was gone he was free to help. This would be his next project, he thought, but for now he watched in distaste as Mrs Hanks seductively unbuttoned her blouse and exposed her very large breasts.

Chapter Sixteen

At 7.30pm Derek opened the door to the living room to tell his mother he was going out.

'You look ridiculous in that get-up,' she sneered. 'A middle-aged man dressed in black leather! And don't go revving that bike outside; it upsets the neighbours.'

'Do you want anything from the garage shop?' he asked, ignoring the ridicule. 'Sweets?'

She shook her head. She usually wanted to know where he was going when he took his bike out in the evening and invariably he told her it was to the garage to fill up the bike with petrol.

'I won't be long,' he said, but already her attention had returned to the television.

With his helmet and black leather motorbike gloves tucked under his arm, and quelling his unease at what he was about to do, Derek went into the garage. It was too small to keep his van in so he used it for his motorbike, stock, and general clutter from the house that they no longer needed but his mother refused to throw out. At the sight of the bike, his confidence grew. It was a big and powerful machine, well respected by other road users. Riding it made him feel important, stand out from the crowd and in control, similar to when he sat at his workstation and viewed his empire of clients. Yes, on the bike he was someone who commanded attention and respect, especially when he opened up the throttle.

He raised the garage door, inserted the key into the bike's ignition, put on his helmet and gloves and then mounted the bike. With a flick of the key the engine roared into life, a deep, resonating throb. He allowed himself one good rev, which he knew his mother would hear, before driving out of the garage, leaving the door open so it would be ready for his return. Once on the road he accelerated away and then out onto the high road. His spirits lifted. It was early evening; the street lights were coming on and the roads were emptying. He drove with purpose: masterful, head held high, but only as fast as the speed limit would allow for Derek always tried to follow the rules.

Five minutes later he entered Coleshaw High Street. Full of shoppers and office workers during the day, the shops and offices were closed now so he was able to park right outside the bank. Switching off the engine, he lowered the kickstand and removed his helmet and gloves. A couple were already at the cash machine and as he waited for them to finish he looked up towards the bank's CCTV camera, aware it would be picking him up very clearly. Evidence, should he ever need it later. He didn't think Paul would do the dirty on him but life had taught him that you could never be sure. If Paul did decide to make trouble for him, he now had some evidence that he was blackmailing him.

The couple finished and walked away, and Derek crossed the pavement to the cash dispenser. Unzipping his leather jacket, he took out his platinum debit card of which he was proud and inserted it into the cash dispenser. The screen showed what he already knew – that although he was allowed to withdraw £1000 in 24 hours, the maximum single transaction was three hundred pounds. He withdrew the maximum three times and then a hundred pounds to make it up to a thousand.

In full view of the bank's camera he took two envelopes from his inside jacket pocket on which he'd already printed Paul's full name and address. He carefully divided the money between the envelopes, counting five hundred pounds into each, and tucked them into his jacket pocket. He placed the receipts in his wallet and put that into his jacket too. Donning his helmet and gloves he returned to the bike, revved and pulled away, trusting it was all recorded on the bank's CCTV.

Using the back streets Derek knew so well, he headed towards Paul's home – about ten minutes away. When Paul had first applied to work for him Derek had spent some time viewing where he lived on Google Earth and Street

View. Then once Paul had begun, he'd made a point of collecting him from home once to take him to a job. He'd done this with all the lads he'd employed so their family could see his work van with the name of his company emblazoned on the side and back doors. It helped reassure them that his was a reputable company and their son would be in safe hands. Most of these lads were straight from school and still wet behind the ears and their parents – especially their mothers – fretted about them in a way his own mother never had. He'd had to go to work when his father had left and that was that.

Not wanting to draw attention to himself, he cut the engine as he entered Paul's road and cruised noiselessly to a halt, parking under a tree a few houses from where Paul lived. The street was quiet and the last vestige of daylight had gone. Derek raised his visor and checked the time. It was now 7.55. He remained astride his bike and waited. Paul had said to post the money through his letterbox at exactly eight o'clock and he would be waiting for it on the other side of the door. Derek assumed that was so none of his family got to the envelope first and began asking questions.

A man walked by with a dog and Derek kept his head down, pretending he was checking his phone. At 7.58 he removed one of the envelopes from his inside jacket pocket and, dismounting the bike, walked the short distance to Paul's house. Dressed all in black with a black helmet, he blended into the night.

There was no front gate, just a gap in the small brick

wall marking the boundary line. Derek went silently up the short path to the front door. The lights were on in the hall and front room. It was now exactly eight o'clock. He gingerly lifted the letterbox with one hand and posted the envelope in with the other. As he did he felt the tug of it being taken on the other side.

He returned to his bike and to be on the safe side texted Paul: *Please confirm you got the £500 just posted through your letterbox.*

Yes, got it came the immediate response. Then: *I want the other £500 as soon as I've spoken to the police.*

Perfect, Derek thought. If ever he needed a bit more evidence that Paul was corrupt and happy to lie to the police he had it in that text. First thing in the morning he'd email Paul's contact details to that police officer, just as she'd asked him to.

Chapter Seventeen

'Interesting,' Beth said, thinking aloud.

It was the following morning and she was at her desk viewing in more detail what Matt had found on the Police National Computer after they'd left Derek Flint's office. Matt was sitting opposite, engrossed in his computer screen and not really listening.

'So he was questioned seven years ago about a break-in at a garage where he'd installed the CCTV,' she continued. 'Not charged though. Someone jumped the cashier at closing time as they were cashing up, having hacked the system's website. Little wonder Flint was edgy when we spoke to him with this and that other incident on file.'

Matt mumbled an acknowledgement but kept his attention on his monitor.

Beth read to the end of the report before closing the file and returning it to the archive. 'I wonder how common

141

hacking into CCTV websites is,' she said, and entered the question into a search engine.

A few minutes later she had her answer. 'Struth! Very common. Matt, did you know it's estimated that fifty per cent of the population never change their default password – on their phone, Smart TV, tablet, router or home security? And before you ask, yes I have changed mine, and so did the Osmans and Khumalos. Derek made a point of telling them to. I guess he'd learnt his lesson from the business at the garage, but it doesn't really advance the investigation.' She glanced up at Matt and he managed a nod.

'The forensic report from the Khumalos' house is back. Have you read it?'

Matt shook his head.

'No fingerprint or DNA match coming from the house or the voodoo doll, so whoever entered the premises and made the doll doesn't have a criminal record. Eight different DNA samples were lifted from the doll itself with three standing out as much stronger – those likely to have been responsible for actually making the doll and handling it once assembled. It wasn't factory made. All are thought to be Caucasian. The cloth the doll was made from was originally sourced from India but then most of our cloth comes from abroad. All the other materials – the stuffing, the string for the hair and buttons for the eyes can be bought in the UK. So it seems that at least three people in this country didn't like Mr K enough to be involved in making the doll. But as he said, what business person would resort to leaving a voodoo doll?'

'Unless whoever he upset paid someone else to do it?' Matt suggested, finally taking his eyes from the screen.

'So you have been listening,' Beth said and he grinned. 'Paid them to put the frighteners on Mr K? I'm sure he knows who's behind this and he's probably already on to them.'

'Remind me again what line of business he's in?' Matt asked.

'Mining and African real estate mainly.'

'I would think there's plenty of dodgy characters tied up in that.'

Beth nodded. 'So unless something fresh comes in I'll be putting this to bed.' She continued through her inbox opening and closing the attachments. 'Nothing new on the stabbing at U–Beat nightclub then, but on a positive note Flint has emailed the details of his last apprentice, Paul.' She fell silent. The minutes ticked by.

'And? What is it?' Matt asked at length. 'The silence is deafening.'

Beth sat upright. 'According to Flint's national insurance contribution record he has employed eighteen apprentices in the last ten years and none has stayed longer than seven months. That's a high turnaround when apprenticeships are expected to last from between one and four years.'

'He said they learnt what they needed and then left to get a better paid job. Having seen his office, I can't imagine he paid them more than he had to.'

'Perhaps, or maybe there's another reason.'

'Like what?'

'I don't know yet but I have a feeling that Flint is hiding something and not just about his past. I'll visit Paul on my way home. Do you want to come?'

'No. I'm meeting someone straight after work.'

'Date?'

'Sort of. An old friend got in touch through Facebook.'

'Have a good evening.'

'I will.' He winked.

'I left because the pay was crap,' Paul said with a deferential glance at his mother. It was nearly 5.30pm and Beth, Paul and Mrs Mellows were in their living room. They'd covered what Paul's role had been while he'd worked at Home Security and the reason for Beth's visit, and had now moved on to why Paul had left. Paul's father, brother and sister weren't home yet.

'How much did he pay you? If you don't mind telling me,' Beth asked.

'The minimum for an apprentice my age, three pounds fifty an hour,' Paul scoffed.

'That's not much,' Beth sympathized, 'although I suppose you were learning a trade.'

He shrugged.

'I said he should have stayed until he got another job,' his mother said. 'A hundred pounds a week is better than nothing.'

Beth could appreciate that at Paul's age he might have acted impulsively.

'I've got an interview lined up for next week,' he said.

'Well done. So while you were working for Derek Flint he taught you all about the business – enough to apply for other jobs?'

'Not about his business, no. He just taught me the job, you know – how to fit the cameras and wire the alarm.'

'Yes, that's what I meant really,' Beth said. 'There was just you working for him?'

'Yes.'

'For five months?'

Paul nodded.

'It's a very small firm. When you applied were you expecting it to be bigger?'

'I guess,' Paul said with a shrug.

'His dad said he wouldn't have let him take it if he'd known it was just him and Derek Flint,' his mother added.

Beth nodded. 'But he treated you well while you worked for him?'

'Yeah, I suppose.' The boy wasn't being very forth-coming, Beth thought. She was getting more from his mother.

'You said earlier that you thought your boss was a bit weird. What exactly did you mean?'

'I dunno. It was none of my business really. He just seemed a bit of a loner. A Billy No-Mates. He rides his motorbike at weekends, otherwise he's always working. He lives for his work and takes it very seriously – too seriously.' It was the most Paul had said so far.

'Paul said he thought Derek liked blokes, not girls, if I'm allowed to say that,' his mother put in.

'What's that got to do with it?' Paul sneered. 'I didn't tell you that.'

'No, but I heard you talking on the phone.'

'You got no business listening to my calls,' Paul snapped, rounding on his mother.

'It's OK,' Beth said. 'As long as he treated you all right. He was in a position of trust and responsibility when he employed you as an apprentice.'

'Yeah. He was just a bit of a loner.'

'I understand. Well, thank you for your help. I think that's everything. If you do think of something else please give me a ring.' She placed her business card on the coffee table.

'So you just wanted to make sure those robberies you mentioned weren't anything to do with Paul?' his mother asked, seeking clarification.

'Yes, that's more or less it,' Beth said, and stood. 'Thank you for your time Mrs Mellows.' Then to Paul: 'Good luck with the interview next week.'

He shrugged dismissively.

'I'll see you to the door,' his mother said.

Beth said goodbye to Paul and followed his mother out of the living room. 'He didn't quit his job,' his mother confided as soon as they were out of earshot. 'Paul doesn't like to admit it but he was fired. No warning, no notice, just out the door. Flint told him business wasn't good so he couldn't afford to keep him, but I overheard Paul tell his mates that he'd upset him by showing him something he didn't know about his business.'

'Do you know what it was?' Beth asked.

'Something about the system failing to send an email when it should have done.'

Beth nodded. 'That makes sense. Thank you.'

'I don't know any more. Paul doesn't confide in me or his dad. But when he came home that day he was furious and I heard him on the phone telling his mates what had happened.'

'Thank you,' Beth said again. 'I hope he gets another job soon.'

'So do I. The devil finds work for idle hands.'

A strange thing to say about your son, Beth thought, as she returned to her car but what she'd learnt was interesting. According to Flint, Paul had left for a better paid job but he hadn't. Paul didn't have a job and had been sacked because he'd pointed out a fault in the system. She could picture Derek Flint flying off the handle and dismissing Paul for identifying an error. His tightly controlled manner suggested a ticking time bomb. A conformist, perfectionist, inflexible and worried about what others might think of him, there was no room in such people for criticism or failure. Beth had seen it before in her stepfather. Charming and obliging to the point of ingratiating himself, unless you crossed him – and then all hell broke loose.

Chapter Eighteen

That evening as Derek returned to his workstation after dinner, his phone bleeped with an incoming text message. It was from Paul.

Police been . . . didn't say anything . . . want the rest of the money tonight.

Was everything OK? Derek texted back.

Yes! Drop off the other £500 at 8pm.

I will.

It was now 6.30pm. Setting aside his phone, Derek clicked on Paul Mellows' file and then made a note of the police visit. He would enter the second payment later when he returned after delivering the money. In preparation, he took the envelope containing the five hundred pounds from the locked drawer in his desk and set it to one side. He had time to check on a few of his clients before he needed to change and leave.

Buoyed up and relieved by the news that the police visit had passed without a problem, he now felt in a better frame of mind to take care of his clients. A quiet confidence of being in control again was starting to return. Soon he would be back in the driving seat and governing those he was responsible for rather than covering his back, which he felt he had been doing for the last few weeks. His place was a leader, a maker of decisions, not someone who was beholden to others or intimidated by the police. He was Derek Flint of Home Security, all-seeing and powerful, almost god-like in his omniscience.

But wait, what was this? His attention went to screen two. The live stream that should have been coming from the Khumalos' cameras wasn't there. The place where the thumbnail image should have been was blank. A sinking feeling hit the pit of his stomach.

Derek clicked the mouse on the spot where the images should have been, wondering if the hide feature had accidentally been triggered, but nothing appeared. It wasn't a technical fault, there was no error message and all the other cameras were functioning as they should. It could only mean one thing: Mr Khumalo had done as he'd threatened to do and gone to another security firm. Once they'd taken over its running they would have created a new password and he'd have been locked out.

He took a deep breath. There was no need to panic. He'd lost a client. It wasn't the end of the world. Mr Khumalo had done what he'd said in his voicemail message. Derek hadn't called him back, so he shouldn't be surprised.

He just hoped he didn't carry out his other threat and sue him for negligence.

The changeover must have taken place while he'd been having dinner or he would have seen the blank space on the monitor when he'd checked before. It was like a gaping black hole in an otherwise starry sky. A void, a chasm. There was no way he could have missed it. Later he'd have to move all the images along to close the gap or the disorder and lack of uniformity would eat away at him. But first he needed to confirm what exactly had happened. The final stage in setting up any security was downloading the software for the customer and changing the password, so there should be a recording up to that point.

Going into the Khumalos' download history Derek rewound to midday, but there was no sign of any engineers and their house was empty. He slowly fast-forwarded and stopped at 12.30 as Mrs Khumalo parked her car on their driveway. He watched her enter the house. A few minutes later her husband returned home. At 1pm a white van with Eagle Eye Securities on the side pulled up outside. He knew the company; it was a large firm with franchises nationwide. They had a reasonable reputation although didn't provide the personal service he did. Two men got out and went up the path to the front door.

Mr Khumalo let them in and Derek watched as he introduced them to his wife. The four of them went into the living room and Derek engaged the microphone on the camera there. The older, more experienced of the two engineers who introduced himself as Tony ran through their printed job description before they began the work. Clicking on fast-forward he watched them take their equipment from the van, and then glanced at the clock. It was now 7pm in real time. He needed to keep an eye on the time. In forty-five minutes he'd have to change into his motorbike leathers to go to Paul's.

Fast-forwarding again he watched the new cameras being installed, each time Tony checked with Mr Khumalo that they were exactly where he wanted them. Then they began checking the existing cameras, their magnified faces suddenly looming at Derek down the lens. 'You won't find anything wrong with my workmanship,' Derek said out loud.

Another glance at the clock and Derek nudged the tape on, but then stopped and reverted to play mode again. Tony was coming down the ladder in the living room having examined the camera in there. He was looking concerned and calling for Mr Khumalo. Derek felt his stomach churn.

'Sorry to trouble you,' Tony said as Mr Khumalo appeared in the living room, 'but I need to check something with you. The cameras you asked us to install are the 3MP HD like the one we showed you? That's what is on the quote.'

'Yes, if that's what we agreed,' Mr Khumalo said. 'Why?'

'It's just that this one in the living room is more sophis-ticated and comes with a built-in microphone. I hadn't realized until just now. It's not something I see much of in private homes unless there is live-in help or a nanny.'

'I hadn't realized there was a microphone either. We never use it,' Mr Khumalo replied.

'OK, that's fine then,' Tony said, clearly relieved. 'I just wanted to check to make sure. It's all up and running now. Five minutes and we'll be finished and I'll get you logged in.'

Derek breathed a sigh of relief and looked again at the clock. He should really be getting ready now but for his own peace of mind he needed to see the next bit. He moved the tape on to where they'd finished running their checks. Tony was sitting in the living room with Mr and Mrs Khumalo while the other guy was clearing up and loading tools into the van. Tony had evidently downloaded the software to access the system on their phones and was now telling them to think of a password. He handed them their phones so they could enter it without him seeing. As they did, the feeds from the cameras to Derek's screen went blank. That would be the last he heard or saw of them. Eagle Eye Securities was now in control.

Mindful he was running late, Derek clicked the mouse to close down the computer and crossed to the wardrobe for his motorbike leathers. He'd need to change quickly if he was going to be at Paul's for 8pm. Opening the wardrobe door, he became aware that something wasn't right. The colour in the room, the shadows, the light coming from the monitors behind him weren't as they should be. He knew the flickering screens of start up and shut down like the back of his hand: the various shifts in greys and blues on the monitors as the programs closed, culminating in four blank screens once the shut down was complete.

He turned. Blast! As he thought, the shut down had frozen part way through. He needed this like a hole in the head! First Khumalo disappearing and now he was going to be late for Paul, but he daren't leave the computer like this. Without being properly shut down the system could reboot, and if his mother chanced to come in, who knew what she might see. He needed to get this sorted before he left.

Throwing his leathers on the bed he slammed the wardrobe door shut and returned to his workstation. The red and green lights on the computer were on which was hopeful. Something must be working. He waited a few moments to see if it would sort itself out and continue the shut down. When it didn't he pressed Ctrl + Alt + Del to end the program and force shut down.

Nothing happened for a moment and then the screens lost their light grey sheen. Thank goodness. Hopefully the shut down would continue. But what was happening now? A new shade of grey on all four screens, then a large eye with a lens for a pupil appeared in the centre. Not that fucking pop-up advertisement again! His anger flared. He'd spent ages sorting all that out before. But then more words appeared at the bottom of the screens:

Watching You, Derek.

Derek! They knew his name. Red in the face and brimming with anger, he yanked out the plug and the image disappeared.

Chapter Nineteen

'Yes, I'm coming now!' Derek shouted down the phone. 'I told you I got held up.'

'If you're not here by eight-thirty I'll tell the police all I know,' Paul said.

'I'll be there, and don't threaten me! You little . . .' He left the sentence unfinished. He needed Paul on his side. 'I'll be there,' he said again and cut the call.

Jabbing the phone into his jacket pocket he stormed downstairs. 'I'm going out!' he shouted to his mother as he passed the living-room door.

'Ooh la la. Someone's in a bad mood,' she returned tartly. 'Don't take it out on me.'

Hot, angry and aware he was losing control again he let himself into the garage, flung up the garage doors and mounted his bike. Calm down, he told himself. It's dangerous to drive while you're angry. Ignoring his own advice, he pulled on his helmet and leather gloves and started the engine. Giving it a good rev he left the garage in a plume of smoke and petrol fumes.

Bloody Paul! Bloody pop-up advertisements! He wasn't sure which was upsetting him the most: Paul threatening to tell the police, or his computer targeted again by malicious spyware. Who knew what information the company had gathered on him or had access to? It was impossible to tell. When he returned home he'd have to install more security software and then spend hours scanning all the files to make sure they were clear of viruses, cookies and so on. Another evening wasted!

It began to rain, a murky drizzle, which added to his gloom. Irritated, he slowed the bike; light rain on a previously dry road made for a slippery surface, especially on two wheels. As for Paul, if he threatened to tell the police again he'd remind him of the text messages they'd exchanged, proof he was guilty of lying to the police, perverting the course of justice, and blackmailing him: all of which carried a jail sentence.

Five minutes later he pulled into Paul's road. Paul had told him on the phone to park right outside his house this time and he'd keep a lookout for him. He switched off the engine; it was 8.35pm.

He glanced up at the house, but there was no sign of anyone although the lights were on in the hall and a bedroom. Perhaps he should text to say he'd arrived.

He flipped up his visor and looked again at the front of the house. As he did Paul appeared at the bedroom window and then disappeared. Derek dismounted, took off his gloves and removed the envelope containing the money from his jacket pocket. It crossed his mind that perhaps he should have called Paul's bluff right at the beginning and never got involved in paying him off, but he hadn't dared take the risk. He'd already come to the attention of the police; he didn't need Paul making trouble for him. One sniff of anything untoward and the police would be visiting him again, possibly at home this time. Better to pay up, although he wondered what Paul's father would say if he knew his son was a blackmailer. From what he knew, the parents seemed decent people.

With his helmet still on but the visor raised, Derek walked up to the front door. He quietly lifted the flap of the letterbox and began to slide the envelope through. As he did it was taken from the other side. He carefully lowered the flap, straightened and returned to his bike. At least that was done and would hopefully put an end to it. As he mounted his bike he glanced up at the bedroom window. Two lads about the same age as Paul appeared at the window and were watching him. Shit. Paul had friends there. That wasn't part of the deal. What had he told them? Snatching his phone from his pocket, he pressed Paul's number.

'Hello, Derek.' He could hear the cockiness in Paul's voice. The other two lads turned from the window so he guessed Paul had just entered the bedroom.

'What do you think you're doing?' Derek demanded. 'This was supposed to be our secret.'

'And so it will be,' Paul said.

'What have you told them?'

'Nothing.'

'So why do they think I'm here?' He could see them looking at him again, then Paul reappeared at their side, the phone to his ear.

'I told them you're my favourite uncle and that you like to bring me gifts,' Paul smirked. 'Don't worry, your secret is safe with me.'

Derek saw the three of them laugh. 'What secret?' he said with a stab of panic.

'I'm sure you don't need me to spell it out,' Paul said, and cut the call. He threw open the bedroom window. 'Night, night, sleep tight, Uncle Derek,' he called down.

'Love the kinky leather!' one of the other lads yelled while the third wolf-whistled.

Derek snapped shut his visor, started the bike and, gripping the handlebars, roared away faster than he should have done on a wet road. Anger and indignation seared through him. How dare those little runts treat him like that! Laughing at him! They were half his age; they needed to show some respect. He hated being laughed at. It reminded him of when his father had ridiculed him. He'd show them. He'd get his own back. No one messed with Derek and got away with it.

Chapter Twenty

'Flint's haunting me,' Beth said when she saw the Home Security logo on the alarm box at the rear of Mr and Mrs Saunders' home. They'd been called here to investigate a burglary while the homeowners had been out.

'But you can hardly blame Flint for this one,' Matt said. 'The alarm wasn't switched on, and it's almost certainly the cleaner. She had keys to the house, knew their routine, and has now disappeared, likely to have returned to her home abroad.'

Beth nodded.

'But I'll tell you what is odd,' Matt continued as they looked around the outside of the property for any sign of a break-in. 'That our Mr Flint installed the cameras in The Mermaid Massage Parlour that was raided yesterday.'

'Why is that odd?' Beth asked, glancing at him.

'The place was empty, not a girl in sight. Just Betty

sitting with a cup of tea in front of the television as if butter wouldn't melt in her mouth. She'd been tipped off.'

Beth laughed. 'Oh, come off it, Matt! And you accuse me of seeing connections where there aren't any! Half the force has visited The Mermaid at some point. It's almost on their rounds. Any one of them could have given Betty the nod. She looks after her girls and they like her. There's a lot worse.'

Matt smiled, a twinkle in his eye. 'I don't know what you're talking about, I thought it was a massage parlour.'

'Of course you did. Anyway, I think we're about done here, aren't we? They haven't even got a photocopy of the cleaner's passport. I'm assuming she gave them a false name so there's little chance of catching her or recovering the stolen goods.'

'I'll let you tell them that,' Matt said, and led the way into the living room.

Mr and Mrs Saunders were sitting side by side on the sofa, he comforting his wife. 'Did you find anything?' she asked hopefully as they entered.

'Nothing to suggest a break-in,' Beth said.

'So it was my cleaner.' Mrs Saunders sighed, pressing the tissue to her face. 'I can't believe it. I trusted her. She was so nice. She showed me photographs of her family and children. Her mother was very ill.'

'They always are,' Matt said sceptically.

'I'm afraid you're not the first person to be taken advantage of like this,' Beth said more sensitively. 'We'll try to trace her with the details you've given us but I have to tell you it's unlikely we'll find her.'

Mrs Saunders gave a little cry and dabbed her eyes. 'The jewellery box was my grandmother's. It had sentimental value. She knew that. She could have just taken the jewellery and left the box. That was so cruel.'

'The box was valuable,' Matt said bluntly.

Beth threw him a look. 'I appreciate how upsetting this is. I think that having your trust taken advantage of is in some ways worse than being robbed by a stranger.'

'It is,' Mrs Saunders agreed. 'I won't ever trust anyone again.'

'We're having extra security installed today,' Mr Saunders said. 'They're on their way here now. They're very efficient and the owner oversees the work personally.'

'Would that be Derek Flint?' Matt asked.

'Yes, you know him?'

'A little,' Beth said. 'We're finished here so if you could send in that description of the jewellery as soon as possible, we'll get it circulated. Hopefully we'll strike lucky and recover some of it if it's being sold here.'

'Thank you,' Mr Saunders said and stood to show them out. As she opened the front door a blue van emblazoned with the Home Security logo was parking in the road. 'Good. Prompt as usual.'

Matt and Beth began down the path. Derek saw them and hesitated, uncertain what to do for the best. As they approached he went to the rear of his van and busied himself with something inside.

'So we meet again,' Matt said, going up to him.

'Oh, hello,' Derek said, turning and feigning surprise.

'Business picking up then?' Matt asked.

'A little,' he replied, flustered.

Beth got into the car as Matt hung around Derek Flint, watching him fumbling amongst the various tools in the back of the van. Taking out a toolbox, he straightened and closed the rear doors. 'Done then?' Matt asked.

'I have to go to my clients. Did you want something?'

'No. Just saying hello. Have a good day then.'

Matt watched him scuttle up the path to where Mr Saunders was holding open the front door.

'Why does he always look so bloody guilty?' Matt asked as he joined Beth in the car. 'You'd have thought he'd pinched the jewellery himself, he's so bloody shifty.'

'It's you, you intimidate him,' Beth returned lightly.

'I hardly said a word!' Matt protested.

'You don't have to.' She fastened her seatbelt.

'Only those with a guilty secret have anything to fear,' Matt said, raising an eyebrow.

Beth paused thoughtfully, staring straight ahead through the windscreen at Derek's van. 'What say we pay him a home visit? See where he runs his business from.'

'What, now?'

'Yes.'

'But he's not there, he's here.'

'No, but his mother should be in. Paul said she rarely goes out. Come on, Matt; keep up.'

'OK, I get it.'

161

Chapter Twenty-One

Half an hour later, Beth and Matt stood on the doorstep of Derek's semi-detached house, waiting for someone to answer the bell.

'Perhaps Mrs Flint has gone out,' Beth said, stepping back to look at the upper windows. All the downstairs windows were covered by net curtains. There was no sign of movement. 'Weird that he hasn't installed CCTV here in his own home, don't you think?'

'Given his track record for it malfunctioning he's probably done himself a favour.' Matt laughed. He lifted the letterbox and peered in. 'Someone is in, I can hear a television. Hello! Anyone there?' he shouted. 'Police!'

'Matt!' Beth admonished. 'You'll scare her.'

'It's worked though,' he said, still looking through the open letterbox. 'She's on her way. I can see a pair of stout legs.' He straightened, releasing the flap with a sharp clang.

A few seconds later a safety chain could be heard sliding into place and then the door opened a few inches. A middle-aged woman with a pale complexion, grey eyes and a severe expression looked at them through the gap. 'What do you want?' she demanded sternly.

'Mrs Flint?' Beth asked.

'Yes. Who are you?'

'DC Beth Mayes.' She held her ID card to the gap. 'And this is DC Matt Davis.' He flashed his ID card. 'Can we come in and have a chat please?'

'Is it about Derek?'

'In a way, yes.'

'What's he done now?' she asked, releasing the chain.

'Nothing, as far as I know,' Beth replied, taken aback that this had been her first thought. The reaction of most mothers to having the police suddenly arrive would have been – *What's happened? Has there been an accident? Is Derek all right?* Not, 'what's he done wrong?'

'Come in before the neighbours see you,' she said, ushering them into the hall. 'They don't miss a thing here.'

With her short grey hair, plain clothes and stern features, she reminded Beth of an old-style retired headmistress.

'What made you think Derek had done something wrong?' Matt asked as they followed her down the short hall and into the living room.

'Because of the last time,' she said bluntly. Picking up the remote control she silenced the television. 'But you're the police, you should know that.'

163

'You mean the break-in at the garage seven years ago?' Beth asked.

'No, that was a misunderstanding.' She hesitated, clearly struggling to choose the correct words. 'The other thing,' she said awkwardly. 'You know, with that man. He hasn't done it again, has he?'

'Not as far as we know,' Matt said.

'Good. I'm glad he learnt his lesson. What do you want then?'

Beth flashed Matt a look. With an obviously homophobic mother it was hardly surprising Derek had resorted to a relationship in a public toilet, for it was doubtful he could ever bring anyone home. 'Can we sit down?' she asked.

Mrs Flint nodded towards the two-seater sofa as she sat in the armchair directly in front of the television, the cushions having moulded to her shape. Beth glanced around. It was a drab room at the back of the house, with faded furniture and little natural light. Only the television was newish. A cold room, isolating, that hadn't seen much fun and laughter, she thought.

'Derek has been helping us with an investigation into a spate of burglaries in the area,' Beth said. 'We saw your son at his office but he said he mainly worked from home. We were hoping to catch him in.'

'Not at this time of day, you won't. He's out working. But that would explain why he's been in such a bad mood recently.'

'Oh yes?' Beth asked, encouragingly.

'Derek takes his work very seriously and personally. He

164

can't stand it when he hears about people being taken advantage of and robbed. That's why he puts in so much time. He tries to protect people. He doesn't talk to me about his worries but I know when something has gone wrong. He's like a bear with a sore head.'

'Very commendable he's so conscientious,' Matt said.

'There's just the two of you living here?' Beth asked.

'Yes, his father left when Derek was in his teens. He took it badly but there was little I could do. Derek hasn't done anything wrong, has he?'

'No,' Beth said. 'Not as far as we know.'

'He won't be back until this evening and it's no good phoning his mobile. He switches it off while he's working. He's very strict about that.'

'A man with principles,' Matt said with an edge of sarcasm, and Beth threw him another look.

'Very much so,' Mrs Flint said. 'Derek has traditional values and principles and detests much of what goes on in society today. That's why he's so good at his job.'

'Do you help him with the paperwork for his business?' Beth asked.

'Good heavens no! He wouldn't trust me with that. It's confidential. When he's working he locks his bedroom door. I'm only allowed in during the day to leave his clean laundry on his bed.'

'So when he works from home it's from his bedroom?' Matt asked. 'Not down here?'

'That's right. I have the television on and he doesn't like watching the soaps like I do. And anyway, he couldn't fit all that equipment down here. He has the largest bedroom and I have the second.'

'I noticed you don't have any CCTV here yourself?' Beth asked.

'No. I wouldn't like to keep seeing myself on the monitor.'

'You could just have an alarm without cameras,' Matt suggested.

'Derek says we won't be burgled, we've got nothing to steal, and anyway I'm in all day.'

'You don't go out much then?' Beth asked.

Mrs Flint shook her head. 'Only to see my sister a couple of times a year.'

The sadness and darkness in the room seemed to grow deeper. Heaven forbid that I ever end up like this, Beth thought. It was depressing. Mrs Flint could only have been in her mid sixties – no age – but looked and acted much, much older.

'So Derek's room isn't locked now?' she asked.

'No, not during the day when he's out.'

'Would it be possible to take a quick look?'

'There's not much to see. All the computers are off when he's out.'

'Even so it might be helpful,' Beth said, aware they were on thin ice. They had no reason to be in the house, let alone search Derek's bedroom. She saw Mrs Flint hesitate before she hauled herself to her feet.

'But he hasn't done anything wrong?' she asked again.

'He's just been helping us with our enquiries,' Matt said relying on the euphemism.

Mrs Flint went first into the hall and taking the handrail began up the stairs, one step at a time. Clearly not in the best of health, she made hard work of climbing and had to stand on the landing for a moment to catch her breath. 'Derek's a good boy,' she said; 'just a bit odd.'

'Odd?' Matt asked. 'In what respect?'

'All of this,' she said, placing her hand on the door handle to his room. 'He never goes down the pub like normal men. It's all work, work, work. Occasionally he goes out on his motorbike, but that's it, really. Don't touch anything, will you?' She opened the door.

Matt stepped in first and whistled. 'It looks like mission control in here!'

'What does he want with all those monitors?' Beth asked as she followed Matt in.

'They're for his work,' Mrs Flint said as if it was obvious.

'But why four monitors and so large?'

'I don't know. You'd have to ask him that.'

The room was meticulously tidy; Mrs Flint had been right when she'd said there was nothing to see. The single bed with two pillows was neatly made, no clothes or shoes had been left out. All the drawers were closed and there was no paperwork – no letters or notes lying on any of the surfaces. The workstation was clear except for the monitors, keypad and printer. The computer unit standing beneath the desk showed no signs of life, only the Internet hub was showing a continuous blue light.

'If I didn't know better I'd say he'd been expecting us,'

Matt said quietly to Beth. Trying a couple of the desk drawers he found them locked.

'He always leaves it like this,' Mrs Flint said. 'What are you looking for?'

'Nothing in particular,' Matt said. He opened the wardrobe door, the only door that wasn't locked.

'I don't think you should do that when Derek isn't here,' she said. 'He won't like it.'

Matt moved aside some clothes and Beth saw Mrs Flint growing anxious. 'Come on, Matt,' she said. Then to Mrs Flint, 'Thank you, we'll be off now.' She began to the door.

'You need to come back when Derek is here,' Mrs Flint said, waiting for Matt to close the wardrobe before she left the room.

'Yes, we'll do that,' Beth said. Matt closed the door and they returned downstairs.

'Thank you for your time,' Beth said as they arrived in the hall.

'I'll tell Derek you were here. If you need to see him again tell him in advance so he can be in.'

'We'll do that,' Matt said, and let them out. 'You could almost feel sorry for Flint,' he said, as the front door closed firmly behind them. 'Not exactly character building when your own mother calls you odd.'

'Agreed. But how odd is he?'

Matt shrugged. 'Perhaps he just takes his work too seriously like she said?'

'Perhaps,' Beth replied thoughtfully.

Chapter Twenty-Two

'I don't believe you could be so stupid!' Derek thundered at his mother. 'After everything I've told you about client confidentiality. I don't believe it!' He threw back his chair and made for the stairs.

'I'm sorry, I didn't think,' she said, going after him.

'No. That's your trouble! You don't think.'

He should have realized sooner something was amiss. She'd hardly said a word since he'd arrived home but had waited until after dinner before telling him the police had been in his room.

'Not only did you let them into the house,' he fumed, flinging open his bedroom door, 'you brought them in here!'

'I'm sorry,' she said again.

He began frantically looking around for any signs that something had been moved or was missing. He'd been late home and hadn't come to his room before dinner.

'But what else could I have done?' she asked, gingerly taking a step into his room.

'Not let them in at all! You had the safety chain on when you answered the front door so when they showed you their ID cards, you should have said I wasn't here. Finished. Period. And told them to go.'

'I did tell them to go in the end,' she said lamely.

'But not before they'd had a good snoop around here.' He was testing the drawers now but they were all still locked.

'They weren't here for very long,' she said, 'and I was here the whole time. They didn't see anything.'

'How do you know what they saw?' he demanded, turning on her. 'If you don't know what they were looking for.'

She bit her lip, all signs of her usual abrasive and caustic manner gone. 'They said you were helping them with their enquires.'

'And you believed them!'

He took a deep breath and tried to regain some control. It wasn't all her fault; they had no business coming in here. But he knew from previous experience how sly and devious these detectives could be. They tricked you into saying things you didn't mean, got you to sign a statement or, as with his mother, had persuaded an old woman to let them in. 'And they definitely didn't say they had a search warrant?'

'No. I would have remembered. They just looked in the wardrobe.'

He checked his clothes, then the corners of the room and under the bed. 'I'll put in a complaint first thing in the morning,' he said, marginally reassured that nothing had been taken. 'You go downstairs now while I get on with my work.'

'I'll do the washing-up tonight then, shall I?'

'Yes, of course,' he said incredulously. 'I'll be busy up here.'

He watched her go, closed and bolted his bedroom door, then felt a pang of guilt. He shouldn't really have gone on at her like that but she could be so daft sometimes, and had given him a dreadful shock telling him the police had been here. His legs were still trembling and he felt hot and clammy. He needed to calm down or he'd give himself a heart attack. He was pretty certain they hadn't seen anything significant – there was nothing to see. But the fact that they'd been here at all, had broken into his fortress, infiltrated his castle and violated his domain made him feel defiled. He could picture the two of them – Mayes and Davis – snooping around, trying to open the drawers to his workstation. Just as well he'd followed his usual practice of locking away all his paperwork and switching off the computer at the mains before he'd left. The only access they'd gained was to his wardrobe and all they'd seen there was a line of neatly pressed clean clothes on hangers with his shoes paired beneath. Of course they'd have seen the monitors but given his job was in surveillance that probably hadn't struck them as odd.

Yet why had they come at all? Had Paul said something

171

to them? No good texting him to ask; he was unlikely to say if he had. Tomorrow morning first thing he'd phone the police station, speak to the most senior person available and get to the bottom of it. But for now he needed to regain control, concentrate on his work and get back in charge.

Trying to calm his racing heart, he sat in his chair before his workstation, switched on the power and drew in a deep breath. As he waited for the system to load he glanced around the room again. He was sure nothing had been touched or removed but to be on the safe side he'd fit a lock so the door could be locked when he left just in case they came back. His mother could leave his laundry downstairs or in the airing cupboard as that was the only reason she needed to come in.

The screens bounced into life and shone their welcome. The thumbnail pictures coming from the live streams arranged themselves across all four monitors and Derek finally started to relax. He took comfort from being with his friends and extended family again. They looked after each other. He knew their routines and what they were doing; pity the same couldn't be said for the police. He didn't have cameras at the police station so he'd no idea what they were up to. It wasn't for lack of trying, but one large firm had the monopoly on installing and maintaining the security systems for most police stations in the UK. He knew because he'd enquired once if he could tender for the work at their local station and was told that the CCTV in police stations never went out to tender.

Having only recently adjusted the rows of thumbnail images after losing the Khumalo contract, he now needed to move them again to accommodate his new client, Mr and Mrs Reed. Derek had been feeling rather pleased with himself for winning the contract when he'd come home. The couple were an ordinary family with two young children and had accepted his quote that afternoon because they liked his personal service and attention to detail. This had pleased him no end – the personal touch was what he prided himself on. There'd been a break-in at the house next door while the family had been asleep upstairs so they were naturally anxious to secure their property as soon as possible. The contract was a good one: installation of an alarm system, four CCTV cameras outside and one in the entrance lobby, with online access, of course. The camera in the lobby would come with the added bonus of a built-in microphone, although Mr and Mrs Reed didn't know that. Like all his other clients he would look after them well, make sure they behaved themselves and came to no harm.

He had a quick look at the images coming from U-Beat nightclub but nothing untoward was going on there, and, as far as he knew, the police were no nearer to catching Kevin's attacker. He doubted they ever would. Then, as he did every night, he began checking his clients, working through them in alphabetical order.

At first glance it appeared that Mr and Mrs Hanks were in the living room having a cuddle on the sofa. A very good sign. Hopefully, she had seen the error of her ways and had stopped inviting that nasty runt of a salesman, Riseman, when her husband was out. But when Derek enlarged the image it became immediately obvious it wasn't her husband she was with but someone Derek had never seen before. Another lover!

His anger surged. 'You cow! You two-timing slut!' His hands clenched so tightly that his nails dug into his palms. Bad enough to be committing adultery with one bloke, but two! The duplicitousness of some women was unbelievable. Did they have no morals?

That was it. Decision made. He couldn't stand by any longer and watch Mr Hanks being taken advantage of. He'd been on the sidelines for too long watching and monitoring, and now he needed to act. If he didn't take up his cause – that of the underdog, the oppressed and lied to – then no one else would. He felt Mr Hanks' humiliation as if it was his own. He knew what it was like to be deceived, ridiculed and laughed at.

And perhaps the indignation he still felt at the police violating his personal space was fuelling his drive for justice too. He needed to prove himself again, assert his authority – and what better way than by exposing Mrs Hanks?

Clicking on the Hanks' file, Derek saw that their preferred method of contact was by email. Launching the firm's email he clicked on the camera warning message, the same email he'd sent to the Williams: *This is an automated message to alert you to a possible breach of security in your surveillance system. Please log in and check your cameras now. If you have forgotten your password, click on the link below.*

He inserted Mr Hanks' email addresses into the *To* box and pressed send, a feeling of deep satisfaction surging through him. He was in charge and in control again – and he was helping Mr Hanks.

He'd no idea how far away Mr Hanks was or if he was in a position to check his messages. He hoped he was close and would be able to read and act on the message straightaway – then there'd be a good chance of catching her red-handed.

Mrs Hanks and the bloke were tonguing now, mouths wide open and lapping at each other like dogs on heat. Disgusting at their age, and all those germs. Derek instinctively wiped his own mouth on his hand. He could almost taste her foul breath just thinking about it. What some people found a turn-on he'd never understand. He'd watched the goings on in The Mermaid, sometimes with excitement but at other times in awe and horror. Sex with a bloke seemed preferable, but he banished that thought.

Mrs Hanks and her new lover seemed pretty settled on the sofa so were probably not expecting Mr Hanks home anytime soon, which was good. Lulled into a false sense of security. Derek briefly wondered what Mr Hanks would do when he found his wife, whom he lavished so much on, cavorting with another man. He was mild-mannered and self-effacing and never stood up for himself or to her. Derek had watched her boss him around, spend his money and then treat him like shit. Now, ironically, the security system she'd insisted on having to keep up with her neighbours was about to be her undoing. Wonderful!

Karma at its best. He just hoped Mr Hanks had the gumption to take the opportunity he was being offered and leave the cow.

Fifteen minutes passed, during which time Derek checked some of his other clients while keeping an eye on the Hanks' home. Mrs Hanks and her lover were still on the sofa groping each other, gradually removing their clothes and working themselves into a frenzy. He had little doubt that before long he'd mount her or she him and they'd copulate like a couple of animals.

But wait. As he looked he saw they'd stopped and were now grappling to sit up. Their faces registering shock and horror, they were looking towards the hall as they frantically tucked in their clothes, she doing up the buttons on her blouse and he the zip on his trousers. Derek quickly changed cameras and saw Mr Hanks letting himself in. Great stuff! Right on cue. Dressed smartly in a business suit, he looked as though he'd come from a meeting. But what was he carrying? What was that in his hand? Derek zoomed in. Something metal; he was raising it up to shoulder height, brandishing it like a weapon. It was part of the jack from a car, the large spanner for undoing the bolts on the wheel.

'No!' Derek cried and watched in horror as Mr Hanks entered the living room, his face red, eyes bulging, completely consumed by anger and hate.

Mouth dry and pulse racing, Derek changed back to the camera in the living room. Mrs Hanks and her lover were on their feet now as Mr Hanks advanced. His wife's lover said something but it was lost in the guttural cry coming from Mr Hanks. Like a wounded animal making its last attack, he rushed at the man with the metal spanner raised high, ready to bring it down. Derek gasped in horror. The man jumped out of its way and the spanner thankfully missed. Grabbing his jacket, he fled the house. Mr Hanks didn't go after him but turned to his wife, pure hatred in his eyes. He was usually so meek and compliant! Derek began to tremble.

'No,' Derek said. Mrs Hanks was backing away, backing herself into a corner as her husband advanced. 'No, don't! Don't hit her with that! You'll kill her!' But he was raising the metal spanner higher. Derek started in horror as Mr Hanks brought the weapon down – once, twice, the full force of it on his wife's head. She fell to the floor, a pool of crimson blood immediately forming around her.

'Jesus! What have you done?'

Time froze. There were a few moments where nothing seemed to happen, as though the couple were actors freeze-framed in a horror movie. Mr Hanks was still holding the weapon, his wife's apparently lifeless body on the floor, oozing blood.

Do something, save her, Derek willed. As he watched, Mr Hanks seemed to realize what he'd done, and his expression changed from hatred to shock to disbelief. The weapon fell from his hand, clattering onto the wooden floor as he dropped to his knees.

'Maggie? Talk to me. Oh, my love. What have I done?' There was no response, her eyes remained closed and the halo of blood pooled as the colour drained from her face. 'Maggie, I'm so sorry. Wake up, please wake up. I didn't mean to hurt you.'

Derek felt his stomach churn and rushed to the bathroom to throw up.

Chapter Twenty-Three

'Then what happened?' Beth asked, pausing again from taking Mr Hanks' statement until he'd recovered enough to continue.

'I called for an ambulance,' Mr Hanks said at last. 'Then waited by Maggie. She was bleeding heavily. I tried to stop it with tissues but they didn't do any good. I went into the kitchen, got a clean tea towel and pressed that to her head. Then I knelt beside her and held her hand, hoping and praying the bleeding would stop and she would wake up and tell me she was all right. But she didn't, she was so still and pale. I thought she was dying in front of me.' He stopped as his breath caught in his throat.

'It was a very deep head wound,' Beth said dispassionately as she wrote. She finished the sentence she was writing on his statement and then looked up at Hanks to continue.

'The ambulance seemed to take ages,' he said. 'I kept the tea towel pressed to her head and talked to her. I told her I was sorry over and over again and that she had to live. I willed her to keep breathing, I'd never have forgiven myself if she'd died.'

'No, and the charge would have been murder,' Beth said dryly. Hanks was obviously distressed and remorseful but that didn't detract from the fact that he'd nearly killed his wife. At least he'd admitted it, had waived his right to a solicitor and was going to plead guilty.

'I never meant to harm her,' he blurted, his brow creasing in anguish. 'Really I didn't. I loved her so much, I still do.'

Beth didn't write this down. He'd said it many times already: that he loved his wife, was usually even-tempered but had lost all control when he'd seen them together, and that he'd never meant to harm her and he was so very, very sorry.

'So while you waited for the ambulance you held your wife's hand, talked to her and kept pressure on the wound?' Beth prompted for him to continue.

Hanks nodded. 'I only left her side when the doorbell rang and I had to let the paramedics in. The police had come too. The paramedics went to Maggie while the police took me to one side and started questioning me. I couldn't tell them much; I was trembling and in shock. They wouldn't let me go in the ambulance with her. That really upset me.'

'They couldn't – you were the attacker – but you've seen her in hospital since?'

'Yes.' His eyes filled. 'They say she might have permanent brain damage.' Beth nodded and slid the box of tissues to within his reach. You could almost feel sorry for him if you didn't know that his wife had a fractured skull and was partially paralysed and unable to speak as a result of his attack. How much recovery she would make wasn't yet known. Yes, she was alive, but what quality of life she would have was doubtful.

'You told me earlier that you had some suspicion your wife might be having an affair,' Beth prompted. 'Why didn't you challenge her sooner? Why not sit down and have it out with her instead of letting your rage build up until it came to this?'

His gaze met hers, hang-dog and pathetic. 'I suppose I didn't want to know,' he said, shaking his head dejectedly. 'We'd been married for over twenty years. There were no children. We just had each other. I needed her and I like to think that in some ways she needed me. I didn't want my marriage to end. I'd have been lost without her. She could have done a lot better for herself than me.'

'What makes you say that?'

'She was an attractive woman, made the most of herself. She could turn blokes' heads in the street. It made me feel proud and grateful to have her on my arm. She was always the sociable one, far more than me. She knew how to talk to people . . . make them laugh; she could be very witty. She liked dinner parties, I never did, but I went to keep her happy. I'm the quiet type, content to come home after a day at work, read the paper and watch television.

I sort of knew I probably wasn't enough for her so I took the view that if she needed an affair to keep her happy and our marriage going, then as long as it was only an affair and she kept it quiet I could ignore it. I expect you think I'm pathetic, but I'd have gone to pieces if she'd left me. I'd have done anything to keep her. But when I saw the two of them together I just lost it.' Full of self-recrimination, he glanced up at the camera that was recording everything.

'And you said you didn't know the man she was with?' Beth asked.

'That's right. I've no idea. I thought she was seeing someone on a Tuesday afternoon, not a Thursday.'

Beth looked up at him questioningly. 'Why?'

'Telltale signs. A gut feeling, I suppose. When you've lived with someone a long time you pick things up.'

'Like what?'

He looked uncomfortable. 'Is this important?'

'Yes. It helps put the crime into context.'

He shifted in his chair. 'Well, for example, she always painted her nails on a Tuesday, and when I came home in the evening she was that little bit more attentive. She looked vibrant too, glowing; fulfilled, I guess, in a way I could never make her feel.'

'But you got it wrong? This didn't happen on a Tuesday afternoon but a Thursday evening.'

'I know. I never normally go out in the evenings without my wife, but a couple of times a year I have to attend a working dinner for our Japanese clients. Wives and partners aren't invited. I told her I wouldn't be home until after midnight.'

Beth nodded as she wrote. 'But you left the dinner much earlier? When you saw the email you claim was sent to you?'

'Yes. My phone was on silent and I felt it vibrate. I read the email, checked my CCTV as the email said, and left immediately. I told the receptionist to let my boss know I wasn't feeling well and I'd gone home. Then I ran to my car and drove back to the house. I was in such a state it was a wonder I didn't have an accident. I was so upset and angry. I realize now I should have calmed down first. But at the time all I could think about were those pictures of the two of them on the sofa in my living room. When I got home I parked out of sight of the house. I got out and took the metal spanner from the boot.'

'So you intended to do them harm before you entered the house? It was premeditated?'

'No!' he blurted with a cry.

'Yet you had the presence of mind to leave a message for your boss at the reception desk, drive home, park out of sight of the house, then quite calculatingly take a weapon from the boot.'

'I wasn't thinking straight. I suppose I wanted to scare them. Perhaps hit him. But I never intended to . . .' He stopped as his eyes filled. 'I loved my wife. I still do.'

Beth waited as he took another tissue. 'Then what happened?'

'I let myself in and went straight to the living room.

There they were, getting dressed. I remember going for him but missing. He ran off. Then I saw her with her blouse undone and her cheeks flushed from what they'd been doing. I just went for her.' His face crumpled. 'I'm so sorry. Really I am. I didn't mean to.'

'It's your wife you need to apologize to,' Beth said quietly. It was difficult to feel compassion for him having seen the state his wife was in.

'I have apologized many times. I don't know if she can hear me or understand. If only I hadn't seen that bloody email none of this would have happened.'

'Yes, I was coming to that,' Beth said. 'We've gone through your mobile phone but can't find any trace of a message about there being a breach of security at your home. The only text message you received that evening was from your sister asking if you wanted to go to dinner on Sunday, and you didn't read that.' Hanks looked puzzled for a few moments but didn't say anything. She held his gaze and felt a small satisfaction that she'd caught him out. He wasn't the victim of his wife's affair but a jealous husband hell bent on revenge.

Then he seemed to understand. 'No, the email wasn't sent to my personal phone but to my work phone. Would you like to see it?'

It was Beth's turn to look confused. 'You have it with you?'

'Yes.' She watched as he delved into his inside jacket pocket and took out the mobile phone.

'And no one here has asked to see this before?'

184

'No.' He began scrolling to find the email.

That none of them knew of the existence of the second phone was an oversight on their part to say the least. If there was an email, it could make a big difference to his defence. It would add credence to his claim that his attack on his wife wasn't premeditated but a moment of madness – a crime of passion – brought on by seeing her with her lover on CCTV. His sentence would be lighter.

'There it is,' he said passing the phone to her.

Beth carefully read the message, a sinking feeling in the pit of her stomach: *This is an automated message to alert you to a possible breach of security in your surveillance system. Please log in and check your cameras now. If you have forgotten your password, click on the link below.* 'So Home Security is the firm responsible for your surveillance?' she asked, suddenly feeling very cold.

'Yes.'

'What was the breach of security? The reason you had to log in straightaway and check your cameras?'

'I don't know,' he said despondently. 'We weren't broken into. I suppose the message was sent in error. But of all the nights for an error to have occurred. What a horrendous coincidence.' He looked at her in utter hopelessness, a broken man.

'It certainly was a coincidence,' Beth agreed, then fell silent. A recognition began to dawn as two half-formed thoughts came together. Coincidence? Chance? 'Mr Hanks, when you logged in to view your cameras on the Internet you presumably had to enter a password?' He nodded. 'Can you remember if you ever changed it from the default password? You know, the one that came with the system.'

He looked thoughtful. 'We must have done. Our password is the first two letters of our names plus the number ten. The guy who fitted the system suggested it so we would remember it. I wish I'd forgotten it, then I'd never have known of my wife's infidelity and we would still be together.'

'Indeed,' Beth said. 'I think we're finished here for now.'

Chapter Twenty-Four

'Flint has put in a complaint,' Matt said as Beth returned to her desk. 'The boss wants to see us at two o'clock sharp. We'd better have a good story ready.'

'About what?' Beth said absently, logging into her computer.

Matt looked at her over the top of his screen. 'About why we searched Derek Flint's house without a warrant, of course. Did everything go OK with Hanks?'

'Yes. We didn't search Flint's house.' She kept her gaze on her screen, scrolling to try to find what she needed. 'We were invited in by his mother.'

'That's what I told boss lady. But she wants to know why we were there in the first place.'

Beth nodded, her thoughts elsewhere.

'You're taking this very well.'

'Yes.'

Matt stood with a sigh and slipped on his jacket. 'I'm going out now but I'll be back well before two o'clock. Let me know what our excuse is going to be, preferably before we go in to see the boss.'

'Yes, see you later,' she said absently.

Beth had found the file she'd been looking for and was now examining the CCTV footage downloaded from the Khumalos' house, a copy of which he'd sent to them. The figure in black moving effortlessly down the garden, across the patio, then up the drainpipe and in through the back bedroom window. No hesitation or looking around as if he knew the layout of the house and gardens very well. Then reappearing and leaving by the same route, out through the gate at the rear and across the paddock where the Khumalos' daughter kept her pony. Beth ran through the recording again, then picked up the phone and keyed in Mr Khumalo's mobile phone number, hoping it wouldn't go through to his voicemail. Her heart was racing; adrenalin had kicked in. She knew this was a long shot, and it was just as well Matt wasn't here, although she doubted she would have shared this with him yet, just in case she was wrong. But there was no point in going back to the hospital to try to interview Mrs Hanks again in her present state. If she was right, then speaking to Khumalo should help.

'Hello, Khumalo speaking,' he said answering.

Good, she thought. 'Mr Khumalo, it's DC Beth Mayes.'

'Hello. Positive news? I trust you're phoning to say you've caught the person or persons responsible?'

'No, not yet, I'm afraid. But I do need to ask you something in connection with the enquiry. Have you got a moment now?'

'Yes, go ahead, although I've told you all I know. I'm sure it's not someone known to me, and my wife gave you the list of trades people who'd visited the house.'

'Yes, thank you, we have that. This is about the message that was sent from the security firm to your phone on the night of the incident, alerting you to the possibility that you had been broken into. Do you still have that message?'

'No, I erased it a while back.' Drat! They should have asked for a copy at the time, Beth thought, but there hadn't been a reason then.

'It was a voicemail message, wasn't it? Not an email or text,' she asked.

'That's right. As I remember the company gave us a choice – as most companies do now – of being contacted by phone, email or text message. I opted for the phone.'

'I don't suppose you can remember what the message said? My colleague and I listened to it on your phone but we didn't take a copy.'

'Not word for word but it was along the lines of: *check your windows and doors. If you find anything suspicious call the police.* But of course I didn't listen to it until the following morning.'

'No, I appreciate that. As I remember it was a digitally recorded voice, not someone speaking.'

'That's right. It was an automated message.'

189

'Triggered by a motion activator on one of the cameras, according to the firm.'

'I think so. I've got a new security company now.'

'Yes, you said you were going to make the change. Mr Khumalo, the password needed to access the surveillance online – did you change it from the default?'

'Oh, yes. Give Derek Flint his due; he was most insistent we changed it straightaway while he was here. It's obviously been changed again since with the new company. I can remember the old password if it's relevant.'

'It might be.'

'It was Anrokh10.'

'You've got a good memory.'

'No, it was the first two letters of my name, my wife's, and our surname plus ten.'

She felt a surge of adrenalin. 'Clever.'

'Yes, Flint suggested it.'

'But you've changed it now?'

'Yes. This new firm are very efficient, far more so than the old one. While they were checking the cameras they found that the one in the living room had an in-built microphone. What a waste of money, fitting it and not telling us! Not that we need it; my wife is here a lot of the time.'

'And you hadn't asked for a camera with an in-built microphone to be fitted?'

'No, I guess it was part of the package. But even it if had been switched on at the time of the break-in, being in the living room I doubt it would have helped identify the intruder. He didn't go downstairs.'

'No, quite. Well, thank you for your time. I'll be in touch if we have any news.'

Beth said goodbye and replaced the handset, trying to quell her excitement so she could think rationally. Two clients, different crimes, but where Flint knew their password. But what did it mean? She reached into her bag, took out a bottle of mineral water, slowly unscrewed the cap and took a sip. Was she on to something? Two examples weren't enough obviously; she needed more.

She took another sip of water, replaced the cap and set the bottle on her desk. Hand on the mouse, she steered the cursor to the Osmans' file with the details of the break-ins at their newsagent shop. They'd had a number of break-ins during the previous eighteen months – these small shops were easy targets – but the last one had happened after a second camera had been installed by Flint at the rear of the premises. She now ran the CCTV footage sent in by the Osmans. A hooded figure could be seen passing in front of the shop and then a minute later entering the back of the premises through a door that had been left unlocked by Mr Osman. The figure looked similar in build to the intruder who'd entered the Khumalos' house, although impossible to identify because of the hood. Mr Osman was insisting it was more than one person who'd ransacked his shop, although that was doubtful.

Picking up the phone again, Beth keyed in the landline number for the newsagent. It rang but no one answered and no answerphone kicked in. Perhaps Mr and Mrs

Osman were both serving in the shop. Cutting the call, Beth entered the number for Mr Osman's mobile phone. He answered on the second ring with a curt, 'Hello!' It was his manner; he always sounded curt.

'Mr Osman, it's DC Beth Mayes.'

'Who?' She could hear background noise but it didn't sound like the shop.

'Beth Mayes, one of the officers who visited you when your stockroom was broken into.'

'Yes, yes, of course, I remember. There's an echo here, I'm in the wholesaler's warehouse. Have you found the people responsible?'

'Not yet, but I need to ask you a couple of questions about the security at your shop?'

'Go on then. My wife is better at Internet things, but she will be busy in the shop.'

'They are straightforward questions. Are you still using the same security firm – Home Security?'

'Yes.'

'When the system was first installed, did you change the password?'

'What password?'

'You can view your system online, right?'

'Yes.'

'It will be password protected. You will have to enter a password to view the stream coming from your cameras.'

'Yes, yes, I know. We were supposed to have received an email when we got broken into but there was a problem and we didn't get it. Their fault. I told the insurance company and they're considering making an ex gratia payment as an act of goodwill.'

'Good. Can you remember if you changed your password from the default? These systems come with a password and it's advisable to change them straightaway. Did you do that?' There was silence. 'If you can't remember, perhaps I can speak to your wife later?'

'I remember, yes. We must have changed our passwords because it's the first two letters of our names and ten.'

'Who suggested that?'

'Mr Flint, I think, so we could remember it.'

'And you still have the same password now?'

'Yes.'

'I think it would be wise to change it. It's advisable to change passwords every couple of months.'

'I'll tell my wife. Is that all?'

'Yes, thank you.'

Beth replaced the phone, took another sip of water and tried to dampen her excitement. Stay with what you know, don't jump to conclusions, she reminded herself, a golden rule of good detective work.

The next case wasn't a break-in but the knife attack at U-Beat nightclub. Still unsolved, apparently motiveless, but the club surveillance had been installed and maintained by Home Security. She opened the file to look at it in a fresh light. Could there be a connection? Concentrating hard on the screen, she ran the CCTV footage from the nightclub on the evening of the attack. She stopped it, first at the place where the figure in black motorbike leathers and a helmet could be seen entering the alleyway, then again when he ran away after the attack. The figure was impossible to identify because of his leathers and helmet, but Derek Flint owned a motorbike and Matt had seen black leathers in his wardrobe.

Chapter Twenty-Five

'Come on! We've got to go,' Matt said. Beth started as he suddenly appeared at her shoulder. 'We need to see boss lady. Now. I'm back later than I thought.'

'Oh! Is that the time?' Beth gasped looking at the clock. 'I haven't even had lunch.'

'No time for that now. We're already five minutes late. I hope you've got our story ready.'

She grabbed the sheet of paper she'd been making notes on and followed Matt across the open-plan office, smoothing her skirt as she went. The DCI's office was through the double doors and on the right. Predominantly glass, DCI Aileen Peters could be seen sitting at her desk studying some paperwork. Beth knocked and she motioned for them to go in.

'Sorry we're late, ma'am,' Matt said straightaway. 'I got

held up at the jewellers that was robbed in the High Street, if you'll excuse the pun.'

Aileen Peters nodded, clearly unimpressed, and looked from one to the other as they stood side by side just in front of her desk.

'As you know,' she said, 'Mr Derek Flint has made a verbal complaint. I'm assuming that some of what he told me was exaggerated and that you didn't terrorize his elderly mother, nearly giving her a heart attack, nor did you ransack his bedroom. But did you search his house without a warrant?'

'No, ma'am,' Matt said quickly. 'Certainly not. We called at his home on the off chance he would be there. He wasn't, but his mother was. She was happy to let us in and then volunteered to show us his bedroom. It seemed an opportunity too good to miss.'

'But why? He has a conviction under the Sexual Offences Act but that was years ago. I also see he was brought in for questioning about a break-in at a garage but never charged. Again, a long time ago. I can't find anything on file that would give you two a reason to visit him now, both at his work place and home. He's claiming harassment, and based on the little I know I'm inclined to agree.'

Matt looked at Beth.

'Ma'am, we believe Derek Flint could be behind a number of thefts and incidents in the area,' she said. 'I've been working on it for the last two hours but haven't had chance to log it on the computer yet.' Matt's jaw dropped in astonishment.

'Go on,' Aileen Peters said.

'Well, ma'am, there appears to be a much higher than average number of incidents on premises where surveillance systems have been installed and maintained by Home Security, Derek Flint's firm. He gives the impression he's running a large company but there is just him and sometimes an apprentice whom he changes very frequently. Our suspicions were raised by chance at the Khumalo residence break-in. Then I went back in our records and found others. I'm up to eleven now where it's highly likely that Derek could have had some involvement in the crime.'

Matt was still staring at her with a mixture of awe and disbelief.

'What sort of involvement?' DCI Aileen Peters asked.

'I'm not exactly sure yet, ma'am, but in all the cases so far the clients could view their CCTV online, not just on a monitor, and Derek knew their passwords so he could log in too.'

'For what purpose?'

'He told them he needed to log in for maintenance but that's not true. All the other firms I contacted don't know their customers' passwords. If they need to log in, they let the customer do it. However, on all the systems Flint installed or upgraded he always insisted the client changed their password from the default to something they could remember. On the surface this appears good advice except Flint always suggested the new password was the first two letters of the client's names, which of course he knew, plus the number ten.'

'So he could log into their CCTV and see everything they could,' Matt put in.

'Yes, I understand that, thank you,' Aileen Peters said impatiently.

'All the clients I've contacted so far had external cameras and some had a camera inside their home too,' Beth continued. 'Flint never just fitted an alarm system without cameras, which is the most common choice. At least one of his clients discovered a camera with an in-built microphone they weren't aware of. I'm almost certain there will be others.'

'So you're suggesting that Derek Flint has been spying on these people and then robbing them?' DCI Aileen Peters said.

'Yes, ma'am, that's part of it. But there's more. I was originally working on a list of incidents – that I ran past you – where victims appeared to have been deliberately targeted in apparently motiveless crimes and where the assailant knew where to find them.'

'Yes.'

'I'm still checking, but I'm certain at least some of those can be linked to Derek Flint. I had the feeling there was something going on with all the coincidences but there was nothing to connect them to Flint then.'

'And there is now?'

'Yes, I believe so. Ron McKenzie is one example. He only went out one evening a month to a Freemason's meeting. While he was out he was broken into and his place trashed. I now know his CCTV was fitted and maintained by Home Security.' Beside her, Matt let out an almost inaudible whistle.

'But some of the incidents you were originally investigating weren't break-ins, but assaults that happened away from the house. The barrister, for example, that was run down by a motorbike. What was his name? Tom Murray.'

'Yes, ma'am; a motorbike mounted the pavement. A witness said it looked deliberate. Derek owns a motorbike.'

Aileen looked at them thoughtfully. 'I'm not seeing the connection here. There was no CCTV in the street where that incident happened, was there?'

'No ma'am, but if Flint had been spying on Tom Murray he would have known his movements from watching him and listening to his phone calls. And the same could be said of Mary Grey, the woman who was abducted,' Beth continued in a rush. 'Whoever snatched her knew exactly where she'd be and that she'd be alone. He also knew her name. She said she had no idea who her abductor was and didn't recognize his voice. He grabbed her from behind, bundled her into a van, blindfolded her, drove her around and let her go. I've spoken to her on the phone again just now, and about six months before the attack she had Home Security fit an alarm and two cameras. She accesses it online and the default password was changed to the first two letters of her first and last name plus ten.'

There was silence. DCI Aileen Peters held her gaze while Matt stood beside her, open-mouthed and incredulous.

'Who else have you on your list?' Aileen Peters asked.

Beth looked at the sheet of paper she'd brought in and read off the names, ending with, 'Kevin Brown, doorman at U–Beat nightclub.'

'You're including him?' Aileen Peters asked, surprised. 'He was knifed in the alleyway at the side of the club.'

'Yes, the club's surveillance system was upgraded a year ago and maintained by Home Security. The attacker seen entering and leaving the alleyway was dressed in motorbike leathers just like Flint owns. I haven't been able to reach the club's office yet to ask about the password but I will do.'

'And motive?' Aileen Peters asked. 'What could Derek Flint possibly have against all these people? You've included Hanks on your list but even if Flint had been spying on them all he didn't beat up Mr Hanks' wife. Hanks has confessed and it is shown clearly on the CCTV he was responsible.'

'That's right, but Flint could be said to have incited Mr Hanks to do it by sending him the email telling him to log in and view his CCTV – at the exact time his wife was on the sofa with her lover. Otherwise it's a hell of a coincidence. Mr Hanks only attends these work do's twice a year; at other times he doesn't go out in the evenings without his wife.'

'But what has Flint got against Mr Hanks or his wife?'

'I don't know yet. I need more time,' Beth said with a small sigh. 'But I'm sure there's a motive somewhere, even if it's only apparent to Flint.'

'Have you spoken to any of Flint's apprentices to see

if they know anything?' the DCI asked. 'Working with him they might have seen something untoward.'

'I have spoken to Paul Mellows. He was Flint's most recent apprentice, but he didn't appear to know anything. We can speak to him again if you like, and contact some of the others.'

'I think that would be a good next step,' the DCI said.

'I'd also like to obtain a list of all Derek Flint's clients,' Beth said. 'Then I can check them to see how many have been burgled or attacked after the security had been installed.'

DCI Aileen Peters nodded. 'Yes, indeed. I told Mr Flint that I'd phone him back once I'd spoken to you both. I'll request a list of his clients in a way that won't raise his suspicions. Once you have enough evidence, apply for a warrant to search his house properly and seize his computers. Make this a priority. If you're right, then he's highly dangerous and needs stopping.'

'Yes, ma'am. Thank you,' Beth said.

'Well done, both of you. Keep me posted, and please log all this; I don't want any more surprises.'

'Absolutely, ma'am,' Matt said. Having taken the few steps to the office door, he held it open for Beth to go first and then closed it again behind them. 'Why didn't you tell me earlier?' he said outside. 'I've been shitting myself all morning.'

Beth smiled mischievously. 'I only made the connections today myself. Hanks triggered it. He said it was a horrendous coincidence that his CCTV system sent a message in error on the very night he was out. That rang bells

201

with the Osmans and other incidents on the list I was investigating. You remember, Matt, the one you mocked and called my giant string theory.'

'I take it all back,' he said, returning her smile. 'And thanks. You didn't have to let me share the credit in there.'

'You're welcome. Now you can help me prove I'm right or you'll look as silly as me.'

Chapter Twenty-Six

Visiting times for the high dependency ward (HDU) at St Mary's hospital were from 2pm to 8pm. Derek planned to arrive at the hospital at 2.10pm, hoping no one else would be visiting Mrs Hanks. If there was anyone there he'd leave straightaway without even saying hello. He had a large box of chocolates tucked under his arm. He had wanted to bring her a bouquet of flowers, bright and forgiving; pink carnations, pale-blue hyacinths, red roses as an apology. But he'd found out while looking for the visiting times on the hospital's website that in line with most hospitals they no longer allowed flowers on the wards for fear of bringing in infection or triggering allergies. So he'd done the next best thing and bought her a box of chocolates. He hoped she enjoyed them.

He felt bad, really bad. He'd never intended Mrs Hanks should be physically harmed. He hated violence, abhorred it; even watching it on the television or Internet made him cringe and turn away. He didn't like to see people hurting each other, he wanted everyone to be kind. In his ideal world there would be no violence and every child would have two loving parents. It was OK to teach someone a lesson as long as it didn't involve violence; that had been his intention with Mrs Hanks. He had wanted to teach her a lesson for all the times she'd cheated on her husband. Never for a moment had he thought Mr Hanks would react as he had, attacking his wife with that large spanner and beating her unconscious. He'd always been so placid and accommodating. It had shaken Derek rigid.

Derek parked his van in the hospital car park and made his way in through the main entrance, hoping Mrs Hanks was making a good recovery. He knew from watching their CCTV that she'd been alive when the ambulance had taken her away. At that point, Mr Hanks had gone with the police, presumably to make a statement. Derek hadn't slept properly since, and not knowing how she was or what Mr Hanks had told the police was becoming unbearable. There'd been a small piece in the local newspaper, just saying that a woman had been found unconscious at her home in Princess Street and a man was helping police with their enquiries. There'd been nothing about how badly she'd been hurt, although being in HDU wasn't a good sign, he thought. When he'd telephoned the hospital to find out how she was, the nurse had said they only gave out information to the next of kin and he should contact her husband. Clearly that was impossible, so he'd decided to visit in person.

The sign next to the lift showed that the HDU ward was on the second floor. With a shudder he got in and pressed for Floor 2. He hated hospitals and usually avoided them. His mother had been in hospital for two weeks when he'd been a child and at the time it had seemed she'd gone away forever. He'd visited her with his father but not every evening. His father wasn't a good man and had resented having to look after his son. Derek remembered how unkind he'd been to him. He now associated hospitals with acute unhappiness and beatings.

The lift stopped and the doors opened. As he got out a woman stepped in. The HDU ward was signposted down a short corridor to his left. He stopped at the security locked double doors to the ward. If they asked who he was he'd have to say a relative. Summoning his courage – he hadn't come this far to turn back now – he pressed the intercom button and waited, the tic at the corner of his eye began to agitate. Nothing happened so he pressed the button again and without any need to identify himself the doors released.

He was in.

The clinical smell of the hospital ward immediately hit him and brought back memories he'd rather have forgotten, so he could have easily turned and run. He breathed shallowly to avoid ingesting the full smell of the ward and went down the corridor, glancing into the rooms on his left and right. Patients were attached to monitors and drips, some awake and propped up in beds of sterile white sheets, others asleep. None looked like Mrs Hanks.

'Can I help you?' A young nurse approached him.

'I'm looking for Mrs Hanks,' he replied, touching his eye to still the tic.

'Room seven, down there on the left,' she said, pointing.

'Thank you.'

She hadn't asked him who he was and he continued steadily along the corridor, then gingerly approached the open door to room seven. He looked in. There were no other visitors, a huge relief, but Mrs Hanks didn't look well at all. She was lying on her back, eyes closed, mouth hung open and a big bandage around her head. A tube ran from her arm to a drip.

'Hello, Mrs Hanks,' he said quietly, approaching the bed. Could she hear him?

There was no response. A dark purple and black bruise was spreading from beneath the bandage across her forehead and around both eyes. In contrast her cheeks were deathly pale, and she was unnaturally still. Her arms lay on top of the covers and were straight at her sides like a soldier lying down on duty, he thought. He'd never seen her so still. She was always on the move, far more vibrant than her husband; phoning her friends and arranging outings, shopping trips, visits to the spa, or entertaining them at home with a coffee or glass of wine. Even when she was alone she was busy, keeping the house nice – dusting, polishing and hoovering. She kept a neat and tidy home, he had to admit. Yet here she was like a corpse. He wished she could be that person again now. He'd have given anything to turn back the clock and undo the harm he'd done.

'I'm sorry,' he whispered. 'I never meant for him to hurt you. Really I didn't. If I'd known this was going to happen I would never have sent him that email.' He waited to see if she'd heard, but there was no reaction. Was she unconscious or heavily sedated?

'I've brought you some chocolates,' he said feebly, holding out the box. 'You'll enjoy these when you feel better. They're your favourites; I know because I've heard you say. I'll leave them here on your bedside cabinet so you can reach them when you wake up.'

He set the box on the bedside cabinet next to a jug of water and looked at her again. It was difficult to know what else to say and he found her unresponsive silence unsettling. When his mother had been ill she'd been sitting up in bed when they'd visited her, giving out instructions, not lying motionless. Only the steady rise and fall of her chest and the line on the pulse monitor showed Mrs Hanks was alive.

He thought about drawing up a chair but decided to remain standing. 'I'm sorry,' he said again, 'but it wasn't all my fault, you know. I didn't make your husband do this. He needn't have hurt you; that wasn't my intention. He should have packed his bags and left. That's what I intended, then you would both have been happy. He could have retrained as a nurse as he wanted and you could have seen your lovers.'

Suddenly she stirred and gave a small moan as if she might have heard some of what he'd said, possibly even knew who he was, but her eyes stayed closed.

'Can you hear me?' he asked. Nothing. 'Are you going to be well again?' She made a noise that could have been 'nurse', then groaned.

'Do you want a nurse?' he asked.

A small movement of her head that he took as yes.

He hurried out of the room and down the corridor to the nurse's station. 'I think Mrs Hanks wants a nurse,' he said, and without waiting for a response turned and headed off.

He'd seen enough and the smell and memories were really getting to him now.

But who was this in the distance? The man coming along the corridor towards him was surely Mr Hanks. He could tell from his outline, the way he walked. He saw so much of his clients that he often recognized them in the street. As he drew closer, Derek saw his grim, haggard expression and could have almost felt sorry for him. His eyes were fixed firmly ahead on the doors to the ward and he took no notice of Derek as they passed. *Well, it was your fault more than mine*, Derek told himself. *You lost control and battered her. If you'd just left like I intended, she wouldn't be in the state she is. You'll have to live with the consequences. Before this you were the innocent party, but not any longer.*

Outside, he breathed in the fresh air and tried to shake off the nauseating smell of the hospital: diseased bodies and disinfectant; it made his stomach churn.

Unlocking his van, he got in and sat for a moment trying to calm his thoughts. It had been unsettling being in the hospital, seeing Mrs Hanks like that, and then passing Mr Hanks on the way out. Although he doubted Hanks had even seen him, let alone recognized him. By the look on his face he was in pieces and barely coping, and even if he did make the connection it wasn't unreasonable for Derek to be there. He could have been visiting someone, or there on work – repairing one of the hospital's cameras. Yes, even if Hanks did recognize him he could come up with a reasonable explanation. Derek was good at explanations, covert operations and covering his tracks. That was what his work involved and he excelled at it.

His phone rang, making him start. The caller display showed a private number. Perhaps another new client? It wouldn't be the first time someone had seen his van parked and noted his contact details.

'Hello, Home Security, Derek Flint speaking.'

'Mr Flint, it's DCI Aileen Peters, returning your call.' Good, about time, he thought. He was looking forward to hearing that those two upstarts had been given a good bollocking. Hopefully even suspended. 'Is it convenient to talk?'

'Yes.'

'I've had a chance to speak to DC Matt Davis and DC Beth Mayes and they want to apologize for any upset they may have caused your mother. That wasn't their intention. The police spend a lot of time building good relations with the public and I am deeply saddened when I hear something has gone wrong. I hope you will accept their apology and pass it on to your mother.'

'Yes, I will on this occasion,' Derek said, his confidence growing from the apology and feeling he had the upper hand. 'But I want your assurance that they won't come near me again, either at my office or home.'

'It shouldn't be necessary to visit you again. They were at your home because they were under the impression that you ran your business from there.'

'I do. But why were they there? I've done nothing wrong.'

'They wanted to ask if you could give them a list of your clients and apprentices for the last five years: their names and contact details. It's in connection with some unsolved crimes in the area.'

Derek smiled. So he had managed to put them off his scent by telling them Paul had been responsible for fitting the surveillance at the newsagent and the Khumalos' house. Now they were investigating his other apprentices for unsolved crimes where he'd fitted the CCTV. Perfect. How easily the police were fooled.

'Yes, of course, I'll see to it as soon as I get home,' he said.

'Thank you, Mr Flint, that's much appreciated. You have DC Mayes' email address?'

'Yes, I do.'

Chapter Twenty-Seven

'Good heavens! Pinch me, I must be dreaming. A box of chocolates from my son!' Elsie Flint scoffed, but Derek could see she was pleased. 'Have you won the lottery?'

'No, Mum, it was just a nice gesture to brighten your day. I've taken on a new client.'

'Good for you. Dinner is ready. I'll dish up.' She placed the box of chocolates on her chair and went into the kitchen.

Derek had to admit that he was feeling pretty pleased with himself. What had started off as a shit-awful day with the Hanks saga looming over him had dramatically improved. He'd done the decent thing and visited her in hospital, convinced himself it wasn't all his fault; had thrown the police off his trail, and then just now he'd taken on a new client – Ms King.

Ms King had telephoned straight after DCI Peters,

saying she wanted to accept the estimate he'd sent her. She lived with her elderly mother and carers came in during the day while she was at work. Her mother was bed bound and Ms King had concerns she wasn't being looked after properly, so wanted cameras inside the house, upstairs and down. This was just the type of client Derek liked. He'd be in their home, living with them and part of their family, and it wouldn't be long before he could provide the information she wanted on the carers.

With so much positive stuff coming his way he'd felt a pang of guilt on the drive home when he'd remembered how he'd spoken to his mother after she'd told him she'd let the police in, so he'd stopped off and bought her a box of mixed chocolates. Unlike Mrs Hanks he didn't know what sort of chocolates she liked or, come to that, her preferences in most things. She was just there – his mother.

Five minutes later, hiding his disappointment at the chicken ready meal she'd dished up, Derek shook out his napkin, picked up his knife and fork and began eating, the weather forecast drifting in from the television in the living room.

'I could take you shopping at the weekend if you like,' he suggested magnanimously.

'Whatever for?'

'I don't know. Whatever you want. New clothes?'

'What would I be wanting with new clothes? Unless you're planning on getting married.'

'Some women like going shopping,' he said, trying to

ignore the slight. But her comment stung now as they always did, for they both knew it was highly unlikely he'd marry. She had a habit of meeting his suggestions with a sneer or a put down. He knew it wasn't what mothers were supposed to do. Many of his clients were mothers and he'd seen how they behaved. He also knew that many women liked to go shopping so it wasn't as ridiculous as she'd made it sound. Mrs Hanks liked shopping. He'd heard her arrange many shopping trips with her friends on the phone; retail therapy, she called it, and he grew sad again at the thought of her lying in that hospital bed.

'All those crowds,' his mother said, 'and the clothes are made for stick insects.'

'It was just a suggestion. Let me know if you change your mind.'

'I won't.'

The meal continued in silence save for the occasional chink of cutlery on china and the background noise coming from the television. Derek was grateful when they'd finished and he could wash the dishes, then escape to his room. As he passed the open living-room door he glanced in and saw his mother sitting in front of the television with the box of chocolates open on her lap, eating them one after another. She was clearly enjoying them, so why not accept them graciously and thank him? It wasn't a sign of weakness. He would never understand his mother, but then neither had his father.

Relieved to be in his bedroom, he bolted the door. He hadn't got around to adding a lock yet and the need seemed to have diminished. His mother had learnt her lesson and wouldn't let anyone in again, and the police were off his trail. He settled into his office chair at his workstation. The first thing to do was to email the list of clients and apprentices to DC Beth Mayes. Then he'd spend the rest of the evening with his clients. He might even finish off the evening with a visit to The Mermaid to relax him before going to bed.

The Windows software loaded and he opened the file on his apprentices. Just as well he was a conscientious and meticulous record keeper, he had all the details he needed and more to hand. Opening a blank word document, he copied in the names and contact details of all his apprentices. That was all the police were having; they could find out anything else they needed about the lads themselves. Then he did the same with the details of his clients. This took longer as there were many more of them. Once complete, he attached both files to an email and typed in the body:

Dear DC Mayes,

Please find attached the information that DCI Aileen Peters requested regarding my clients and apprentices. I would point out this information is highly confidential and must be treated as such and stored securely.

Yours faithfully,

Mr Derek Flint

Proprietor Home Security

He added his company sign-off and pressed send.

Now to business.

Launching the live streams coming from his clients' cameras, he relaxed back in his chair. The thumbnail images began to appear in their neat rows across all four screens. But what was this? Some were missing. There were blank spaces where they should have been. Leaning forward, he waited to see if they would load; perhaps the software was running slow this evening? But no more images appeared. Perhaps a reboot would sort out the problem? It was always the first option. He shut down the system and rebooted, mildly irritated he was wasting time. The Windows screen appeared followed by the thumbnail images but the gaps were still there, exactly where they had been before. Blast! He'd had more problems with his computer in the last two months than he'd had in the previous ten years! What the hell was going on?

He counted ten gaps in all dotted randomly across all four monitors. He clicked on a couple of the blank spaces, hoping the images might appear but nothing did. Could all ten CCTV systems be down together? It had never happened before and why hadn't the clients contacted him reporting a fault? Unless their systems had only just gone down? That might explain it. His heart sank. It was Friday and U-Beat nightclub's busiest evening. They might not open with their CCTV down.

Quickly bringing their file on screen, he keyed in the number of their office phone. It rang for some time before it was answered.

'U-Beat nightclub,' a man said gruffly.

'Sorry to disturb you. This is Home Security. Are your cameras working?' he asked anxiously.

'I think so, just a minute. I'm in the office, I'll check on the monitor.' A pause, then, 'Yes, they're all working.'

'Oh. I see. Good.' Derek thought for a moment. 'Has anything been changed today on any of your settings?'

'Not as far as I know but I've only just come on duty. Oh, hang on, there's a note been left on the desk.' Derek waited as he read the note. 'The password was changed earlier today, but that's all.'

That would explain it. 'Why was it changed, do you know?'

'No idea. I've just come on duty. Everything is working. Is that all you want?'

'Yes. Thank you.' He said goodbye and replaced the receiver.

The change in password had locked him out just like it had with the Khumalos. It wasn't a big problem; he'd pay them a routine maintenance visit and learn the new password. Firms were happy to tell him their login details for everyone trusted their security firm. Yet while this explained why he hadn't been able to access the cameras at U-Beat nightclub, it didn't explain the other nine systems that were down. Too much of coincidence that those clients had suddenly decided to change their passwords all on the same day! He'd once had two changes within twenty-fours after a television programme about hacking, but ten at the same time was unheard of.

He now brought up the Osmans' file – another one that was missing and whose contract he'd been lucky to keep after the last break-in – and keyed in the telephone number for their shop. It was answered on the third ring by Mr Osman in his usual brusque manner.

'Osman speaking.'

'Good evening, Mr Osman,' Derek said, at his most conciliatory. 'Derek Flint from Home Security here. Sorry to disturb you but are your cameras running?'

'As far as I know. Why shouldn't they be? You haven't got another system error, have you?'

'I don't know. Could I ask you to check please?'

'My wife will do it. She's on the laptop now.' Derek then heard him say, 'It's the bloke from the security firm. He wants you to check the cameras are working.' He waited. Mr Osman came back on the line. 'Yes, they're working,' he confirmed.

'Good. Have you changed your password?' He knew he couldn't ask too many questions as it would start to sound suspicious and further undermine his efficiency.

More muffled voices and then Mr Osman again. 'My wife changed the password after the policewoman phoned. They haven't caught anyone yet for the break-ins but she advised us to change all our passwords. She said it was good practice to change them every few months.'

'Yes, indeed, thank you. I'm pleased everything is functioning as it should be.' He said goodbye and ended the call.

Derek sat back for a moment and thought. Another

change of password but with a reasonable explanation. Even so that still left eight unaccounted for. He'd have to contact them all, go through them alphabetically, starting with Mr and Mrs Abbot.

He tried their landline and got no reply, then both their mobile numbers went through to voicemail. He didn't leave a message. Curtis was next and thankfully, he answered.

'Mr Curtis, Derek Flint from Home Security. Sorry to disturb you. I'm checking to make sure your CCTV is working. We've experienced a few minor technical problems today. I wanted to make sure your system was fully operational.'

'Yes, it's fine, thank you, but it's a coincidence you've phoned now.'

'Is it?' Derek asked, trying to keep the edge of anxiety out of his voice. 'Why?'

'The police phoned earlier about the break-in we had last year. While we were talking, the officer mentioned that we should change our passwords, so I did. I thought that's why you were calling, to check I had.'

'Yes, that's right. I was. Good. Thank you. Glad everything is as it should be.'

Saying a quick goodbye he hung up and tried to settle his racing heart. Coincidence yes, but not in the way Mr Curtis had thought. Three passwords changed on the same day, two after a call from the police. There was something going on here, but what? A knot formed in his stomach and he took a sip of water. There was nothing else for it: he'd have to try to contact all those whose cameras were down to see if they had changed their passwords too. Mary Grey was next and he knew he needed to tread carefully as understandably she'd become very nervous since her abduction.

He entered the number of her landline and it rang a couple of times before she picked it up. A pause, and then her timid voice: 'Hello? Who is it?'

'Miss Grey, it's Derek Flint from Home Security.'

'Who?'

'Derek Flint. I fitted your alarm system.'

'Yes, what do you want?'

'This is a courtesy call to check that your system is working.'

'Yes, it is. I'm watching it on my television now.' She hadn't been able to afford a separate monitor so he'd connected the cameras to a channel on her television. 'And you can see all the cameras?'

'Yes.'

'Have you changed your password today?'

'Yes. Did the police tell you?'

Derek felt an icy chill run down his spine. 'About your change of password?'

'Yes – Beth, that nice lady detective, phoned me about the investigation into my kidnap and said I should change the password on my surveillance system.'

'That's right.'

'Can you tell her I have done so?'

'I will. Why were you viewing your cameras just now when I phoned? Is there a problem?'

'No. I often look at them, it makes me feel safe.'

'That's fine then. That's what they're for. Take care.'

He said goodbye, set down the phone and stared straight ahead, trying to calm his thoughts. Was he overreacting? Becoming paranoid? Or was there something going on he didn't know about? Another password had been changed after a call from the police. This time he knew it was Beth Mayes who'd phoned. He hadn't thought to ask the others who had called them. Could it simply be a police initiative to keep people safe online? It was feasible, he supposed. The police ran crime prevention drives every so often – road safety, keeping children safe, saying no to strangers and so on. Was that what was happening? He sincerely hoped so.

The next client he phoned didn't answer but the next two did. Twenty minutes later he had succeeded in contacting another six and all had said they'd received a phone call from DC Beth Mayes updating them on the police's investigation and recommending that they change their passwords. He was now struggling to know what exactly to make of this.

It was perfectly reasonable that she should be updating the victims about their investigations into the crimes against them, and if they were running a campaign for online safety then it made sense to tell them to change their passwords at the same time. Yet it still seemed a coincidence – a big one – that this was all happening now. Perhaps this was the end of it and no more of his clients would change their passwords and disappear from view. Even so Mayes had created a lot of extra work for him; he'd have to visit all these clients now to gain their new passwords on the grounds of a routine maintenance check.

While he'd been making the phone calls a couple of emails had arrived in his inbox. The first was from a new customer thanking him for the 'great job' he'd done, which was always good to receive. The second had the subject as *security update* and he opened it.

> Dear Mr Flint,
>> Have you thought about updating your security?
>> Kind regards,
>> Watching You

His delight at receiving the first email vanished as his indignation and his anger flared. The bastards were still targeting him and telling him of all people to update his security! There was no unsubscribe link, which he knew was illegal. He closed the email but didn't delete it. When he had more time he'd examine the code behind the email and hopefully get to the bottom of it. But not now. Now he needed to spend time with his extended family and friends. It had been a stressful week and he needed their reassurance and comfort more than ever.

Chapter Twenty-Eight

'Absolutely nothing,' Matt said frustrated, setting down his desk phone again. 'I'm over halfway through Flint's list of apprentices and not one of them knows anything about his business, let alone saw anything suspicious. However, contrary to what Flint told us, he didn't teach them so well that they left to get better jobs. They all left because he taught them bugger all. They seem to have spent their entire time sweeping up, cutting wire, and occasionally being allowed to tighten a screw. I'll continue through the list, but I'm not hopeful. I take it you're having more luck?'

'Not too bad,' Beth said, glancing up at Matt over her computer screen. 'So far a dozen of the clients I've contacted changed their passwords on Derek's suggestion, all to the first two letters of their names plus 10. So we know for sure he could access all those systems. When I asked them to check their cameras for a built-in microphone, they all discovered at least one of their cameras had a mic. None of them had been aware of it.'

'But that doesn't prove he was spying on them,' Matt said. 'The mic might have come as standard as it does on most laptops now.'

'I know, I need more. The Mermaid Massage Parlour is the next on my list, although I'm expecting the same there.'

'It might be better if I visited them in person?' Matt offered with a suggestive wink. 'You know, the hands-on personal touch.'

'Just concentrate on your work,' Beth chided with a smile. 'I'm quite capable of managing this.'

She keyed in the phone number for The Mermaid and the phone was answered by Betty.

'Hello, it's DC Beth Mayes at Coleshaw police station.'

'Your lot were only here last month. I can't be due for another raid yet?'

'No. I need to ask you a few questions about your surveillance system.'

'OK. What about it?'

'I understand it was fitted by Home Security?'

'Correct.'

'Can you tell me how many cameras you have and where they are situated?'

'We have one in the entrance and one in each of the rooms.'

'Do you know if any of the cameras have in-built microphones?'

'Yes, they all do,' she said matter-of-factly.

Beth was completely thrown. It wasn't the response she'd been expecting. 'And the microphones are switched on?' She saw Matt watching her, intrigued.

'Yes. It helps keep everyone safe.'

'Does anyone else have access to your surveillance system apart from you?'

'Why?' she asked suspiciously.

'It's part of an investigation into online safety.'

'I doubt it, but there's no reason why you shouldn't know. Me and the guy who fitted the system have access to it.'

'Derek Flint?'

'Could be.'

'Is it?'

She sighed. 'Yes.'

'So he knows your password?'

'Yes.'

'Do the girls know he can watch them?'

'Of course. They don't mind if it keeps them safe.'

'Does he ever visit The Mermaid in person?'

Betty gave a hearty laugh. 'No love, of course not. He's a voyeur like so many of them online. They like to watch but don't touch. It's not an offence if the person knows they're being filmed.'

'I know. OK, Betty, thank you for your time.'

'Always glad to help the police,' she said with only a hint of sarcasm.

Beth replaced the handset and looked at Matt. 'Well, well.'

'I told you he was weird,' Matt said, aware of the gist of the conversation.

'Each to his own, I suppose. But I still need to prove he was spying on his clients to gain information to commit the crimes.'

Beth put a C and a tick beside The Mermaid Massage Parlour on her list, denoting that Betty knew the cameras had built-in microphones and they were in use. All the others had a C and an X, showing there was a mic but they weren't aware of it and it wasn't in use. She now phoned the next on the alphabetical list Derek Flint had emailed.

It was a long day but by five o'clock Beth had come to the penultimate name: Mr and Mrs Williams. Stiff from sitting at her computer, she stood and stretched. Matt had left an hour before to visit Paul to see if he could jog his memory. As the most recent of Derek's apprentices he was the most likely to remember something. She stretched again, took a sip of mineral water and returned to her chair, considering what she knew. All the clients she'd contacted so far had changed the default password on Derek's instructions and at least three had found in-built microphones they weren't aware of, but it still didn't prove Derek was spying on them and gaining information to commit crimes. Only his computer would reveal that and at present they just didn't really have enough evidence to bring him in and seize his equipment.

Beth dialled the Williams' house and with a stab of

horror recognized the address. It was the same family she and Matt had visited a few months back after a break-in had gone horribly wrong and resulted in Mr Williams being viciously attacked. They must have installed CCTV subsequent to the attack, but in choosing Home Security had they become any safer? Not if her suspicions were correct.

Julie Williams answered.

'Hello, DC Beth Mayes here from Coleshaw police station.'

'Hi. How are you?' she said, recognizing her name. 'Have you caught the person who broke in?'

'Not yet, I'm afraid, but we're still working on it.'

'We had the CCTV put in like you suggested. Even so, it was a long time before we felt safe in our home again.'

'I'm sure it was. How is Mr Williams now?'

'He's made a full recovery, thank you.'

'Excellent. I'm actually phoning about your security. Could you answer a few questions?'

'I'll try.'

'Am I right in thinking that you have used the firm Home Security?'

'I'm not sure, there's a sticker on the monitor in the hall. Shall I check?'

'Yes, please.'

She was gone a moment. 'Yes, it is Home Security. I remember now, a man called Derek Flint. He was very efficient and got everything done in a day. We were so relieved.'

'Do your cameras have in-built microphones, do you know?'

'I don't think so. Should they?'

'No.' Beth put a question mark beside their name. 'Did you change the password from the default – the one it came with?'

'Oh yes. Mr Flint was very insistent on that.'

'Do you still remember it?'

'Yes, it's easy, a combination of our names plus the number ten.'

'Thank you. Have you changed it recently?'

'No.'

'I think you should. It's a good idea to change passwords every few months.'

'I'll do it later when my husband comes in. It needs to be something we can both remember so we can log in and check when we're out.'

'Do you have to check it often then?'

'We have been doing after the business with our babysitter. We've got a new sitter now but I wouldn't trust anyone after that.'

'What happened with the sitter?' Beth asked.

'We caught her in our bed with her boyfriend.' Beth suppressed a smile. 'It was pure luck that we received the email when we did or we would never have known.'

'What email would that be?' Beth asked, her interest piqued.

'It was an automatic email sent by the security firm, but it turned out to be an error. Russ and I were out for a meal when we received it.'

Beth felt the hairs stand up on the back of her neck. 'What did the email say?'

'I can't remember exactly something like there may be a security issue and to log in and check the CCTV cameras.'

'Then what happened?'

'We did as the email said and logged in while we were still in the restaurant. We'd just finished eating. We saw our babysitter and her boyfriend go into the living room tucking in their clothes. We had no idea he was there. We went straight home. Later, when we played back the CCTV we discovered they'd gone upstairs and presumably used our bed. One of my kids woke and she just got ignored. Thank goodness we took Mr Flint's advice and had a camera in the house as well as those outside or we'd never have known.'

'That was very fortunate,' Beth agreed, trying to keep the excitement from her voice. 'What was the security issue?'

'There wasn't one. Mr Flint said that sometimes the auto alerts go off unnecessarily as the system is very sensitive to any disturbance. It was a lucky coincidence that it happened when it did.'

'Yes, a very lucky coincidence,' Beth said. 'Well, thank you for your time. I'll be in touch when I have some news.'

'Is that all you wanted to know?'

'For now. Thank you. And don't forget to reset your password.'

'I won't.'

Beth set down the phone and punched the air. 'Yes!

Got you! One too many coincidences, Mr Flint! Your luck has just run out.' She scooped up the paperwork she needed and went in search of the DCI. Surely they had enough to bring him and his computer in now?

At 6.30pm Derek logged on to his computer, and, to his horror, saw that virtually all four screens were empty. Only five live streams remained. For a brief moment he thought it must be a software problem for so many to be down, but then quickly realized that he'd sent Beth Mayes his list of clients. He'd been tricked. She was responsible; she must have gone through the list, contacted them and told them to change their passwords. Worrying enough, but what else had she said to them? What questions had she asked and, more importantly, what had they told her?

As he stared at the nearly blank screens, the Williams disappeared too.

Panic gripped him. His stomach churned and his throat closed. The police were onto him, they must be. Time was running out. He clicked the mouse to bring up the files and began deleting them. Rows and rows, column after column. Hundreds of documents, all neatly filed in order, his life's work. He'd destroy anything that could incriminate him. But it was taking too long so he began deleting indiscriminately, complete folders: information on clients, spreadsheets, photographs, live streamed videos. As he deleted them, they were automatically sent to the trash bin, which he emptied every so often. *Are you sure you want to permanently delete 1000 files?* the message box kept asking him. He clicked *Yes*. Only of course he knew it wasn't a permanent, complete deletion; nothing is ever completely deleted on a computer. All the files and folders would still be in the coding on the hard drive, and with the right technology they could be retrieved. But at least they weren't obvious now and deleting them might have bought him some more time.

He unlocked the top drawer of his workstation and removed the two portable hard drives on which he backed up all his files – more incriminating evidence. Plugging in the first, he began deleting files and folders, trying to wipe it clean. The front door bell rang and his hand momentarily froze. Don't panic, it's probably a charity collector or double glazing salesperson, he told himself, and continued frantically clicking and deleting.

'Derek! Door!' his mother shouted from downstairs. He kept going and heard it ring again. 'Derek!'

'Answer it, you silly cow,' he cursed, clearing the trash bin again. He heard the front door open and voices in the hall. Then footsteps on the stairs, more than one. He highlighted another line of folders and pressed delete.

'Police! Open the door.' He kept quiet. 'Derek, we know you're in there.'

A hard double rap and the doorknob turned and rattled, the small bolt keeping them out for now. Perspiring heavily, Derek continued to delete. They were trying to force the door now; the bolt wouldn't hold for long. In a frantic last ditch attempt he cleared the trash bin and switched off the computer. Another thud against the door and the bolt gave way. The officers poured in. He stood and turned to face them, four in all. One stepped forward and began handcuffing him.

'Derek Flint, I'm arresting you for aggravated burglary and grievous bodily harm with intent. You do not have to say anything. But, it may harm your defence if you do not mention, when questioned . . .'

And, as the police officer continued to read him his rights, he looked past him to his mother who was standing on the landing, weeping.

Chapter Twenty-Nine

'But why would I want to harm Kevin Brown?' Derek asked, perspiration glistening on his forehead. They'd been in the interview room for over an hour and seemed to be going round in circles. 'It's ridiculous. I wasn't even there!' He looked at the solicitor they'd provided, who'd advised him not to admit to anything at this stage.

'You tell me why you wanted to harm Kevin and the others on this list,' Beth persisted, tapping the crime sheet on the table between them. 'The motorbike in your garage, registered to you, is the same model as the one seen leaving the area after the stabbing at U–Beat nightclub. And the man caught on CCTV running from the alleyway was wearing motorbike leathers and a helmet identical to the ones found in your wardrobe at home.'

'Lots of bikers have them,' Derek said.

'Added to which,' Beth continued, 'the description given

by the witness who saw Tom Murray run down by a motorbike matches you too.'

'I've already told you I didn't even know the guy, apart from fitting his CCTV.'

'That's probably sufficient,' Matt put in, seated beside Beth; they'd decided that Beth would lead the questioning.

'What motive did I have then?' Derek asked. His solicitor cleared his throat as a warning not to be drawn in.

'Revenge? Jealousy? Paranoia? I'm not sure yet,' Beth said. 'But I will find out. Just as I'll find out why you kidnapped Mary Grey, held her hostage and terrorized her.'

'I didn't!' Derek squealed, the tic on his eye flickering. 'Why should I do that?'

'The thrill of it? Power? Hatred of women?' Beth said, holding Derek's gaze. 'I think you like to see women suffer. You don't get on with your mother, do you, Derek?'

'Who told you that?' he demanded.

'It's obvious,' Matt said, leaning forward and folding his arms on the table. 'Your father left when you were a child and you blame her. That's why you watch the girls at The Mermaid rather than going in person.'

'Stuff you,' Derek cried. 'You're not a bloody shrink.'

'Charming,' Matt said leaning back.

'Can we move on, this isn't really relevant,' the solicitor put in.

'The voodoo doll,' Beth said, glancing at her notes. 'You left it on Mr Khumalo's son's bed; I assume it was to get back at his father. What exactly had he done to you?'

'Nothing. I didn't. No comment.'

'Was it intended for the child then?' Beth asked repulsed.

'No, of course not! It wasn't me. I wasn't there.'

'The intruder knew the layout of the Khumalos' house and grounds in detail. So well, in fact, that he knew which bedroom the child slept in. You are one of the very few people outside their family who would have had access to that information.'

'Of course I knew the layout of their fucking house, I fitted their CCTV! Just as I did all the others on your list. It doesn't prove I committed any of the crimes you're accusing me of.'

'Not by itself,' Beth agreed. 'But forensics lifted a lot of DNA from the doll and I'm expecting some of it to match yours.'

Derek stared at her aghast and it was some time before he said, 'No comment.'

'Why did you fit cameras that had in-built microphones but never told the clients they had them, apart from those at The Mermaid Massage Parlour?'

'No comment.'

'I'll tell you why,' Beth continued. 'It was to allow you to spy on these people to gather the information you needed to commit the crimes. The circumstantial evidence is overwhelming. For example, Ron McKenzie only went out in the evening once a month and during that three-hour time slot his home was broken into and trashed. Far too much of a coincidence. A note was left that said "payback time". What was the payback for, Derek? What had he done to you?'

'Nothing. No comment.'

Beth took a breath but maintained eye contact. 'Similarly, you knew when Mrs Hanks would be seeing her lover because you had been spying on them for months. You sent an email alerting Mr Hanks to his wife's infidelity, for what reason?'

He paused, touched his eye before saying, 'No comment.'

'Then there is the matter of Mr and Mrs Williams' babysitter who invited her boyfriend in when she was supposed to be babysitting. You were watching them and emailed Mr and Mrs Williams alerting them, didn't you?'

'Well, she was supposed to be looking after their children, for God's sake!' Derek cried. 'Little Phoebe was only four.'

The silence in the room was deafening.

'Go on,' Beth encouraged.

'My client is due for a break,' his solicitor put in.

'In ten minutes?' Beth asked. He nodded.

'You were saying?' Beth prompted.

'No comment.'

'You're a man with very high principles, aren't you, Derek? And you didn't like it that little Phoebe was neglected – perhaps it brought back unhappy memories of your childhood – so you took it upon yourself to teach their babysitter a lesson. Just like you taught Mrs Hanks, Ron McKenzie, Tom Murray, Mr Khumalo, Mary Grey and all the others on this list a lesson.'

'Ridiculous! No comment.'

'OK,' Beth said, taking a different tack, 'let's go back

seven years to the robbery at Meekers garage. You remember it?'

His solicitor nodded at Derek to answer.

'Yes,' he said.

'The thief jumped the cashier at the exact moment she opened the safe to put in the day's takings. During the police investigation, it was discovered that someone had hacked into their CCTV so they knew exactly when to strike. You were questioned at the time as your firm installed the CCTV but there wasn't enough evidence to charge you. I think we can safely say that with what has come to light, there is now.'

'They are two different crimes!' Derek thundered, clenching his fists. 'Don't you know anything about the Internet? They were hacked. They were using the default password and someone hacked into their system. It happens all the time. I don't hack, I know my clients' passwords.'

'Precisely,' Beth said, pleased. Finally they were getting somewhere. 'So you were able to log in and watch them when you wanted for as long as it took to gather the information you needed to commit the crime – whether it was burglary, kidnapping or GBH. Your computer is with forensics now and you know as well I do that it will prove what I'm saying is true, despite you trying to delete the files.'

Derek stared at them, the colour draining from his face, then held his head in his hands.

'It's time for that break now,' his solicitor said.

Beth nodded and began gathering up the paperwork. 'Is a quarter of an hour long enough?'

'I would think so,' his solicitor replied, glancing at his client.

'I don't want a break,' Derek said, head still in his hands. 'I want to go home.' He looked up at his solicitor. 'They've got my computer; it's only a matter of time before they find out. I want to tell them what really happened so I can go home.'

'I recommend we have a break and you discuss this with me first,' his solicitor said, clearly worried.

'I didn't mean her any harm,' Derek said, ignoring him and looking at Beth. 'It was a mistake, and now I'm being blamed for all those things I didn't do.'

'You need to discuss this with me before you say anything further,' his solicitor reminded him.

Derek shook his head.

Beth waited, senses alert and tingling. She saw Matt give her the thumbs-up sign out of sight below the table. Derek was about to confess. But whether he told the truth or not was another matter.

A few moments passed and then Derek straightened in his chair, took a breath and steeled himself for what he was about to say. 'You're right, I did watch and listen to my clients and I have been doing so for many years. I did it to protect them, to look after them and make sure they were all right. I looked upon it as part of my job, my role in life. They became my friends, my family although they didn't know it. But I was only trying to protect them, I'd never harm them and you're wrong about my mother. I don't hate her, I love her, although she's a difficult woman sometimes.' His eyes glistened and he swallowed hard.

'I understand,' Beth said gently. His solicitor began making notes.

'There were no automated messages,' Derek continued after a moment, his voice unsteady. 'I made them look as if they were automated. I sent them as and when necessary, either by email, text or voicemail. It made me feel important, in charge and needed.'

Beth nodded as the solicitor wrote and the camera above recorded the interview. 'Going back, how did you choose your clients originally? One of your apprentices said that you didn't give quotes to everyone who contacted you.'

'The clients had to want cameras, not just alarms, and want their system online, otherwise there'd have been no point. I wouldn't have been able to log in and join them. I had to like them too. I wanted them to be good people, like families should be, which is why I got upset when they behaved badly. But I never intended Mrs Hanks should come to any harm.'

'So what did you expect to happen when you sent that email alerting Mr Hanks to his wife's affair?' Beth asked sceptically.

'That he would go home, pack a bag and leave. He wanted to retrain as a nurse and I was giving him the chance to leave and start a new life.'

Beth looked at him incredulously. 'And you didn't for one moment think that Mr Hanks might be angry seeing his wife of twenty years with another man?'

'No, he wasn't like that, not at all aggressive. He was always so meek and mild and never stood up for himself.'

'They're often the worst,' Matt put in.

'I thought I was helping him; honestly I did,' Derek said helplessly. 'I helped Mr and Mrs Williams and lots of my other clients. None of them got hurt. I can't believe what Mr Hanks did. I went to the hospital and apologized to Maggie – Mrs Hanks.'

'You've visited Mrs Hanks in hospital?' Beth asked, astounded. Matt and the solicitor were looking at Derek. The only person in the room who didn't seem to think his behaviour was odd was Derek.

'I took her some chocolates, her favourites,' he said. 'I hadn't realized she was so ill. She was asleep or unconscious, I don't know which, so I told her I was sorry and left the chocolates on her bedside cabinet. Do you know if she's had some?'

Beth stared at him, amazed that he could be so naïve. 'No, I don't know.'

'I passed Mr Hanks on the way out but he didn't see me,' Derek continued. 'He looked very worried.'

'Are you surprised?' Matt asked.

'It's not a good idea to go to the hospital again,' his solicitor said. Then to Beth and Matt, 'I will advise my client accordingly.'

'Thank you,' Beth said, then looking at Derek, 'How many of your clients do you think you have "helped", as you put it, since you set up your business ten years ago. Approximately?'

'I know exactly. It's all on the spreadsheet. I'm a conscientious record keeper. Ninety-eight. It was ninety-nine but I crossed off Mr Hanks after what happened.'

'Where is this spreadsheet?' Beth asked.

'On my computer.'

'Did you cross off McKenzie, Brown, Murray, Khumalo and Mary Grey too? Or do you consider you helped them?'

There was a moment's silence when Derek's jaw tightened in anger before he suddenly exploded. 'You're not fucking listening to me!' His fist crashed onto the table. 'I keep fucking telling you I didn't have anything to do with them! Kevin Brown was a nasty bit of work and needed to be taught a lesson, but I didn't do it. I was at home watching him on CCTV, so how could I be there?' His solicitor touched his arm to silence him.

'Your mother told us that you often go out on your motorbike late at night without saying where you're going,' Beth continued.

'I don't have to tell her! I'm not a fucking child!'

'We'll have that break now,' his solicitor said, and Derek nodded.

At home Elsie Flint had recovered from the shock of Derek's arrest and was now giving her third interview of the day. What had started off as a local news story had developed into national news, and a camera crew was in her front garden. She was standing outside her front door, wearing her best dress and bright red lipstick. Neighbours, many of whom she'd never seen before had gathered on the pavement to watch. She'd never been so popular and had risen to the occasion.

'So what sort of child was Derek?' the reporter asked, holding the microphone just out of sight of the camera.

'Quiet, shy, a bit of a loner,' she replied, looking directly into the lens. 'A nervy child. He didn't make friends easily. I think his dad leaving left its mark. He never really got over it.'

'And that isolation continued through to his teenage years and into adulthood?'

'It got worse,' she said. 'He never really had mates to go out with. He sits in his bedroom all evening with his computers.'

'Which the police think were used for spying on people and committing crimes. Ordinary people who'd done nothing wrong and were unaware your son was watching them – sometimes in quite intimate situations.'

'I never knew what he was doing up in his bedroom until the police came. They've taken away all his computer stuff. I don't know what he'll find to do in the evenings now. He doesn't like watching television.'

The reporter suppressed a smile.

'But it wasn't just watching people, was it, Mrs Flint? Bad enough he broke their trust by stalking them, but Derek is now being questioned in connection with a number of unsolved crimes in the area, including the stabbing of the doorman at U-Beat nightclub.'

'I suppose they think he can help them with their enquiries.'

'Or possibly the police suspect he was involved?'

'Do you think so?' she asked naïvely.

'Mrs Flint, as Derek's mother do you feel responsible for what he's done?'

'Good gracious no! The reporter from the *Sun* asked me that this morning. I told her I brought him up as best I could without a father. She wanted some old photographs of him so I found some. It seemed only right as she was paying.'

'How much have you been paid for your story?'

'Ten thousand pounds.'

A murmur rippled through the crowd of neighbours watching.

'So although you brought up Derek alone you don't feel any responsibility for his crimes?'

'I've already said no.' There were more mutterings from the crowd and some were now pointing at her accusingly.

'Do you feel sorry for the victims?' the reporter asked.

'I suppose so, although I didn't know them.'

'But your main sympathy lies with your son, despite what he is accused of?'

'Yes.' A roar went up from the crowd.

'Is there anything you would like to say to the victims of your son's alleged crimes or to their families?'

'No, thank you.'

The crowd booed and Mrs Flint looked surprised. 'You're as much to blame as he is!' someone shouted.

'I'm going in now,' she said and immediately turned.

The camera panned so she could be seen running

indoors as the reporter wound up with the crowd jeering in the background.

'As you can see, although Derek's mother doesn't believe her son has done anything wrong, her friends and neighbours here clearly think differently. Sandy Smith reporting for Channel News.'

Chapter Thirty

'We've had to bail Flint pending further enquiries, ma'am,' Beth said to DCI Aileen Peters.

'And he's admitted to what so far?' she asked rhetorically, looking at the report. 'Filming people inside their homes without permission. So a breach of privacy at least.'

'Yes, ma'am. And once forensics have finished taking apart his computer and running the DNA checks on his van, bike and office we'll have him for most – if not all – of the other crimes on the list.'

'But you won't be able to use anything his mother has said now she's sold her story to the press.'

'I know, ma'am.'

'Well done. You put a lot of work into this and it has reaped rewards.'

'Thank you.'

'OK. Go home now; it's gone seven. Get some sleep

over the weekend and on Monday I want you to join the team investigating the Kingsberry rapist. They desperately need another pair of hands. Matt will keep you informed on any developments with Flint. You're aware of the basics of the Kingsberry rapist case?'

'Yes, ma'am. Two rapes and five indecent assaults in the last nine months, all on young women in their twenties while they slept in their beds.'

'And the residents of Kingsberry are asking why he hasn't been caught yet. Familiarize yourself with the details over the weekend so you're ready for off on Monday.'

'Yes, ma'am. Will do, thank you.'

'Have a good weekend.'

'And you.'

Beth left the DCI's office with a frisson of excitement. It was always nice to be congratulated on a job well done in addition to the personal satisfaction gained. She collected her bag from the now near-empty office and went down the stairs to the car park.

It was a sign of the confidence being placed in her that she would be working on the Kingsberry rapist case and it would be a welcome change after all the weeks of tracking down Flint, although she'd still be involved until he was convicted.

His solicitor was already making noises about a psychiatric assessment. Mad or bad? It was the old argument and often it turned out to be a bit of both. Derek appeared deluded, possibly psychotic, and a certainly a misogynist who'd had an unhappy childhood and resented his mother. But, like many criminals with personality disorders, he'd also had the presence of mind to plan and execute his crimes. That they'd had to let him out on bail for the time being was worrying, although without any of his computer equipment he was hopefully now impotent to harm anyone else.

Outside the evening was still pleasantly warm and banishing further thoughts of work, Beth started her car, switched on the air con and headed for home. The weekend beckoned and she was looking forward to it: relaxing with a glass of wine tonight and a day trip to the coast with three friends tomorrow. Then a lie-in on Sunday morning while she read the files on the Kingsberry rapist so she was prepared for Monday. It would be a feather in her cap if she could add something to this inquiry; a fresh pair of eyes sometimes did the trick. After all, if she hadn't revisited the cases of Ron McKenzie, Tom Murray and Mary Grey and spotted the links with Derek Flint he would still be out there working his evil. But here she was thinking about work again! Reining in her thoughts, she concentrated on driving and the weekend ahead.

Chapter Thirty-One

Beth arrived in the office on Monday morning, refreshed from the weekend and ready to start, but knew straight-away something bad had happened. The air was charged. DS Hannah Grove, her immediate senior on this case, approached her.

'There was another rape in the early hours of Saturday morning,' she said. 'Looks like the same attacker but he's changed his patch. Mansion Gardens in Prospect Road, a small block of privately owned flats.'

'I know it,' Beth said.

'Lorrie Gates, twenty-five, a junior school teacher,' she continued, bringing Beth up to speed. 'She lives in a downstairs flat with her boyfriend but he was away for the weekend. Her attacker got in through her open bedroom window but it was security locked – which we're hoping will prove to be his downfall. We're checking with the manufacturers to see how many windows had the same key, and speaking to any workmen who had access to her flat. Nothing useful from forensics so far. As usual the rapist wore gloves and a balaclava helmet and used a condom – so no sperm DNA. However, on a positive note the whole building was covered by CCTV so hopefully it will have picked up the attacker going round the back of the building. I want all the CCTV they've got asap. We haven't been able to contact the firm yet. Collect it in person if you need to.'

'Certainly, Sergeant. I'll get straight to it.' Beth took the printout Hannah now gave her. What a start to a Monday morning but if felt good to hit the ground running. She'd already had a few thoughts about the case over the weekend, which she would share with her boss when she had the chance. Beth picked up the phone from her desk and looked at the number she was supposed to call in respect of collecting the CCTV footage.

'Serg!' she called standing and rushing to her. 'This phone is already with digital forensics in connection with an investigation into Home Security.'

'I thought the name sounded familiar.'

'This is Derek Flint's phone number; he's the owner of Home Security. It's a one-man operation. I helped bring him in. He'd been using the cameras he installed to spy on his victims. All his computer equipment is here too.'

'Now that's a happy coincidence. Two birds with one stone. I suppose it would be asking too much to hope he is our rapist?'

'He hasn't raped before that we know of,' Beth said.

'OK. Let me know if you find anything useful on the CCTV footage.'

'Yes, Serg.'

Beth returned to her desk, her thoughts racing. They were looking for a serial rapist, yet, had this crime been a stand-alone and taken place while Derek Flint was still able to work his evil, Beth would have almost certainly added it to her list. The similarities between this case and those Flint was accused of were striking – apart from the rape. The CCTV installed and maintained by him, the attacker aware of the victim's movements – that Lorrie was alone that weekend. When digital forensics examined Flint's online activity for Mansion Gardens would they find he'd been spying on its residents just as he had with all the others? But how? This attack had happened in the early hours of Saturday morning when Derek had been without his computer equipment for over forty-eight hours. A nasty feeling began to settle in the back of Beth's mind as she picked up the phone and dialled forensics to say she was on her way.

Derek Flint sat at his empty workstation, staring into space. No computer, no monitor, no portable hard drives, no van, no motorbike and no phone. The police had taken the lot. His life's work was on his computer, his reason for living all gone, as were his friends and extended family, and he'd no idea when any of them would return. He was a broken man and all because he'd tried to help people lead better lives.

A small knock sounded on his bedroom door. It was his mother again, trying to make amends. 'I've brought your dinner on a tray,' she said in a tiny, subdued voice. It was the third time she'd come up with his dinner, her way of apologizing for selling him out. She didn't attempt to come in though despite the broken bolt.

'I'm not hungry,' he said as he had before, his voice tight.

A few moment's hesitation and he heard her footsteps on the stairs, taking his dinner back down, probably to reheat and return again later. How many more times was she going to do it? It was almost comical, except Derek didn't feel like laughing. He was upset and angry with her. When he'd first arrived home she hadn't realized the damage she'd done in selling her story and talking to the media. She'd been glued to the television, watching herself being interviewed, channel-hopping so that as the news finished on one station she could see herself again on another.

'We're famous!' she'd said, more animated and happy than he'd ever seen her before.

'You silly cow!' he'd thundered. 'You've no idea what you've done, have you? Not only have you sold me out but yourself too.'

'I didn't, I just answered their questions honestly,' she said taken aback.

He threw up his arms in despair. 'You made me sound like a complete psycho and you a cold, heartless bitch. Have you seen what's on our front door? No, of course you haven't because you've been sitting watching yourself on that fucking television! Well, enjoy your five minutes of fame because you've destroyed us both!'

He'd stormed upstairs to his room where he'd remained since. He'd heard her scrubbing the front door trying to remove the spray-painted words: *Nutters Inc. Monster House Schizo ward*. He doubted she'd shift the paint; it was gloss. He'd have to see to it tomorrow; he'd have nothing better to do.

Ridiculously she'd made dinner at the usual time and called up to him that it was ready, but when he hadn't gone down she'd started bringing it up on a tray. Every half an hour he heard the microwave ping, then her footsteps on the stairs and her slight voice at the door. 'Derek, I've brought your dinner on a tray.' Yes, it would be comical if he wasn't so upset.

And angry. He was angry with her, and with the police for taking away all his computer equipment, stripping him bare. It was like a rape, he thought, the police taking all he had, going through his private records stretching back years and years. Emails – personal and work, files on those he knew, video recordings, notes he'd made on his clients, apprentices and others. His movements tracked, his innermost thoughts and feelings shared, scrutinized for evidence and probably ridiculed and laughed at. It shouldn't be allowed. Their behaviour was worse than the crimes of which he was accused.

And as bad and worrying as the police raiding his life and what they might find was that his friends and family were out there now, unaware that he couldn't join them.

Not only because of the loss of his computer but because they'd been persuaded to change their passwords by Mayes. Of course if you were a hacker the lack of a password didn't stop you. A hacker would have been in, viewing the live streams coming from the cameras in no time. But hacking had never been his thing – his modus operandi. He wasn't a hacker by nature; there'd been no need.

But then again the situation had changed, hadn't it?

He paused thoughtfully for a moment and then straightened in his chair. He'd played fair in the past and look where that had got him. His clients still needed him and he needed them. What had happened didn't necessarily mean the end for his life's work, did it? More a change in working practice. He'd no idea how long the police would keep his computer so tomorrow he'd buy himself a new one, a laptop would do for now, then set about hacking into his clients' CCTV, and anything else he fancied. Why not? What did he have to lose? With his knowledge of coding and the way computers worked online it shouldn't take him long to master the skills, and what he didn't know could be learnt from one of the hacking communities online.

A new world had just opened up and Derek's spirits lifted. The next time his mother came up with his dinner he accepted it and ate it in his room while making notes on what was needed for the following day.

Chapter Thirty-Two

Beth read the forensics report handed to her by Matt. He'd highlighted the salient points and was now standing beside her, his expression as sombre as hers.

'I don't believe it,' Beth said as she turned to the final page. Then again as she came to the end. 'I don't believe it. No DNA match with Flint? To the voodoo doll, his van, motorbike, office or any of the crime scenes! In fact no DNA match at all. How can this be?'

Matt shrugged. 'Search me.' There was silence as the enormity of what this meant hung between them.

Beth looked at him, her brow furrowing in contemplation. 'Unless Flint has an accomplice? Someone he sends in to do his dirty work. Flint plans the crimes and the other guy executes them, which would explain the lack of DNA.'

'It would,' Matt agreed, 'and if so Flint could still be

held accountable for the crimes, but as yet we have no evidence for that. All we can do him for at present is filming people inside their homes without permission and possibly – in the case of Hanks – incitement to commit a crime.'

Beth nodded thoughtfully. 'But for that to work we'd have to show that when Flint told Hanks to view his wife on their CCTV it was with the intention that Hanks would commit the crime. At present he's saying the opposite. He's adamant he had no idea Hanks would react in the way he did because he'd always been so meek and mild.' She let out a heartfelt sigh. 'What about the digital team? Have they come up with anything?'

'They're still trawling through Flint's computer and external hard drives. He deleted a lot of files so they're having to dig quite deep to retrieve them.'

Beth nodded. 'I saw them yesterday about the Lorrie Gates rape case. Believe it or not Flint was responsible for the CCTV covering the flats where she lived – Mansion Gardens.'

'You're joking!'

'No. And you know what, I've just had a thought that would add to the theory Flint had an accomplice.' She held his gaze.

'Go on,' Matt prompted.

'The CCTV footage I viewed yesterday of Mansion Gardens shows the attacker going around the back of the building and entering the flat. He can't be identified; he's wearing a balaclava helmet. But it definitely isn't Flint.

The person seen on the CCTV is slightly built, more like a lad in his twenties, which I'm now thinking could be Flint's accomplice.'

'That would work except we'd already seized his computer when the rape took place.' Matt pointed out.

'Yes, I know. But the digital forensics guy I spoke to yesterday said Flint had been watching Mansion Gardens for eight weeks prior to the attack. He's got all the dates and times Flint logged in. Flint could have set it up ready to go, and might even have been there out of sight of the cameras. He'd know the range of the cameras because he installed them. Derek Flint wasn't the rapist, but his accomplice was. A leap, I know, but it's all we've got and maybe not such a big jump when you know how much Flint loves to watch.'

'Something else occurs to me,' Matt said, warming to the theory. 'You remember the CCTV footage we took from the Khumalos' home?' Beth nodded. 'The person seen entering their house was thought to be a lad in his twenties.'

'You're right. I wonder how many times he features in the footage we have of the other crime scenes on the list. We need to re-examine them all.'

'I'll make a start,' Matt said.

'Thanks. I'll join you as soon as I'm finished here, and have told the Serg what we've found. She's going to love this!'

Chapter Thirty-Three

Derek greeted the new day with tempered enthusiasm. While not wholly forgiving of his mother's actions he was marginally more tolerant of her. He didn't bring up the subject of what she'd done again or actively avoid her as he had been doing the night before. She made him a cooked breakfast as a peace offering while he'd fetched a tin of paint from the shed and painted over the graffiti on the front door. He even found it within himself to say goodbye to her before setting off for the retail park and she'd called goodbye too.

Thankfully there were no bail restrictions other than he mustn't leave the country, although he had to use the bus as the police still had his van and motorbike. He hated every minute of the half-hour journey. All those people invading his personal space. Much better to keep them at a distance and view them through their CCTV. He was relieved when the bus pulled into the retail park and he could get off.

My Computer World advertised itself as stocking everything anyone could possibly need in computing, claiming its 'specialist staff' were on hand to help and advise its customers. Derek wasn't impressed. The assistant who intercepted him at the door soon proved he had no technical knowledge of the products beyond knowing the manufacturer's name, the size of the laptop and how many photos it could hold. Derek's patience quickly evaporated and he asked to speak to a more senior sales person, who turned out to know little more than his assistant. Derek sighed repeatedly as he talked to him about the products, shook his head and then finally snapped that the colour of the case was immaterial, and to leave him to choose a laptop for himself.

Two hours later he came out carrying a store bag containing the fastest, most reliable laptop with the biggest memory the store sold, two portable hard drives and a mobile phone. The return journey was more bearable as he held his precious purchases on his lap and looked forward to arriving home and getting started. Soon he would be on the path to retrieving what he'd lost and more. The omniscient, all-seeing and powerful protector of the innocent and punisher of evil would be back in business – despite the police.

Alighting from the bus at the stop nearest to home, Derek walked swiftly along his street, keeping his head down and away from the prying eyes of the neighbours. Thankfully no more press had arrived on his doorstep and no new graffiti had appeared. He took out his key ready, and quickly let himself in. Odd, he thought straightaway. The house was silent. Too quiet. No sound was coming from the television, and when he went into the living room it was empty.

'Mum!' he called upstairs. No reply. 'Mum!'

Where on earth was she? She hardly ever went out alone. With mounting concern he went into the kitchen and found a handwritten note on the work surface: *Gone to stay with my sister for a few days. Mum.*

'Oh, I see,' he said out loud, surprised. She stayed with her sister a couple of times a year but usually spent weeks trying to decide when to go, then asked him to buy her train ticket, take her to the station and see her to the correct platform. Never before had she just gone like this. He'd phone her later and make sure she'd arrived safely and was all right, but for now he had more pressing matters to attend to.

His stomach grumbled, reminding him it was well past lunchtime so he made himself a ham sandwich and a mug of tea and took them upstairs with the bag containing the laptop. In his room Derek set the mug and plate to one side and with mounting anticipation carefully unpacked the laptop and placed it in the centre of his workstation. He manoeuvred his chair directly in front. The laptop looked a bit lonely all by itself after all the equipment that had been there, but that would change over time. This was just to get him going again, the beginning, and his excitement grew.

Taking a bite of the sandwich and a swig of tea, he plugged in the laptop and watched it boot, a warm feeling coursing through his veins. He had to admit he often felt more relaxed and in tune with computers than he did with people. You knew where you stood with them. He typed in his name when prompted and five minutes later the installation process was complete and his new laptop was ready to go. He took another bite of sandwich and drawing in his chair, set the security level to high before connecting to the Internet. As he did, emails rushed into his inbox, uncollected while he'd been without a computer or phone. He ran his eyes down the list. Nothing urgent, he'd read them later. For now he wanted to get on.

Standing, he crossed to the wardrobe and took out a concertina folder from the bottom containing his clients' invoices. The police hadn't been interested in these and had left them where they were. More fool them, he thought. What they hadn't appreciated was that the invoices, as well as showing his clients' names and contact details, included the make and model numbers of the cameras he'd installed and the router they'd been connected to. In fact everything he needed to hack in.

Returning to his workstation, he typed 'hacking' into a search engine — always try the obvious first — and sure enough pages of websites appeared. Set up supposedly to help keep people safe online by showing how hacking worked, but detailing how to hack, assuming you had a bit of technical know-how. They included coding and even links to software programs that could identify your targeted equipment, with disclaimers stating that the website owners were not responsible for any misuse of the information supplied on the website. Derek smiled, found the software he needed and downloaded it, then took the invoice for Mr and Mrs Abbot from the folder. With mounting expectation and a little anxiety he entered their details and within seconds the IP address for their router appeared.

Now for the password to log in. He tried variations of their first and last names as the website suggested and eventually he struck lucky and was successful.

'Yes!' he cried, elated. He was once again looking through the Abbots' cameras just as he had before. If it worked for one it should work for the others.

Barely able to contain his excitement, he finished the last of the sandwich, typed their new password into a spreadsheet, then created a thumbnail of the live stream coming from their cameras, before returning the Abbot invoice to his file.

Now to his next client, Andrews. Same process, and having identified their router he found to his delight that they too had used a combination of their names for their password. Most people did, even when they changed it. With rising joy he entered their password, created a thumb-nail and set it on screen next to the Abbots, then backed up on the portable hard drives.

Just like old times, he thought.

The next password took longer to crack; they hadn't used a combination of their names. Eventually he found it was the name of their street plus 10. So he hadn't been completely forgotten! Creating another thumbnail he decided to spend a little time revisiting his old friends and family – the three he had so far. A warm feeling of contentment ran through him. It felt good, really good to be with them again. He'd only been away a few days but even in that time things had changed, their lives had moved on, and he caught up a little before going to the next.

Time passed, the evening drew in and more thumbnail images were added. The laptop screen was small compared with what he was used to. Goodness knows why the police had taken away the monitors, they didn't store information as the computer and hard drives did. He assumed it was out of ignorance or to stop him from working. Well, he'd certainly got the better of them now.

Evening turned to night and the natural light faded. He reached out and switched on the lamp. An hour later he stopped to use the bathroom and fetch a glass of water, and realized he hadn't phoned his mother. It was after ten now and too late; he'd phone her in the morning. It was strange without her in the house, he had to admit; unnaturally quiet without the television on, and of course he hadn't had dinner. No time for that now, he'd make up for it in the morning. There was always bacon and eggs in the fridge.

Returning upstairs he continued with his work and at 3am he'd reinstated all but four of his clients whose passwords he simply couldn't crack. Interestingly three still had the old password he'd suggested, presumably because Mayes hadn't been able to contact them. Or they'd ignored her advice or hadn't got around to changing it yet. He'd keep a close eye on them. Tomorrow was a new day and it held the promise of things to come. Why stop at hacking into his clients' CCTV when a whole world lay out there? Some of his clients had changed security company but that hadn't stopped him. But now for some sleep. He disconnected the two portable hard drives and then tapped the touchpad on the laptop to start the shutdown. He'd read all his emails in the morning. He was too tired now.

The screen began to fade but then stopped as a personalized pop-up advertisement appeared.

Hello Derek!
  We've just sent you an email on a product we thought you'd be interested in.
  Kind Regards,
  Watching You

What the fuck! Derek fumed, balling his fists. How dare they! He'd only had the laptop a day and already they were spamming him with their bloody advertisements. Well, he'd have them this time for sure. He was just in the mood. Wide awake now and shaking with fury, he pressed to reboot the laptop. As soon as it loaded he connected to his email and sure enough, at the top of the list of unopened emails, was one from Watching You. Sent an hour earlier, with the subject line: *A Product For You.*

He opened the email and stared in disbelief and shock. Not a promotion or recommendation for surveillance equipment but a photograph of two men, one sodomizing the other.

And worse, beneath the photo was the first paragraph of a newspaper article from nine years ago: *Local man, Derek Flint, pleaded guilty in court today to the charge of gross indecency after a member of the public reported him and another man to the police.*

The blood pounded in Derek's head and a strange buzzing noise filled his ears. Fear and anger coursed through him as he stared at the screen, trying to make sense of what he was seeing. Who exactly had sent this and why? What did they want? His first thought was that someone working at the company Watching You had discovered his past and was now playing with him, but he dismissed that idea – the tone of the wording wasn't funny, and whoever had found the online article must have dug deep. It was nine years old! And while he knew that nothing was ever completely erased from the Internet, he also knew it would have taken a lot of effort to find it.

His next thought was that a journalist had discovered the article while researching after his recent arrest. That seemed more likely. It might have gone unnoticed had his mother not broadcast his arrest to the world. But this wasn't from a journalist but a company – Watching You – that purported to be selling surveillance equipment. And of course he'd been receiving their pop-up advertisements and emails long before his arrest. Yet the content of the email wasn't that of a company pushing its wares. It was sexually suggestive and vindictive. Someone had unearthed his past and was now using it against him. What did they want? Was it blackmail? Hardly; the information they had – his past conviction and recent arrest – were already known. He studied the photograph of the two men, possibly male models, his heart drumming wildly. Someone was out to get him, but who – and why?

Chapter Thirty-Four

Sleep would be impossible until he discovered who was responsible and what they wanted. Derek drained the last of his water and typed 'Watching You' into a search engine to check what companies, if any, had that name. Up came pages of web addresses where those two words appeared in the description of the website but no actual companies. He looked as far as the fifth page but only found a film and a book with that title. He checked Companies House but there wasn't a company registered with that name, so whoever it was must be an individual working alone, which made him feel very uneasy.

It must be someone with a grudge who wanted to get their own back. Perhaps someone he'd upset? Obvious contenders were Khumalo and Hanks, but Khumalo didn't seem the type and had reacted by getting angry and changing security company, while Hanks would surely be too worried about his wife to engage in a prank like this? Added to which neither of them, as far as Derek knew, had the technical skills needed to mount this sort of vendetta. This was someone who was well versed in computing knowledge like himself.

With the email open, Derek selected *options* from the dropdown menu and a display box opened showing the coding path the email had taken, all the way from the sender to him. There were lines and lines of code, which to the uninitiated made no sense at all but to Derek contained a route map.

Very soon he found that whoever had sent the email hadn't used a virtual private network, which would make tracing them easier. Then, with the same ease he saw that the Internet service provider responsible for sending the email was a large firm based in the UK. He continued checking the code. If he wasn't sure of a piece, he copied and pasted it into one of the online code breakers run by hackers.

Dawn broke and finally he had what he needed: the sender's unique IP address giving the location of his computer. Not the actual street but the area of the town. To Derek's amazement the sender lived a mile away on the other side of town. The only person he knew living in that area was Paul Mellows, his last apprentice. He began to relax. Of course, it made perfect sense. Paul had been angry when he'd let him go and despite paying him off with £1000, he'd clearly decided to get his own back and wage this ridiculous war.

He sat back and allowed himself a few moments of satisfaction. He had what he needed, and knowing who was behind it reduced the threat. He wasn't afraid of Paul, the little runt. He'd go and see him later and make it clear he wasn't paying any more and if he continued to harass him or demanded more money – which Derek assumed was what this was all about – he'd have no hesitation in going to the police. He had nothing to lose now his illegal online activities had been discovered, but Paul had plenty to lose and Derek had proof of his previous blackmail.

It was nearly 5am now, too early yet to go knocking on his door and wake his parents, and he needed to eat first; he was starving.

More confident than he'd been for some time, he went downstairs, took eggs and bacon from the fridge and threw them into a frying pan. He warmed a can of baked beans and boiled the kettle, and began humming Mozart's *The Marriage of Figaro*, a favourite of his. The theme of the opera was of revenge, which seemed appropriate given what he had on his mind. He took his plate of food and mug of tea into the living room and sat on the sofa. He hardly ever used this room when his mother was here; she and the television dominated it. But now the television was off and her chair was empty it seemed to have become neutral territory, although it remained a cold, friendless room with little natural light and not one he'd want to spend a lot of time in.

Plate and mug empty, he left them on the coffee table, then rested his head back and allowed his eyes to close.

It had been a long night and soon a full stomach combined with exhaustion and he fell asleep.

He awoke to the sound of the neighbour's dog barking and looked at the clock on the mantelpiece. Drat. It was eight o'clock.

He immediately stood. He'd slept longer than he'd intended. He wanted to catch Paul before he left for work and he was going to have to use the bus again. Never mind, he consoled himself, if Paul wasn't in he'd leave a message telling him to contact him as soon as possible. He'd know what it was about, and would do as he asked if he knew what was good for him. Derek was in charge again.

Not wanting to delay leaving he quickly brushed his teeth but left showering and a change of clothes until he returned. He took his house keys and wallet from the hall table and went out the door, deadlocking it behind him. He walked swiftly along the street, keeping his eyes down and away from the prying busybody neighbours as he headed for the bus stop. A woman who lived a few doors away was already waiting but she turned her back when she saw him approach, which suited him fine.

Five minutes later the bus arrived and he went to the very back, which was empty and well away from the woman. He looked out of the side window as the bus began its stop-start journey, still feeling pretty pleased with himself. He had successfully been reunited with his friends and extended family all but three, had identified Paul, and later when he returned home he'd get down to the business of finding evidence to help his solicitor defend him as he'd asked him to. Against his advice Derek had confessed his crimes to the police, but he wasn't going to take the blame for every unsolved crime in the district simply because he'd fitted their CCTV. True, it was a worrying coincidence that so many of his clients had become the victims of crime but that wasn't his fault. He'd done his best to protect them but people did silly things and left themselves vulnerable.

The bus finally jolted to a halt at the stop he needed and he began towards the road where Paul lived. He knew his way. The first time he'd been to Paul's house had been when he'd collected him as a new apprentice and the last when he'd dropped off the second instalment of £500 hush money. He'd had two mates with him and they'd shouted abuse and tried to make him look foolish; well, the boot was on the other foot this time. Now who was going to look foolish? It vaguely crossed his mind whether Paul's two friends were in on this too, in which case he'd have them all.

He went up the short path, pressed the bell and heard it ring inside. A few moments later the door was opened by Paul's mother.

'I'm sorry to disturb you,' he said politely. 'Can I speak to Paul?'

'He's not here,' she said, eyeing him up and down.

'Can you tell me when he'll be back? I need to discuss something with him.'

'I can but who's asking?' she said. They'd never met but Derek knew who she was from his research.

'Sorry, I should have introduced myself. I'm Derek Flint. Paul used to work for me.'

'In that case, he's left something for you,' she said curtly.

'He has?' Derek asked, surprised.

'Wait there . . .'

He stared after her as she disappeared down the hall, not knowing what to make of it. Paul had left something for him? What on earth could it be? He hadn't known he was coming, had he?

Returning, she passed him a piece of paper. 'That's the address where he's working. He said if you came here to tell you to go find him there.'

'He was expecting me?'

'Apparently. What do you want to see him for anyway?'

'It's a work matter,' Derek said.

'Is that everything then?'

'Yes, thank you.' He returned down the path as the front door closed sharply behind him.

He read the address as he walked: 35 Bushmead Close, Cranberry Gardens. It was an estate, about a fifteen minute walk away. Slightly uneasy that Paul appeared to be one step ahead of him again, he tucked the note into his trouser pocket and began in the direction of the estate, deep in thought.

Had Paul assumed that sooner or later he would find out who was behind his silly *Watching You* prank and come looking for him? He must have done. It was the only explanation. It crossed Derek's mind as he walked that he could have asked Paul's mother when he would be back and visited him at home, but that would have meant more tedious trips on the bus and further delay. This nonsense had been going on for long enough; better to confront Paul now and put an end to it, then he could concentrate on more important matters like gathering evidence for his defence. He was pleased Paul had found another job and was working again, it should help sort him out.

Derek knew the location of the estate but wasn't familiar with its actual layout. He'd been asked to quote for work there a couple of times in the past but those quotes hadn't been accepted. Most of the Cranberry estate was social housing and part of it was due for redevelopment, so the residents had neither the money nor inclination to pay for surveillance.

Ten minutes later he arrived at the main road leading to the estate, hot and sweating from the walk. The day was warm, he should have brought a bottle of water with him but he hadn't expected to be walking this far.

'Excuse me,' he said, stopping a man. 'Could you tell me where Bushmead Close is?'

'Follow this road round the edge of the estate to the far end,' he said pointing. 'It's the last road on your right.'

'Thank you.' Derek headed off in the direction the man had pointed.

It certainly wasn't a very salubrious area, he thought grimly as he went, rows of identical, tired-looking terraced houses and three-storey concrete flats. The buildings would have been drab and unimaginative when first built but now with years of weathering and the accumulation of general muck and grime they were positively depressing. Quite a few appeared to be empty while many others had been badly neglected, with torn curtains hanging at grubby windows. It wasn't the sort of place Derek usually visited nor liked to be associated with. No, his clients were professional people who had nice homes and kept them well maintained.

The road ran right around the edge of the estate as the man had said and at the furthest point he saw Bushmead Close on his right. Another jungle of concrete flats, odd numbers to the right, he noted, and evens to the left. He crossed over and began along the right-hand pavement, the flats rising above him, pressing in, and even more suffocating and desolate in the narrow confines of the close. Some of the ground-floor flats seemed to be for the elderly with wheelchair ramps and handrails. A dog barked and a baby screamed from an upper floor.

He found that number 35 was in the last block at the far end of the close. He pushed open the outer door and went in. A flight of grey metal steps rose in front of him. Checking the flat numbers, he deduced that 35 was on the top floor and, avoiding touching the grubby handrail for fear of germs, he started up, his footsteps echoing on the metal steps.

What work would Paul be doing here? he wondered. Certainly not upmarket surveillance. Probably a more basic trade like plumbing or electrics; everyone needed those services at some time. Yet he would have expected to see a trade's van outside.

Arriving at the top floor he found that 35 was at the back of the building. It was very quiet up here and had an empty feel to it. No doormats, outdoor shoes or children's toys left by front doors, and no noise or cooking smells coming from the flats. The door for 35 was dark green and in need of a repaint like the others. The bell was taped over so Derek assumed it hadn't worked for a while. Lifting the small metal doorknocker, he gave a double rap. No sound came from within. He knocked again, this time more loudly. Silence, then he heard the door chain rattle and a key turning in the lock. Why would workmen lock themselves in, he wondered with a stab of unease.

But then the door was opened halfway by Paul, who was smiling. 'Hello, Derek, glad you could make it. Do come in.'

Dressed in black jeans and a black T-shirt bearing the *Watching You* logo, it was a moment before Derek knew what to say.

'So you're not going to deny it was you,' he began.

'Of course not.' Paul laughed and pointed to the logo. 'But don't stand there, come on in and I'll explain everything.'

Not wholly reassured but needing to know and have it out with Paul – the reason he'd come here – Derek cast aside any doubts. As Paul opened the door wider, he stepped in. The hall was very dark; he could hardly see a thing. All the walls appeared to be painted black and the small single bulb hanging from the ceiling at the far end gave virtually no light at all.

'Are you working here?' Derek asked cautiously.

'In a manner of speaking, yes,' Paul said, and closed the door behind him.

'What's that smell? Is something burning?'

'That's very perceptive of you, Derek,' Paul said cockily. 'We've just been smoking a joint. You can have one if you like.'

'No. You know I don't smoke.'

He heard the key turn in the lock behind him.

'Why are you locking the door?' he asked, spinning round.

'Just a precaution.'

Derek hesitated. He didn't like Paul's manner, it was unsettling.

'I think I should go,' he said, taking a step to the door.

'But you've only just arrived. Come on in.'

Derek remained where he was. Something wasn't right here. Smoking a joint when he was supposed to be working? And why was it so dark?

'We can meet later, another time,' he said and took another step towards the door. Paul stood in his way.

'What are you doing? I'm going now, unlock the door please.'

'No. I can't.'

'Why not?'

'You'll see.'

Fear gripped Derek. He made a lunge for the door but Paul grabbed him.

'What's going on? Let me out now!' He tried to grapple with Paul but he was younger, stronger and fitter. Derek was no match.

A chilling laugh came from the hall behind and Derek spun round. Out of the gloom a ghoul-like figure appeared, its face deathly white, sightless eyes staring at him, and fanged teeth stained with blood.

'What the fuck is this! Let me out!' Derek cried again, and with renewed strength managed to push Paul out of the way. He groped in the dark for the key but it had gone from the lock. He hammered on the door with both fists. 'Help! If you can hear me, call the police!'

A movement from behind him, then a sharp pain in his upper arm followed by a metallic taste, dizziness and falling. His arms flayed the air as he went down. Down, down, collapsing in a heap on the floor. The last thing Derek saw before unconsciousness engulfed him was the grotesque face of the ghoul leering over him, holding a syringe.

Chapter Thirty-Five

Where was he? Derek's head throbbed, his arm ached, and as he slowly regained consciousness he realized he couldn't move. His eyes flickered open and images swam in and out of focus. He was on his side on the floor, his arms tied painfully behind his back and his legs tethered at his knees and ankles. He tried to straighten but the cord binding his legs to his knees held him firmly. His mouth was dry; he could barely swallow or part his lips. He peered into the gloom. He seemed to be in a sort of cave. Large grey rocks rose up in front of him with dead bats caught in netting, and a life-size human skeleton was slumped against one rock. He must be trapped in a nightmare.

He groaned and swallowed the bile rising in his throat.

'I think he's waking,' he heard a half-familiar voice say.

'Where am I?' Derek whimpered, his voice rasping.

'In hell,' someone said, and laughed.

'Who are you? What do you want with me?'

'All will be revealed in time.' Paul's voice. Then a light tapping that he recognized as a computer keyboard.

The fog clouding his vision slowly began to clear and the nausea settled a little. He struggled onto his back. His knees stuck up, the cord that bound them to his ankles making it impossible to straighten his legs. The room was dark like the hall. He remembered now coming to see Paul at 35 Bushmead Close, a run-down deserted block of flats on the estate. But where was he now? Still in the flat? He supposed so, in a room that seemed to be decorated for Halloween. He remembered the ghoul in the hall and trying to get out of the front door, then the sharp pain in his arm.

'Did you inject me with something?' he asked, still on his back, his eyes adjusting to the dark.

'Yes, with a date rape drug, but don't worry, we didn't rape you. You're not my type.' It wasn't Paul's voice but it was followed by more laughter.

He peered into the gloom, then forced his head further to the left and saw Paul with two others, dressed in black jeans and *Watching You* T-shirts. They were grouped around a computer, concentrating on the screen. Only Paul wasn't wearing a mask. The ghoul he'd seen earlier in the hall had been joined by a zombie, the mask showing the side of a face slashed open with a row of rotting teeth and congealed blood around the wound.

'Why are you dressed like that?' Derek croaked, his throat parched.

No answer.

'Why are you keeping me here? What do you want with me?' he asked.

'Shut up! I'm trying to concentrate,' the zombie snapped, his gaze on the screen.

Derek struggled, pulled against the cord but nothing budged. It was knotted too tightly at his back. He stared around the room for any means of escape. Terror welled; he needed to get his bearings, but he couldn't. All the walls and windows were painted black so it was impossible to make out where they were.

'What is this place? Why am I here?'

'I thought I told you to shut the fuck up!' Zombie barked.

'I need to use the bathroom,' Derek tried. He did.

'Tough,' Zombie replied. He seemed to be the leader; he was the one issuing orders and working the computer while the other two stood either side of him, watching.

'You have no right to keep me here,' Derek said, making his voice as authoritative as possible. 'If you don't let me go, I'll tell the police.'

'Contradiction in terms,' the ghoul sneered. 'You can't tell the police if we don't let you go.'

Zombie stood, and for a moment Derek thought he was going to release him, but coming over he raised his booted foot and kicked him in the side. A cry escaped Derek's throat.

'Now will you shut the fuck up?' Zombie snarled, and returned to his chair at the computer.

'Just keep quiet and you won't get hurt,' Paul said.

'Yet,' the ghoul put in with a laugh.

Derek lay on his left side facing them, his ribs throbbing from the kick. What the hell was going on? What were they doing and why was he here? Clearly he'd been lured into a trap. Paul wasn't working here and why were they wearing those masks and in a room that looked like Halloween? He really did need to use the bathroom, urgently.

He caught glimpses of the screen between them. It looked like they were tracking using street CCTV, but he couldn't be sure. Perhaps it was some sort of sophisticated online game, there were plenty on the market, but that didn't explain what had happened to him. Zombie and Ghoul could have been the same lads who'd been with Paul when he'd dropped off the second £500, Derek thought. They were the same build and their voices sounded familiar, but he couldn't be sure. Had Paul told them about the money? Was that what all this was about? Blackmail? If so it would make some sense.

'Do you want money?' he asked. 'Is that why I'm here?' No one answered; they were concentrating on the screen. 'It's no good trying to blackmail me if that's the reason; the police know everything about me.'

'What the fuck is he rambling on about?' Zombie demanded.

'I've no idea.' Paul shrugged.

'The police know all about what I've been doing with my cameras so you can't blackmail me. But I'll give you money, if that's what you want to let me go.'

'Shut him up before I do,' Zombie hissed at Paul.

Paul came over. 'Be quiet, Derek, do as you're told.' He returned to stand beside Zombie at the computer.

It was almost farcical, Derek thought, as if he was caught up in some macabre game or play. But there was no humour in what had happened to him: injected to render him unconscious, then tied up and assaulted. Perhaps they were all mad?

He couldn't just lie here and do nothing, so he allowed a few minutes and then tried a different tack.

'My mother hasn't got any money if you're thinking of holding me for ransom. And she's disabled. She needs me. If you let me go I won't tell anyone I was here. It will be our secret.' He knew he was babbling but he was scared and he could hear the tremor in his voice.

No one answered; they were all too engrossed in whatever they were watching on the screen. Derek's anger and terror rose. 'You can't keep me here!' he shouted. Then immediately regretted it.

Zombie jumped up, sending his chair crashing to the floor. 'I thought I told you to shut the fuck up!' he shouted, advancing towards him. Through the slits in his mask Derek caught a glimpse of the hatred in his eyes as he towered over him and raised his boot. He cried out in pain and tried to roll away as he kicked him once, twice, three times. Then came a sickening thud to his head and Derek passed out.

When he awoke, the room was empty and with horror and shame he realized he'd wet himself.

Chapter Thirty-Six

'It always feels hotter in the south,' Derek's mother remarked as she climbed out of the cab.

'Spoken like a true southerner,' the cab driver returned, taking her case from the boot.

She gave him the fare plus a tip.

'Thanking you,' he said. 'Do you want a lift in with your case?'

'No, it's only light. I can manage, thank you.'

'Enjoy the rest of your day then,' he said, and returned to his cab.

Front door key ready, Elsie Flint pushed open their garden gate. Taking a cab from the station had been a real luxury; she couldn't remember the last time she'd caught a cab, perhaps never. Neither had she ever just upped and left before but she'd needed to get away after all the trouble she'd caused. Clearly Derek was still annoyed with her because he hadn't even telephoned her. But the three days she'd spent with her sister had done her good. She felt revitalized and more confident. It had been a complete change of scenery and mixing with others had helped, although three days had been enough. Her sister had quizzed her about what exactly Derek had been up to, to the point where she'd had to tell her firmly that she didn't know any more than what had been reported in the news. Added to that, her sister had moved since her last visit and now lived in block of retirement flats that had a busy social scene: organized activities in the communal lounge and neighbours stopping by for coffee. It wasn't what Elsie was used to so while she'd enjoyed it, a few days had been sufficient.

Her front door was double-locked so Derek must be out. Elsie let herself in and set down her case in the hall for unpacking later. She picked up the mail scattered across the floor and tucked it on the hall table, again for seeing to later. Derek must have gone out early before the mail had arrived, suggesting he was working again, which was a good sign. Presumably the police had given him back his van, motorbike and computer, so he should be in a better mood when he returned. First things first, a cup of tea, then unpack and catch up on the television she'd missed. There'd been no time for watching television at her sister's and she didn't like soaps anyway. Slipping off her jacket, Elsie hooked it on the hall stand and went into the kitchen.

A frying pan with a thick layer of white bacon fat and

a saucepan containing dried baked bean sauce greeted her. She tutted as she carried them to the sink; Derek might have a least put them in to soak. She made tea and took it through to the living room where she found his dirty plate and mug on the coffee table. Admittedly he didn't know she was coming home today but he might have cleared up. Sometimes it was like having a teenager in the house, having to clean up after him. Never able to relax with dirty dishes in view, she took the plate and mug into the kitchen and left them in the sink, then returned and made herself comfortable in front of the television, mug of tea in her hand. It was good to be back. She'd phone her sister to say she'd got home safely just as soon as she'd caught up on EastEnders.

An hour later the clock on the mantelpiece struck six o'clock and Elsie heaved herself out of the chair and went into the hall to phone her sister. Why they didn't have a phone in the living room like her sister did, she'd no idea. Her sister's answerphone cut in so she left a message saying she was home and thanking her for a nice time. Then she took her case upstairs to set about unpacking. Derek would be home for his dinner before long and she'd need to check what was still in the fridge and freezer as she doubted he'd restocked it while she'd been away. She and her sister had ordered a Chinese takeaway one night, which her sister did at least once a week. She and Derek never had takeaways; perhaps she'd suggest it for tonight. But then again Derek was very conservative and set in his ways when it came to food, indeed as he was in most things so probably wouldn't like Chinese.

Elsie returned her empty case to under the bed, dropped her dirty washing in the laundry basket in the bathroom and went downstairs. Opening the freezer door, she found to her small surprise it was still fully stocked; none of the meat or ready meals she'd left for him had been touched. She took out a steak pie for them to have and then looked in the fridge to see what vegetables were left. All of them, and the cheese, yogurts and cold meats were untouched too. What had he been living on? A couple of eggs were missing and a few rashers of bacon, hence the dirty pans. She looked in the bread bin and saw the packet of six rolls and the small loaf she'd left for him for sandwiches were untouched. Her puzzled expression gave way to a wry smile. Was it possible Derek had finally found himself a girlfriend and he'd been seeing her while she'd been away? Well, well, who would have thought it? She couldn't think of any other rational explanation as to why he hadn't been eating here, and if she was right she couldn't wait to tell her sister. Derek was normal after all!

At seven o'clock there was still no sign of him so a little miffed, Elsie sat at the table to eat alone. Once she'd finished she washed the dishes and returned to the living room and the television. An hour passed and when Derek still hadn't arrived home or thought to phone, Elsie was more annoyed than worried. He was probably with a client or his new girlfriend. If he was going to eat with her then she needed to know so she didn't waste any more good food. His mobile number was in their address book on the hall table. Elsie seldom needed to use it as Derek was such a creature of habit. Silencing the television, she went into the hall, found his number and keyed it in. A recorded message said straightaway: 'This phone is switched off, please try again later.'

Strange, she thought. She'd never known Derek to switch off his phone before. If he was at work it went through to voicemail. Must be with the girlfriend. She'd leave it half an hour and try again.

Picking up the pile of mail from the hall table, Elsie now took it into the living room to sort through. There was quite a lot and as usual most of it was for Derek, mainly circulars in connection with his work. She set his mail in a pile to one side and opened the first of her letters. It was from her doctor reminding her it was time for another well-woman check-up and to phone the surgery to make an appointment. The second was an electricity bill which she put in Derek's pile; although it was addressed to her he took care of all the bills and paid them online. The last of hers was a postcard with a photograph of a dog on the front, its large doleful eyes gazing out imploringly. Another appeal from the animal charity she supported. She turned it over and read the dog's tale of woe and that they were asking for another £15. Her gaze slid across the card to the pretty commemorative stamp with her address below. It was a wonder the card had been delivered at all, the franking machine had missed the stamp and obliterated the first two lines of the address.

It was then she noticed that the card had been stamped three days before – the day she'd left. Why had Derek left it lying on the floor all this time? He was usually very particular about opening the mail each day. She checked the dates on the other envelopes and realized that this was three days of mail, all left untouched in the hall.

Had Derek been with his girlfriend all that time? Moved in with her without telling her? Had he now left his mother for good? Was that why he hadn't phoned? The air around her chilled. Surely he would have said something or at least left a note? They had their differences and snapped at each other sometimes but Derek wasn't the type to just up and leave her, was he? The last time she'd seen him – on the morning she'd gone to stay with her sister – he'd appeared in a better mood and seemed to have forgiven her for talking to the press. Yet now he had gone and a feeling of unease stirred within her.

She went upstairs to his bedroom, out of habit knocking on the door before going in. His computers weren't there – the police must still have them. She crossed the room. A brand-new laptop sat on the workstation with a mobile phone still in its packaging beside it. That could explain why he wasn't answering his phone. Kneeling on the floor she looked under the bed; his suitcase was still there.

She straightened, crossed to the wardrobe and opened the doors. If he had taken any clothes it couldn't be many, as it was still full. She went into the bathroom, saw his toothbrush in the mug, then lifted the lid on the laundry basket. It contained only her washing, none of Derek's. It didn't make sense unless his lady friend had been doing his laundry, but why were all his belongings still here?

With mounting unease Elsie returned downstairs and opened the interconnecting door to the garage. Derek's motorbike wasn't there. Either he'd taken it with him or the police still had it. But his van wasn't outside and why leave his new laptop and phone here? It really didn't add up and she suddenly felt very alone and abandoned.

Closing the door, she went round the downstairs, switching on all the lights and drawing the curtains. Alone in the house, it felt safer with the curtains closed now it was dark outside. She shuddered as another thought struck her. Perhaps Derek had been arrested again? That could explain why he hadn't taken his belongings, and his computer, motorbike and van were still missing. Three days' mail suggested he'd been arrested again on the day she'd left and he'd been there all this time. Her breath caught in her throat.

But what was she supposed to do about it? She'd no idea. She'd seen episodes of soaps on television where one of the characters had been arrested, but they always seemed to know what to do and phoned their lawyers to get them off. But as far as she knew they didn't have a lawyer and she hadn't a clue how to go about finding one. It was at times like this – when there was a problem – that she relied on Derek to take control and sort out what needed to be done – which gave her an idea. She could telephone the police station and ask to speak to Derek, then he could tell her what she needed to do to bring him home.

Her spirits lifted slightly and she gave herself a mental

pat on the back. This certainly seemed the right thing to do and she went to the telephone in the hall again. It wasn't a 999 police emergency so she'd need the number of their local police station. Derek usually found any telephone numbers they needed on the Internet, but that wasn't an option for her. She didn't know how to use a computer. She remembered that he'd written the number for directory enquiries in their address book in case she needed it during the day when he was out at work. She opened the address book and turned to D for directory enquiries. Taking a deep breath to calm her nerves she keyed in the number, then told the operator she wanted the number for Coleshaw police station.

'Connecting you now,' the operator said a few moments later.

She heard it ringing and her heart began to race. She'd never phoned the police before.

A rather stern male voice answered. 'Duty sergeant.'

'I'm sorry to trouble you, but could you tell me if my son is there please? I need to speak to him.'

'You think your son is being held in custody here?'

'Yes.'

'His name?'

'Derek Flint.'

'The name doesn't ring a bell, but I've just come on duty. I'll check.' She waited for what seemed like ages, then, 'No, he's not here. What made you think he was?'

'He's not at home and I don't think he's been here for three days. I don't know where he is.'

'How old is he?'

'Forty-one.'

She heard his pause and guessed what he must be thinking — over-protective mother. 'Have you tried phoning him?'

'Yes, his phone is switched off. I thought he might be with his girlfriend, but I don't think so now.'

'That's the most likely reason for a man of his age to be away from home. Either that or he's out with his mates on a jolly.'

'He doesn't have any friends.'

'Do you want to report him missing?' the officer asked, an edge of impatience in his voice.

'I don't know. I thought he'd be there.'

'I'm sorry, ma'am, we're very busy. I suggest you give him a bit more time and try his phone again. If he doesn't return and you're still concerned you can phone back and report him missing.'

'Yes. I'll do that. Thank you.'

Elsie ended the call and tried Derek's mobile again but the message still said the phone was switched off. She returned to her chair in the living room. It was unlike Derek to cause her so much worry. Surely he would phone her before long? If only to tell her he wasn't ever coming home again.

Chapter Thirty-Seven

'Not one lad, but three,' Beth emphasized as she and Matt looked at the report from the forensics team. 'That comes from analysing the CCTV footage from all the crime scenes you sent them. They can tell the sex and approximate age of the suspects from their body structure and movements. These lads are likely to be in their early to mid twenties.'

Matt peered at Beth's computer screen, taking it all in.

'From the dates on the recordings,' Beth continued, 'it seems that one of the lads was involved until about six months ago, then he doesn't appear again on any of the more recent footage. The other two are constant throughout, going back eighteen months – as much footage as we have.'

'Is there anything to suggest they knew each other?' Matt asked.

'Not as yet, but my hunch is they do. And between them they could have been responsible for at least twelve of the crimes on our list, possibly more, including both break-ins at the Osmans' newsagents, the voodoo doll left on the child's bed at the Khumalos', and the rape of Lorrie Gates. Forensics are still working on it but they have matched a footprint found beneath Lorrie Gates' bedroom window with some found in the garden at the Khumalos. No match on the PNC yet though.'

'Pity. With no previous convictions, all we have to work on is that they are lads in their twenties and wear balaclavas when committing their crimes. Doesn't exactly narrow it down. Do we know if any of them have a connection to Derek Flint?'

'None found yet but I'm sure there will be before long. The digital team are still ploughing through Flint's computer. By the way, he can have his van and motorbike back now. Forensics have finished with them.' Matt nodded. 'But look at this,' Beth said, opening another document. She began slowly scrolling down, allowing Matt time to read.

He whistled. 'Flint's been amassing data on everyone he knew. Not only his clients and apprentices but neighbours, an aunt, his father! Look, there's a record of our visits.'

'He's completely obsessed with watching others and collecting data on them. See this column here with the row of dates and times,' Beth said, pointing. 'That's when he was online and watching his clients – every evening until midnight, sometimes all night, and most weekends.

All good evidence, and of course while he was watching he couldn't have actually been there committing the crimes, which adds to our accomplice theory.'

'Great stuff.'

'And look at this,' Beth continued in a flourish of delight, opening another document. 'You remember when you went to see Paul Mellows he told you he hadn't had any contact with Derek after he was sacked?'

Matt nodded.

'He was lying. This is a list of text messages the digital team found on Derek Flint's phone. The first text is from Derek to Paul: *Please confirm you got the £500 just posted through your letterbox.* Then Paul's reply: *Yes, got it. I want the other £500 when I've spoken to the police.*'

'Wow!' Matt exclaimed.

'I've checked and this exchange of texts happened later on the day we visited Flint at his office after the break-in at the Khumalos' house. We thought we'd spooked him, he was very agitated, and we were right. There's more,' she said, moving the cursor up the page. 'After I visited Paul at his home with his mother he sent this text to Derek: *Police been. . . didn't say anything. . . want the rest of the money tonight.*'

'Shit!' Matt exploded. 'He was blackmailing Flint.'

'Exactly. Then Derek replies: *Was everything OK?* And Paul responds, *Yes! Drop off the other £500 at 8pm.* And Derek says, *I will.*'

'Talk about incriminating evidence!' Matt exclaimed with a deep sigh of satisfaction.

'There were some phone calls between the two of them too around the same time but obviously we don't know what was said.'

'It almost doesn't matter. This alone is pretty damning stuff.'

'And if we needed any more evidence we have it,' Beth said with delight, clicking the mouse. 'As you know Flint is a meticulous record keeper. Look at this entry in Paul Mellows' file.' Beth waited while Matt read. His face was a picture.

'He's actually logged it all! Would that all criminals were so helpful! The dates and times of our visits, the payment demanded by Paul, and when he dropped off the money in two lots of five hundred pounds. Thank you, Mr Flint!'

Beth smiled. 'Flint's bank account shows he withdrew a total of one thousand pounds at the ATM in the High Street twenty minutes before he texted Paul to confirm he had the money.'

'Well done, you!' Matt said, glancing admiringly at Beth. 'So Paul Mellows was one of Flint's accomplices. It's likely the other two lads on the footage were the others.'

Beth nodded. 'The digital team will find the link eventually but there's so much stuff on Flint's computer and hard drives it will take time. They found a lot of pornography but it's legal stuff. Adult, no paedophile activity. Mainly footage from The Mermaid and some gay sex.'

Matt nodded. 'I wonder why he fell out with Paul?'

'No idea, but I'm going to bring Paul in for questioning, and Flint back for further questioning. I've briefed the

Serg and the DCI, and she said you should come with me.'

'Suits me, I could do with some proper action.'

Matt went to his desk to collect his jacket from the chair back and as he did the telephone on Beth's desk rang.

'Just let me get this first,' she called. 'It might be digital forensics with something new.' Then speaking into the handset: 'Mayes here . . . Oh, I see . . . OK. Yes . . . I'll deal with it. Thank you.'

She replaced the handset and looked at Matt. 'That was the duty sergeant. Derek Flint's mother has telephoned and reported him missing. She said she hasn't seen him for four days.'

'He's made a run for it?'

'Looks like it.'

'We'll visit Mrs Flint first and then bring Paul in.'

Chapter Thirty-Eight

Derek lay on his back on the hard floor, narrowing his eyes and trying to focus. The cave swam unsteadily around him but he could see it was empty and the computer was off. One of the lenses in his glasses had been broken during the last beating but he thought most of his lack of vision was due to the drug they kept injecting him with. Every night before they left him or if he made a fuss, the ghoul gave him a shot in the arm to keep him quiet. He doubted his mind or body could take much more. He felt constantly sick and shivery and had begun hallucinating as reality steadily retreated.

The flat seemed to be empty at night, although he couldn't be completely sure. They left him with his arms and legs securely tied behind his back, even during the day, except when Paul took him to the toilet or brought him food, when he untied his hands so he could eat or take a piss. It was Paul's job to take care of him. Zombie issued the instructions and Ghoul and Paul followed his orders. Derek still didn't know who Zombie and Ghoul really were. They always wore their masks in the room. As well as concealing their identities he'd come to learn it was part of the online game they were playing on the dark web – devil-like creatures who committed evil acts in an Internet underworld.

He'd tried talking to Paul when he took him to the bathroom – the only time he was alone with him. He'd tried appealing to his better nature but Paul had told him to shut the fuck up. He thought Paul might be the weak link and possibly his only hope of survival. Ghoul and Zombie were completely cruel and heartless and took pleasure in goading and humiliating him and watching him suffer. If he could get to Paul, then perhaps he could persuade him to help him escape. Perhaps. Although he didn't have a plan and hope was fast running out. He was finding it increasingly difficult to think logically – from weakness, the beatings and the drugs. He stank too; he was still in the same clothes he'd arrived in and the urine from when he'd wet himself had dried, making his pants stiff and rancid. 'Smells like a rat's died in there,' Zombie had laughed, poking his crotch with the toe of his boot.

Derek had no idea what day or time it was and it hardly mattered. Time and the life he used to have had blurred and receded. He knew he was quickly reaching the point where nothing would matter and he would give up and die. They were going to kill him anyway, Zombie had said so. He just hoped it would be quick and painless, although from what Zombie had said that wasn't likely. 'Do you know what they used to do with queers in Medieval times?' he'd asked him, dropping his trousers and shoving his bum in Derek's face. 'Ramrod them up the arse with a really sharp pole. It takes three days to die, and no one will hear you scream in here.'

The flat seemed very quiet at present, as though it could be empty, but they only usually left him alone at night, injecting him before they left. It was impossible to separate night from day with no natural light but his body clock seemed to think it was afternoon or early evening. Yet there was no sound. Usually when they were in he could hear them moving around. A door opening or closing, the toilet flushing, water running, even the kettle boiling. It was strange listening to these little noises of domesticity – reminders of a normal life – when everything around him was abnormal. Surreal.

He'd given up trying to get out of the room when he thought they'd left him during the day, bound but not drugged. He'd tried a number of times, hauling himself painfully across the floor but the door was always locked. If they heard him, Ghoul or Zombie came in and gave him another beating. His whole body was cut and bruised and he thought some of his ribs were broken. His hands were lacerated from where he'd tried to defend himself from the whip, and he knew his face was a mess. Paul hadn't been in the room during the last beating and had winced when he'd seen him. Now Derek kept very quiet and still so he didn't attract attention.

Sometimes they seemed to forget he was there when they were completely engrossed in their macabre online game. He had some idea of what they were doing on the dark web from snatches of conversation and glimpses of the screen. It was an interactive game but instead of using avatars they were using real people to act out their evil fantasies. Members of their online community were the hunters and their targets were innocent victims whom they assaulted, terrorized, kidnapped, even stabbed and raped to build up points and move to different levels. They were committing real crimes in real life, some of which he recognized from the list of incidents the police were blaming him for. He knew extremely violent games existed on the dark web but these people had taken it to a whole new level, hacking into computers, CCTV and phones in search of their prey.

He heard a movement, so the flat wasn't empty, then a hand on the door. He raised his head and Paul came into the room carrying a sandwich and glass of water.

'What time is it?' Derek rasped, his throat sore.

'Two o'clock.'

'In the afternoon?'

'Of course,' Paul laughed.

Derek knew the routine: Paul set the plate and glass on the floor by the door while he closed and locked the door, then he came over and placed them beside him. He untied his hands and left them free for the length of time it took

Derek to eat and drink and then retied them before leaving. Derek cooperated fully now and did as he was told; he knew that if he didn't, the food and water would be taken away again, and despite everything he was hungry. He'd once tried jumping Paul but Ghoul had heard the commotion and had rushed in and beat him senseless.

'Thank you,' Derek said politely, struggling into a sitting position. He drank the water first before picking up the sandwich.

Paul always stayed in the room while he ate – the glass and plate could have been smashed and used as a weapon – either watching him or wandering around, or as he was doing now, sitting in Zombie's chair at the computer.

'It's quiet here tonight,' Derek said, trying to engage Paul. 'Are they on a mission?' Paul nodded. A mission was the term they used when they were out committing one of their evil acts. Sometimes they went alone and at other times in pairs. As far as Derek knew, Paul hadn't gone with them since he'd been here but had been left to guard him, and Derek sensed he was starting to resent it.

'And they might have gone too far this time,' Paul added quietly, his gaze remaining on the screen.

Derek stopped eating and looked at Paul's profile from across the room. Was this the first sign of dissension? A chink in his armour that he could exploit? He needed to handle it carefully. He shook his head and tried to clear his thoughts.

'What are they doing that you don't like?' he asked.

'None of your bloody business,' Paul snapped.

Derek waited a moment before trying again. 'You know, Paul, you were one of my brightest apprentices. I always considered you one of the best. Why did you get in with this lot?'

'Because you pissed me off!' he retorted. 'I wanted to get my own back after you sacked me.'

'I didn't sack you. I let you go,' Derek said pathetically.

'Whatever. I knew you were up to something dodgy, and when I joined *Watching You* they made it easy to find out the rest. They can hack into anything, as you found out. It's been fun watching you.' Paul gave a low, humourless laugh.

'Why send me all those advertisements and emails? You must have known I'd trace you eventually. If you hadn't sent them I might never have known my computer had been hacked. Why bring me here and make yourself known?'

Paul laughed again while concentrating on the screen. 'We couldn't believe how long it took you to rumble you'd been hacked.'

'But why tell me and lead me here?' he asked again. 'It doesn't make sense.'

'My initiation,' Paul said. 'To become a full member of the *Watching You* online community, you have to complete a task decided by the other members. Something fitting and appropriate. As you were responsible for my joining the group, it seemed appropriate that bringing you here was my initiation. The kidnapping of Mary Grey and the stabbing of that bouncer at U-Beat nightclub were some of the other group members' initiations.'

Derek stared at him, horrified, and pushed his half-eaten sandwich away.

'So this group of yours has been hacking into my computer for their victims?'

Paul nodded.

'How many crimes are they responsible for?'

'Not sure, but quite a few of the ones the police want you for. We had a right laugh about that. Online stalking is so easy now, as you know. You watch and track them through their computer, tablet, phone and CCTV, then spot the perfect time to strike. I'm just a newbie, you wouldn't believe how much this lot are responsible for.'

'But I just watched,' Derek said plaintively. 'I tried to help them. I didn't commit any crimes.' He felt sweat trickle down his back, although it wasn't hot in the room. 'So what is going to happen to me?'

'That's for the other members to decide. But they're obviously not going to let you go, you know too much.'

'I only know who you are,' he blurted, panic stricken. 'What if I promise not to tell anyone? If you let me go I could say you wore a mask too and I'd no idea who any of you were.'

'As if you are going to do that!' Paul sneered. 'You're too fucking self-righteous. The reason you watch and monitor people is to make sure they're behaving them-selves. You've created a fantasy world – just as we have. You'll go straight to the police and tell them who is really responsible for those crimes.'

'What if you left the group and stopped playing their

horrific games?' Derek tried. 'Then I could report them without you.'

'No one leaves this group once they've joined. The guy I replaced wanted out and was found floating in the canal.'

'You were responsible for that?' Derek asked, appalled.

'Not me personally. I hadn't joined then, but the other two were. Sorry, Derek – you're in as deep as me.'

'You're going to let them kill me because I sacked you? You're sick in the head.'

'No, I don't let them kill you. I have to do it, it's one of the rules of the game. Whoever brings in the victim finishes them off.'

Chapter Thirty-Nine

The door opened to the length of the security chain and Mrs Flint peered through the gap.

'DC Beth Mayes and Matt Davis,' Beth said, flashing her identify card. 'We visited you before.'

'I remember,' she said, but didn't open the door further.

'You've reported Derek missing. Can we come in?' Beth asked.

'I got into trouble the last time I let you in.'

Matt sighed. 'Mrs Flint, Derek has jumped bail. We can talk inside or at the police station.'

'We want to help him,' Beth added, trying to be more conciliatory.

'I don't know where he can be,' she said her voice breaking. Unhooking the chain, she let them in.

'We'll take some details and start looking for him straightaway,' Beth said. They followed her into the living room, gloomy and chilly even on a fine day. 'Can we sit down?'

She nodded to the sofa, and, having taken a tissue from her sleeve, dabbed her nose and sat in her armchair.

'When did you last see Derek?' Beth asked, as Matt took out a notepad and pen.

'On the morning I went to stay at my sister's.'

'And when was that?'

'Five days ago, I think; yes. When I got back I thought he must be out for the day. Then I thought he could be with his girlfriend.'

'Does he have one?' Matt asked, pausing from writing and unable to hide his surprise.

'I don't know. It was just one of the reasons I thought for him not being here.'

'Has he ever said he had a girlfriend?' Beth asked. The girlfriend's or boyfriend's home was always the first place they looked for a missing person.

'No.'

'He's never brought her home?' Beth asked.

'Good gracious no.'

'What about talking to her on the phone? Have you heard him speak to her?'

She shook her head.

'So a girlfriend is just something you surmised?' Matt asked. Mrs Flint looked confused.

'You wondered if Derek might have a girlfriend because he wasn't here, but he's never talked about her so you don't know for sure?' Beth clarified.

'That's right.'

Matt didn't comment but continued to write.

'Are any of Derek's clothes missing?' Beth asked, going through a mental check list of questions to ask in a missing person enquiry.

'Only what he was wearing.'

'Which was?' she prompted.

'Grey trousers and a navy shirt and jumper. Same as usual.'

'Was he wearing a jacket?'

'I don't know, I wasn't here when he left.'

'Is there one missing from his wardrobe, do you know?' Beth asked.

'No, but his navy zip-up jacket isn't on the hall stand where he keeps it so he must have it with him. His suit-case is still here though.'

'What about his passport?' Beth asked. 'Do you know if that's still here?'

'He doesn't have a passport. We don't go abroad, and he'd tell me if he was going away.' Her face clouded. 'But there's none of his washing in the laundry basket; that's why I know he hasn't been here.'

'I see,' Beth said. 'Try not to worry, I'm sure he's fine.' Given that Derek was on bail it was most likely he'd done a runner rather than coming to any harm.

'I've been phoning his mobile but it's always turned off,' she said, wiping her nose again.

'It would be,' Beth said. 'We still have it at the police station, together with all the other things we took from

305

here. When Derek returns he can collect his van, motor-bike and office keys from us. We've finished with them.'

'So you think he'll come back?' Mrs Flint asked, bright-ening a little.

Beth nodded positively. 'Once his details are circulated I'm sure someone will spot him.' She omitted to say that when Derek was found, having jumped bail, he'd be taken straight into custody.

'I do hope so. I'm worried, I miss him.'

Beth smiled reassuringly. 'Is there anything else that makes you think he hasn't been back here while you've been at your sister's?' she asked, aware that absconders often returned home for food and clothing as they had nowhere else to go.

'He only had one meal, bacon and eggs. I know by the dirty plate and what's missing from the fridge. Derek has a good appetite and likes his food.' Her face clouded again. 'And one of my neighbours said she hasn't seen any lights on. She thought it was strange. Since all the trouble with his computer, and you lot and the press being here, the neighbours don't miss a thing.'

'One advantage of nosy neighbours then,' Matt put in. Beth threw him a warning glance.

'Is his wallet here?' Beth asked.

'It's not on the hall table where he usually leaves it so he must have it with him.'

'What about his front door keys?'

'He must have those too. When I came back from my sister's I found the mail on the floor from all the time I'd

306

been away, so I know for sure he hasn't been back or he would have picked it up.'

'OK, thank you.' It was looking increasingly likely that Derek had been missing for the whole period. 'We'll check his bank account, but do you know how much he had with him? Roughly.'

'No.'

'Credit cards?'

'I think he has one, he keeps it in his wallet. Why? Is it important? He can't spend money if he's had an accident.'

'The hospitals will be checked when his details are circulated. But you can't think of anywhere he might have gone? A relative or friend?'

'No. Our only relative is my sister and he's not there.'

'His father?'

'No.' Elsie turned her nose up. 'There's been nothing from him since he left when Derek was a teenager.'

Beth nodded. 'Are his motorbike leathers here?' she asked. If they weren't it was a possibility he'd bought himself a new motorbike to make his escape.

'I think they're still in his wardrobe but I'd need to check.'

'We'll come with you,' Beth said. 'We'll need to see his room and check the rest of the house.'

'Why?' She stood.

'It's standard procedure in a missing person. Shall we start down here?'

'If you like.'

She went with them into the kitchen-cum-dining room, and then unlocked the door to the integral garage for them to go in. She watched them carefully, making sure they didn't touch anything as they looked around; there was nothing that should interest them in here.

'Thank you,' Beth said as they came out, and closed the door behind them. She and Matt then waited while Mrs Flint relocked the door, then followed her upstairs.

'I'm not really supposed to let you in here without a search warrant,' she said, reluctantly opening the door to Derek's bedroom.

'It's different for a missing person,' Matt said.

Beth went in first and immediately spotted the laptop and phone lying on the workstation.

'When did he buy these?' she asked, going over and lifting the lid on the laptop.

Mrs Flint shrugged. 'I don't know. After I went to stay with my sister. I didn't see them before.'

The laptop had been left in sleep mode and came back to life now the lid had been lifted. Beth watched as the screen saver loaded, while behind her Matt opened the wardrobe doors. 'His motorbike leathers are here,' he said, checking through the rail of clothes.

'I told you,' Mrs Flint said. 'Derek hasn't taken any clothes, only what he was wearing.'

Matt checked the rest of the wardrobe for anything that might help and then looked in the drawers that had been left unlocked, and under the bed.

'It all pretty much as we left it after the warrant search,' he said to Beth, joining her at the laptop. Software icons now filled its screen. 'Looks like he's been pretty busy.'

'We'll take this and these two portable hard drives, Mrs Flint,' Beth said, closing the lid.

'We'll take the phone too,' Matt said, picking it up. 'It's brand new, not even out of its box.'

'Derek will be annoyed if he comes back and finds all that gone.'

'It might help trace him,' Matt said. 'We'll send you a receipt.'

There was nothing else of interest in the room and Beth began towards the door. 'We'll have a look around the rest of the upstairs, and leave you in peace.'

Mrs Flint followed them out, and waited on the landing as they went in and out of the other two bedrooms and the bathroom. 'I take it you didn't find anything,' she said.

'Nothing that will help,' Matt replied, then stood aside to allow her to go downstairs first.

'Now what happens?' she asked as they arrived at the foot of the stairs.

'We'll circulate Derek's details and keep you informed,' Beth said. 'Obviously if he does contact you please let us know immediately. One last thing: did Derek ever talk about the apprentices he employed?'

'Not really; he moaned about them sometimes not doing their jobs, but he never discussed his work with me. It was confidential, all those CCTV cameras in people's homes.'

'Yes, quite,' Beth said. 'Does the name Paul Mellows mean anything to you?'

'I think he might have been one of his apprentices but I couldn't be sure.'

'So Derek never brought him or any of the other apprentices home?' Matt asked.

'No, of course not. Derek keeps his work completely separate from his private life. Why should he bring them here?'

'No reason,' Matt said.

'OK, thank you,' Beth said, and opened the front door.

'What do you think has happened to him?' Mrs Flint now asked anxiously, her brow creasing.

'I'm sure he's fine,' Beth said. 'Try not to worry. We'll do everything we can to find him.'

As soon as they were outside, the door was shut and locked behind them.

'You have to feel sorry for her,' Beth said as they returned to the car. 'As far as she's concerned, Derek's a missing person. It's never occurred to her he's jumped bail and done a runner.'

'But is she telling the truth about when he left and not knowing where he is?' Matt said.

'I think so, or she wouldn't have reported him missing, would she? Unless it's a smoke screen. But it's odd he left his new phone behind and his laptop on standby. It's as though he just popped out and planned on returning later.'

'Perhaps Paul Mellows can shed some light on that?'

Chapter Forty

As Beth drove through the rush hour traffic, Matt contacted the station and put out an alert to bring in Derek Flint, then got put through to a colleague and asked her to check Flint's bank account for any recent activity. The bank details were already on file because of the ongoing investigation into his criminal activities, but Matt couldn't access them from the car and it needed senior approval. While he waited for her to return the call, he took Flint's new phone from its box and switched it on. A welcome screen appeared.

'As we thought, the phone is brand new,' he said to Beth. 'He hasn't even started a contact list. The store's sticker on the box should help identify some of Flint's movements if his bank account doesn't. The purchase will have been logged on their computer so they should be able to tell us the day and time he bought it. If Mrs Flint is telling the truth it will be sometime on Tuesday.'

Beth nodded. 'Ask them if he bought the laptop at the same time.'

Matt returned the mobile to its box as the car's phone bleeped with an incoming call. He pressed the speaker button.

'Hi Matt, Beth. It's Sue here with the information you wanted.'

'Thank you. That was quick,' Matt said.

'I'm a fast worker,' Sue quipped and Matt smiled. 'Flint has used his debit card once this week. On Tuesday morning. The transaction was timed at eleven-fifty am at My Computer World on the Coleshaw retail park. It was for three thousand five hundred and sixty-eight pounds drawn from his current account. He also set up a direct debit at the same time for twenty-one pounds a month for a mobile phone contract. Prior to that he withdrew one hundred pounds in cash the week before at the ATM of his own bank at 153 High Street. There is a standing order on his account for gas and electricity, which is due to come out tomorrow. The balance at present stands at two thousand one hundred and forty pounds, sixty-eight pence. I checked his credit card and that hasn't been used since Christmas, and has no outstanding balance.'

'Thank you. Any other accounts?' Matt asked.

'Just a savings bond but he hasn't made any deposits or withdrawals this year.'

'That's great. Thanks.'

'Thanks, Sue,' Beth added.

'You're welcome. Have a good day.'

Matt cut the call and glanced at Beth. 'So that confirms where he was on Tuesday morning and answers your question about the laptop being bought at the same time. But where did he go after that?'

'I saw an icon on his laptop marked "diary",' Beth said. 'Long shot but have a look to see if he recorded anything in it. Given his obsession for record keeping it's possible he might have started logging his movements again.'

Matt opened the laptop as Beth concentrated on driving. The Windows welcome tune sounded and the screen again filled with icons. 'Top row, fourth from left,' she said, glancing across.

'Got it.' He opened the file and read out: '"Bought a decent laptop, two hard drives and a phone this morning. Might send the bill to the police!" So he has got a sense of humour,' Matt said.

'Is that all there is?'

'"Mother is staying with her sister for a few days, which will allow me to get on and work." That's it. The rest of the week is blank.'

'Given how meticulous he was in keeping his diary on his last computer I think it's reasonable to assume he intended to continue with it but something stopped him,' Beth said. 'What "work" do you think he's referring to?'

'His home security business, I suppose. Let's see what else is on the laptop.' Matt closed the diary folder and began studying the other icons. 'He's so precise, I mean how many people arrange their desktop icons in alphabetical order?' He paused. 'Now what have we here?'

Beth again glanced from the slow-moving traffic ahead to the laptop screen as Matt opened another folder. 'Clients. Wow! I don't believe it!'

'Abbot, Andrews, Brown . . .' Matt read. 'They're all his old clients.'

'Perhaps they've remained loyal to him,' Beth said. 'After all, he hasn't been charged with anything yet. He's just helping the police with their enquiries.'

'No, these aren't their accounts. These are live streams coming from their CCTV. He's up to his old tricks again!'

Beth braked as a car in front suddenly stopped.

'Are you sure? I telephoned them all and told them to change their passwords. Did none of them do it?'

Matt was silent for a moment as he opened and closed a few of the files. 'Couldn't have done. These are all live streams. Here's the one for The Mermaid Massage Parlour!'

'You don't need to check that,' Beth said with a laugh. 'Betty was the only one of his clients who gave permission to be viewed.'

'Spoilsport.'

'Have a look in the properties of some of the files to see when they were created. We'll have digital forensics go over it properly but it might help to know what he was up to before we interview Paul.'

Matt fell silent again as he concentrated on checking the properties of the clients' files he selected at random. 'From a quick look it seems they were created from Tuesday afternoon through to the early hours of Wednesday morning. I haven't seen any before two pm on Tuesday or after four am on Wednesday morning. He appears to have worked through the night so whatever he was up to was urgent.'

'Can you phone a few of the clients who have live streams and ask them if they changed their password? He seems to be using the same filing system so their contact details will be on a spreadsheet in their files.'

'He's nothing if not predictable,' Matt said, and opened the first file.

Beth concentrated on the road ahead. The traffic was clearing now and moving faster so they should be at Paul's in about ten minutes.

'I may as well keep to his order so the Abbots first,' Matt said. He pressed the speaker button on the car phone and entered the Abbot's home phone number. The call went through to their answerphone, but he didn't leave a message.

'Andrews next,' he said closing one file and opening the next. 'Preferred contact is Mr Andrews' mobile.' He keyed in the number.

'Clive Andrews speaking.'

'Good afternoon, Mr Andrews. DC Matt Davis here from Coleshaw police station. It's a routine call. My colleague Beth Mayes contacted you a few weeks ago in respect of your CCTV, and advised you to change your password. Did you do so?'

'Yes. Why? Is there a problem?'

'No, it's just part of our ongoing "keeping people safe online" campaign. Did you inform Home Security of your change of password?'

'No. Of course not. We changed our security company too after what we saw about him on the television and in the press.'

'Thank you for your time.'

Matt said goodbye and ended the call. 'Well, that's interesting. Let's try the next.'

The result was the same, password and company changed, Home Security not informed, but nevertheless Derek had managed to log in to their cameras. The third had stayed with Home Security, presumably unaware of the story in the press, but had changed the password and not informed Derek Flint. All very puzzling.

Beth pulled into the road where Paul lived and parked out of sight of his house.

'So how the hell has he been getting into their accounts?' Matt asked.

'Try phoning one of the clients who doesn't have a live stream and see if there's a difference. Then we'll collect Paul.'

She watched as Matt opened the relevant spreadsheet and keyed in the number. The call went through to voice-mail. 'I'll try another one, there's only four without live streams. They live in Southfields; nice area, must have some money.' The call connected after a few rings.

'Mrs Rudd?' Matt asked.

'Yes. Speaking.'

'Sorry to trouble you, it's DC Matt Davis here from Coleshaw police station. A routine call. My colleague Beth Mayes contacted you a few weeks ago in respect of your

CCTV and advised you to change your password. Did you do so?'

'Oh yes, straightaway with a high-strength password. My husband's company's website was hacked a few months ago and lots of employee details were stolen. As soon as your colleague phoned we changed it. We also changed the password on our router at the same time, and when the news broke about Home Security we changed company.'

'Thank you. That's most helpful. I assume you haven't told anyone your new passwords?'

'No, and neither would we. Can I ask why you want to know?'

'It's just part of our ongoing campaign to keep people safe online.'

'That's very reassuring. There is so much online fraud now with websites being hacked. You can't trust anyone. It's good to know the police are running these campaigns and advising people.'

'Thank you, Mrs Rudd.' Matt cut the call and turned to Beth. 'Do you think that could be it? That their password strength is high enough to keep Flint out, and they changed the password on their router too?'

'It's certainly possible,' Beth said. 'Most people leave their default password in place, especially on their router. But that would mean Flint has changed his tactics and widened his field and is now hacking into websites rather than learning the passwords from his clients. Let's see what Paul has to say for himself. Best hide the laptop and phone.

We'd look right fools if we came back to find the car window smashed and them gone.'

Matt leant behind and secreted the laptop, phone and portable hard drives under his jacket on the rear seat, then opened his car door and got out. Beth joined him on the pavement.

'We're taking him in for questioning, right?' Matt confirmed.

'Yes.' She followed him up the path.

He pressed the doorbell but no one answered. He pressed again. Still no answer and none of the windows were open. The front door of the house on the right opened and a woman came out.

'They're all at work,' she said. 'Mrs Mellows is usually back first.'

'Thank you. When will that be, do you know?' Beth asked.

She looked at her wristwatch. 'In about half an hour, usually around six. Then her husband comes in around six-thirty. No telling when her kids will be back now they're older.'

'Thank you, that's very helpful,' Beth said. 'You know the family well, do you?'

'No, not really. Only to say hello, but I see them coming and going, like I do most in this street. Did you want anything in particular?'

'It's just routine. Thank you anyway,' Beth said. She and Matt returned down the path and to the car.

'Mrs Flint's not the only one with nosy neighbours,' Matt remarked as they got in.

'And doesn't it make our lives easier! We might have just gone away. Now we can wait for Paul's mother to come home and tell us where he is.'

'May as well put the time to good use,' Matt said, retrieving the laptop from the rear seat.

'I'm impressed.' Beth stifled a yawn. 'To be honest I'm knackered. It's been a long week and it's not over with yet.'

Matt studied the screen of the laptop. 'He's set up an email account,' he said presently. 'Let's take a look at who he's been emailing.' Beth watched as he clicked on the email icon. There was nothing in the sent box but a dozen or so emails in his inbox, only some of them read. Matt began opening and closing them.

'Anything of interest?' Beth asked after a moment. She was looking through the windscreen for any sign of Mrs Mellow's return.

'Not so far. A notification from his energy supplier that the direct debit will be taken from his account within the next few days. Another is confirmation of the direct debit he set up for the new mobile phone. Then a product of interest email from Amazon. More junk mail.' A pause then: 'Bloody hell, Beth! Hide your eyes!'

Beth immediately looked at the screen. 'Struth! That's a bit graphic,' she said. 'Naked men sodomizing each other.'

Matt read out the writing beneath the photograph: '"Local man, Derek Flint, pleaded guilty in court today to the charge of gross indecency after a member of the public reported him and another man to the police." The writing seems to be an excerpt from a newspaper article from nine years ago but with a different picture.'

'Who sent the email – Paul? Given we know he's been blackmailing Flint he'd be my first guess.'

'No, it's from an organization called *Watching You*, whoever they are. It's not asking for payment.'

'I'd put money on Paul being behind it though,' Beth said. 'It's easy enough to set up an anonymous email account. Digital forensics should be able to trace the sender but there's no one else been blackmailing Flint as far as we know.'

'I wonder if receiving this email has anything to do with Flint suddenly taking off?' Matt said, looking at the other emails. 'This is the last one he read, all the others are unopened.'

'It's possible.' Beth paused and looked sombrely at Matt. 'I hope Flint hasn't done something daft.'

'What, like suicide you mean?'

She nodded. 'It would explain why he's missing. Perhaps he hasn't jumped bail and done a runner; perhaps his body is lying somewhere, as yet undiscovered.'

'I'm not sure,' Matt said doubtfully. 'This is old news. He must have realized it couldn't do him much harm now.'

'Who knows what went through his mind. He's pretty screwed up and doesn't have friends who can support him through a difficult time. I can't imagine he confided in his mother. Perhaps the pressure built up. He's being investigated by us and Paul ups the blackmail and it all becomes too much.'

'You could be right, I suppose, but I'm not convinced.' Matt looked up through the windscreen. 'Isn't that Mrs Mellows coming down the road?'

'Yes.'

Matt tucked the laptop under the passenger seat and followed Beth out.

'Mrs Mellows,' she called, catching up with her on the garden path.

'Oh, hello. You were here before.'

'That's right. DC Beth Mayes and DC Matt Davis.'

'If it's Paul you've come to see, he's not home, and I'm not expecting him until much later.'

'It was,' Beth said. 'Does Paul have a job then?'

'Yes, then he's meeting up with friends later, so it's likely he won't be back until well after midnight.'

'I don't suppose you know where he is now?'

'Not when he's out with his mates, no,' she said with a caustic smile. 'He's a bit old to be telling his mother.'

'And when he's working?' Matt asked. 'Where's that?'

'On Cranberry estate. Maintenance. It gave me great pleasure telling that Derek Flint Paul was working again after the way he treated him.'

'You've seen Derek Flint?' Beth asked, astonished.

'Yes, he came here on Wednesday morning. Quite early on; I was getting ready for work but Paul had already left. I don't know what Flint wanted, but Paul seemed to think he might come round and had left the address of where he could be found.'

'I don't suppose you remember it?' Beth asked.

Mrs Mellows thought for a moment. 'Bushmead Close. But I should think he's finished work for today.'

'Has Paul mentioned what Derek Flint wanted with him?' Matt asked.

'No. But I didn't ask. I've never liked that bloke and after hearing on the local news what he'd been up to, it rather confirmed I was right not to trust him.'

'Do you have Paul's new mobile number?' Beth asked. 'The one we have is no longer in use.'

'He lost his phone and bought a new one. Come inside while I find the number.'

They followed her into the hall, then waited as she retrieved her mobile from her handbag and scrolled down the list of contacts. She read out Paul's number as Matt made a note. 'Thank you.'

'I'll tell Paul you were here then.'

Beth thanked her and they left. In the car Matt immediately tried Paul's mobile number but it went through to his voicemail and he didn't leave a message.

'That would have been too easy,' Beth said. 'It seems we've got two choices: sit here all night until Paul returns or drop Flint's laptop off so forensics have it over the weekend. Then pick up Paul first thing on Monday.'

'Definitely the second option,' Matt said. 'It's not likely to make any difference, and Flint might have reappeared by then, saving us an awful lot of work.'

'Agreed.'

Chapter Forty-One

Derek supposed there came a point when a hostage gave up all hope and resigned themselves to certain death. The news sometimes featured people who'd been taken hostage in lawless and war-torn countries, and previously other than feeling some sympathy for the family as they made an emotional plea for their loved one's safe return, he'd never given much thought to the actual captive, and how they must be preparing for death. Now he had first-hand experience and it was terrifying.

Possibly if you were religious, and believed you were going to a better place, then death didn't hold the same horror. Although it was the actual dying he found more frightening than death itself. But try as he might, he couldn't summon the belief he needed to ask God to help him through it, and knew that when the time came he wouldn't be brave, but would scream and cry like a baby.

The long lapses into unconsciousness were a welcome relief. There was a cosy feel in being enveloped by darkness, like the embracing hug of a loving parent. But as soon as he woke, his fevered brain took over and tortured him with thoughts past and present; there was no future to worry about. Dying was a great leveller, he'd found; it had forced him to see what he'd done wrong in his life – just when it was too late to do anything about it. His mother, for example; his eyes filled every time he thought of her. He should have been kinder to her, more understanding and patient. He should have spent time with her rather than shut in his room with his clients as his family. Little wonder she'd taken solace in the television; it was all she'd had. What the hell had been so important that he'd spent all those years immersed in his clients' lives rather than his own mother's? She was his family, not them, but ironically it had taken his impending death to see that, and he was truly sorry.

Derek also thought about his father, whom he'd succeeded in tracing many years before but had never had the courage to confront. Given the chance, would he visit him as he'd envisaged doing so many times over the years? Turn up on his doorstep and say, 'Hi Dad, remember me? I'm your son?' Would he? Given the opportunity? No. Because any visit would be fuelled by bitterness, recrimination and resentment, which only now he saw he needed to let go of. His father had left him and he had to accept it, painful though it was.

Acceptance, physical weakness and delirium from the accumulative effect of the drug they kept injecting him with made him shout out things he quickly regretted. He called them names: scumbags, tossers, pathetic cowards. They beat him for it and he laughed. 'You can't reach me now,' he said, and they beat him again, but it didn't matter. He was just one step closer to the end. There was no escape and he'd overheard them talking, sometimes arguing, about the best way to dispose of him.

Through the darkness in the room he could see them grouped around the computer, busy planning their next 'mission'. The challenge had been set by someone in the Far East and it involved all three of them this time. He learnt it was a high-status challenge, where, if successful, the points they earned would take them all to the next level.

It was the abduction and gang rape of a fourteen-year-old girl on her way home from school, and they were going to live-stream it onto the dark net for others to 'enjoy'. They'd been planning it for some days now, stalking her through the webcam on her laptop and the CCTV at her parents' home. He'd heard it going on in the background as he'd lapsed in and out of consciousness. But when he realized who the victim was, he exploded into anger and found the strength to shout at them again.

'You fucking depraved idiots! Leave her alone. She's done nothing to you.' He knew her and her family; they'd been clients of his. He cursed and swore at them even as they beat him senseless.

When he'd come to, his mouth had been taped shut with heavy-duty parcel tape, which no one bothered to remove to let him drink. So he knew it wouldn't be long. You couldn't go for many days without water.

Chapter Forty-Two

'Good weekend?' Matt asked, as Beth climbed into the passenger seat of the unmarked police car.

'Slept for most of it,' Beth said. 'What about you?'

'Same. Although I did play football yesterday morning. The first time in ages.' Matt waited while she fastened her seat belt before pulling away. They'd arranged for him to collect her as it was on their way to Paul Mellows' house and they wanted an early start. They should be there by 7.30am, hopefully before he left for work. They would take him in for questioning so the rest of the day was pretty much mapped out.

'Still no sign of Flint then?' Matt said as he drove.

'No, no sighting since Wednesday. I'll phone Mrs Flint when we've finished here and tell her we're doing all we can to find him. Also, as soon as we've got Paul, I need to update the boss. The DCS is involved now.'

The traffic kept moving and they arrived at Mellows' house on time. Matt parked right outside as there was no need for subtlety now. They were going to arrest Paul. The front bedroom curtains were open and a light was on in the hall. 'Someone's up, then,' he said, opening his car door.

They went quickly up the garden path and Matt gave the doorbell one long, hard push. It was answered almost immediately by Mrs Mellows, dressed ready for work and looking anxious.

'Paul's not here,' she said. 'He hasn't been back all weekend.'

'Where is he?' Beth asked.

'I've no idea.'

'Has he phoned?'

'He's been texting. His work clothes are here. I don't know what he thinks he's playing at.'

'Can we come in?'

She opened the door wider to allow them in. A teenage girl still in her nightwear crossed the hall behind her on her way upstairs. 'You need to be out of here in fifteen minutes,' Mrs Mellows called after her. 'I don't want you being late too.'

'Does he often stay out?' Matt asked.

'Sometimes the odd night, but not the whole weekend without letting me know where he is.'

'Can I have a look at the text messages?' Beth asked.

'Come through.' They followed her into the living room where they'd previously seen Paul. Mrs Mellows took her mobile from the coffee table and handed it to Beth. She angled it so Matt could see too as she scrolled down. Most of the messages were from Mrs Mellows as she'd grown increasingly worried, starting on Saturday morning.

Paul, it's 8am. Where are you?

No reply. She sent a similar message again at 11.45am. Still no reply.

At 2pm she texted: *Paul can you please phone or text to let me know you're OK.*

He'd replied an hour later: *be back later or first thing in the morning.*

At 7am on Sunday she'd texted: *where are you?*

No reply.

At 11.15am she'd texted: *I'm worried. Phone or text please.*

At 12.23pm he replied: *I'm staying rest of weekend with friends. Will be home Monday.*

'I've tried phoning this morning but it just goes through to his voicemail,' she said, with a mixture of exasperation and concern.

'Does he have a girlfriend he could be with?' Beth asked, handing her back the phone.

'It's possible, that crossed my mind. Paul finished with his last girlfriend a few months back – or rather she finished with him. But he hasn't mentioned that he's seeing anyone new.'

'Could we take a look at his room?' Beth asked.

'I don't see why not, although it will have to be quick as I've got to leave for work soon. You don't think anything has happened to Paul, do you?'

329

'I'm sure he's fine,' Beth said. 'He's been in contact.'

On the landing a shower could be heard running from the bathroom. 'Hurry up!' Mrs Mellows called to her daughter through the door. Then with a sigh to Beth, 'There's no way she's leaving on time.'

A normal family at the start of the working week, Beth thought. Why had Paul gone off the rails and turned into a blackmailer? Greed? Drug money? He wouldn't be the first. Or was it for another reason they had yet to discover?

Mrs Mellows opened Paul's bedroom door. The room contained the usual detritus associated with a young single man living at home. His bed was unmade, a used mug, plate, and glass were on the bedside cabinet, and the chair and floor were clearly used as wardrobe.

'I make no apology for the mess,' Mrs Mellows said. 'It's his space so his responsibility.'

Beth smiled. But in contrast to the shambles of an unkempt room, an expensive and new high-tech Smart TV with a sophisticated gamepad controller stood against one wall.

'Nice,' Matt said, going over for a closer look. 'Wish my salary could stretch to one of these. Birthday present?'

'No, his new job is paying well,' Mrs Mellows said.

Matt threw Beth a doubtful look.

An older laptop, closed, lay on the bed beside a pile of unwashed clothes, which spilled onto the floor. 'I do his laundry,' Mrs Mellows said, following Beth's gaze, 'but I'm not his servant. He seems to think his dirty clothes will

330

find their own way to the laundry basket.' She gave a small humph.

Beth went to a pile of T-shirts. One in particular had caught her eye and she picked it up. 'You're brave touching his dirty washing,' Mrs Mellows said.

'Where did this come from?' Beth asked, holding it up so Matt could see the design on the front.

'Internet, I suppose, or The Mall,' Mrs Mellows replied. 'There's a stall there that prints T-shirts with whatever you like.'

'Do you know what *Watching You* is?' Beth asked.

'I assume some sort of boy band? Why?'

'It came up recently in another context. Must be a coincidence.'

Mrs Mellows nodded. 'Look, I'm sorry to rush you but I really do need to leave for work. Could you come back this evening when Paul's here?'

'Yes, of course. We won't keep you; thank you for your time,' Beth said.

They went out of the bedroom and downstairs.

'Try his mobile, you may have more luck,' she suggested as she saw them out. 'Although it's likely to be switched off if he's working.'

'We will. Thank you.'

'I've never heard of a band called Watching You,' Matt said as they returned to the car.

'Neither have I, and it would be too much of a co-incidence if they both used exactly the same logos – the eye with a camera for the lens. It was identical to the one on the email on Flint's laptop. Which rather confirms Paul was behind that email. But why go to the trouble of having a T-shirt printed?'

'No idea. Let's try his phone as his mother suggested,' Matt said, settling into the driver's seat.

Beth made the call. It went straight through to voice-mail and she didn't leave a message. 'I think we should try the estate where he's working and see if we can pick him up there. There can't be that many trade vans in Cranberry Gardens. Flint is still missing and it now appears Paul could be too. Anyone can send a text message. It might not have been Paul, and Flint wouldn't be the first person to murder his blackmailer.'

'The worm turned,' Matt said. He started the engine and pulled away. 'And if he's not there then we come back here later with a warrant so we can take Paul's laptop and search the house.'

'Agreed.'

The morning rush-hour traffic had built so it was 8.50am by the time they pulled into the estate.

'The area hasn't improved since the last time I was here,' Beth said, glancing out of her side window. Matt turned into Bushmead Close. 'This part is due for regeneration; I think most of the houses and flats are empty now.'

Matt nodded and cruised slowly down the close with both of them looking out. It was deserted. 'No sign of any trade vans or workmen,' Matt said. He did a three-point turn at the end and then drove slowly back.

'I think Paul has been giving his mother a load of bull about working here,' Beth said. 'There's no building work going on at all. In fact it looks like most of it is ready to be demolished.'

'Back to the station then?'

'Yes.'

Matt pulled to the end of the close and turned left. As he did the car phone rang and Beth pressed the speaker button.

'Good morning, Beth, Matt.'

'Good morning, sir,' she said, automatically straightening in her seat. It was the DCS.

'What's happening with you two right now?' he asked.

'We're just leaving the Cranberry estate, sir, on our way back. Paul Mellows wasn't at home and there's no sign of him where he's supposed to be working so we'll pick him up later with a search warrant.'

'Fine, but don't come back here. I need you to go to Flat 28, Fell Court. A community police officer has just called in with a suspected child abuse case. Matt can go with you.'

'Very good, sir. We're on our way.'

'Thank you.' The line went dead.

Beth pulled a face. 'Just what we needed to start the week off.'

Matt sighed and turned the car around, as disconcerted as Beth at the prospect of investigating a child abuse case. No police officer relished investigating child abuse; it got to you in a way that other investigations didn't. The details lingered and tormented you in the early hours. The look on the child's face, lost and frightened, as they used childish language to describe what had been done to them. It definitely wasn't a good start to the week. Flint was still missing, Paul had vanished, and now this.

Chapter Forty-Three

Derek peered into the darkness. His legs and feet were numb and he was lapsing more and more into unconsciousness, with no idea of what day it was. He knew their evil plan was reaching fruition; there'd been a lot of activity recently. They'd hired a van which he'd heard them say was to be used to rape their victim, Nicole, in. And they'd bought extra condoms to do the job. They'd laughed over Ghoul's choice of colour and taste – black cola.

Zombie and Ghoul had raped before but this was to be Paul's first time. Derek sensed some uncertainty when they'd talked him through what would happen, describing it in graphic detail then repeating it for Derek's sake. Two would hold her down while the third raped her. They'd all have a turn but as it was Paul's first time he would be going first to prove himself. Derek gagged when he'd heard what they would do to her and had to stop himself from throwing up. With the tape stuck over his mouth he would have drowned in his own vomit.

He'd also learnt that once they'd finished raping Nicole and had dumped her in Coleshaw Woods they were going to come back and dispose of him. Bound and gagged, Paul was to put him in a sack weighted with bricks and throw him in the deepest part of the canal.

'Just like I did with your predecessor,' Ghoul laughed.

Derek thought that if there was a God and he could only save one of them then he wanted it to be Nicole. She was young, fourteen, with her whole life ahead of her – a good, kind girl who wanted to be a doctor.

'Take me but leave her,' he tried to cry out, 'and please look after my mother.'

'Did it speak?' Zombie growled, advancing towards him. But Derek was already safe again in the depths of unconsciousness so didn't feel the blows.

Chapter Forty-Four

It was after 1pm by the time Beth and Matt left Fell Court where they'd been investigating the suspected child abuse, and they were emotionally drained. Thankfully it wasn't the worse case they'd come across, not by a long way, but even so it was worrying. A neighbour had reported hearing a child screaming and crying for help on a number of occasions. They'd interviewed the neighbour and the child's parents who claimed the neighbour was racist and that their daughter had been having nightmares – even in the day. Aged six, and with English as her second language, the child had nodded agreement with her parents, although to Beth her eyes told a different story.

They'd taken statements and waited for the social worker to arrive. It was the first time the family had come to the attention of the social services so it was likely they'd be given the benefit of the doubt and be monitored for now.

But Beth was sure there would be a next time. The haunted look in the girl's eyes had said it all.

The fresh air outside was a welcome relief. Matt opened the car and automatically climbed into the driver's seat.

'My chauffeur,' Beth teased.

'You can drive if you want to?'

'No, it's fine. I need to return the call from forensics. John texted while we were in there.'

Beth keyed John's number into the car phone as Matt dove in the direction of the police station. 'We'll pick up something to eat on the way,' he said.

Beth nodded. 'Hi John, Beth here returning your call.'

'What kept you?' he said disgruntled. 'I thought you said you wanted the stuff on Flint's new laptop urgently. I worked on it over the weekend.'

'Sorry, John. We got held up. Thanks for putting in the extra hours. What have you got for us?'

'I'll email you the full report but I thought you'd want to know my findings so far.'

'Yes please.' John was very good at this job and he often held the key to solving a case, or at least providing suffi-cient evidence to take the case to court. He liked the detectives to acknowledge that. 'Thank you,' Beth said again.

John cleared his throat. 'You were right when you said Flint had recreated the live streams on his new laptop, but it was through a mixture of hacking and password guessing. As you surmised, the ones he couldn't get into had high-strength passwords not derived from their names, streets, or date of birth. They'd also changed the password on their routers.'

'Well done us,' Matt said.

'It's pretty basic stuff for a hacker,' John added. Matt looked deflated. 'People make it too easy for hackers,' John continued. 'However, what you weren't to know, and I'm sure Flint didn't know either, was that despite installing good virus software his laptop had been hacked, as had his other computer.'

'Really?' Beth said. 'When?'

'At least ten months ago on his old computer, and as soon as he went online with this laptop. Flint didn't practice what he preached, and not realizing he'd been hacked once, he used the same login and password, so they already had the details they needed.'

'I see,' Beth said thoughtfully. 'So it was by the same person or persons.'

'Yes. I'm still checking what exactly they accessed but in theory it could have been all Flint's files and folders. So they would know everything Flint did about his clients, and about him too.'

There was a moment's silence as the full implications sunk in.

'Struth!' Beth said.

Matt let out a long, slow whistle. 'That could put a different take on things.'

'There's more,' John said, his excitement palpable. 'Not only did they hack in, but they'd been goading Flint and leading him on for many months using the dark web. You're familiar with that term?'

Beth was about to say they were, but John continued with his explanation anyway.

'The dark web is a collection of websites that use an encryption tool to hide their IP addresses so you can't find them on a search engine. It needs specific software and configurations to use. The fact that these people need to hide their identities and their activities says it all. It's used by terrorist groups, whistle-blowers, black market sales, paedophiles and weirdos who think it's fun to play sadistic interactive games. Flint was computer savvy but I'm sure he had no idea who was targeting him and how serious it was until they sent him that final email.'

'What email is that?' Beth asked.

'The one that was sent to his laptop on Wednesday morning from a group calling themselves Watching You. They didn't use a VPN so Flint was able to trace them. It was probably then that the penny dropped and Derek realized at least some of what was going on.'

'And then he suddenly disappears,' Beth said.

'Who are they? What do you know about them?' Matt asked.

'Not a lot at present. They're well hidden on the dark web. From the little I've seen so far they really are a nasty bunch. But it's very time-consuming trying to keep track of these buggers and sift through all the data they generate, and there's just me been working on it.'

'Thank you, John, it is appreciated,' Beth said. 'Tell us

when you have more. I don't suppose you know where the group is based?'

'Like most of these groups they're global, the Internet is worldwide, after all – hence www: world wide web.'

'Yes, but was there a UK branch?' she asked.

'It's not that simple. These dark web groups subdivide into smaller groups, sometimes down to two or three members, so there can be many all over the place.'

'And the group that's been targeting Flint has how many members, do you know?'

'There is evidence of four but one's been sleeping by the look of it.'

'Sleeping?'

'A non-active member. He was involved until about six months ago, then disappeared and another guy took his place. There's quite a hierarchy in these groups and they give themselves identities, like Devil's Child, Hell's Fury and so on.

'So when will you be able to give us the location of the group that's been linked to Derek Flint?' Beth asked, glancing at Matt.

'I can do that now. I made it a priority. As I thought, the group that's been targeting Flint is the nearest group geographically to him. They are operating from a computer at 35 Bushmead Close. You'll have to look up the post-code.'

'No need,' Beth said as Matt screeched the car to a halt and began a U-turn. 'We know where it is.'

'They've been active this morning until about half an

hour ago. If you'd returned my call sooner, you might have caught them red-handed.'

'Thank you, John. We're on our way there now,' Beth said.

'I'll email my full report when it's complete, but you realize the connotations for your case against Flint?'

'Yes,' Beth said. She disconnected the call and turned to Matt. 'It's been blown wide apart.'

Chapter Forty-Five

Fifteen minutes later, the unmarked police car sped onto the Cranberry estate and continued around the ring road. Matt turned right into Bushmead Close and then drew to an abrupt halt outside the block of flats at the far end. They jumped out, crossed to the entrance of the block and ran up the first flight of metal stairs. The place was deserted.

'I wonder if John made a mistake with the number of the flat?' Matt said as they continued round the landing and to the second flight of stairs. 'The only flat that seems to be occupied in this block is that one on the ground floor. Thirty-five is at the top.'

'Let's try thirty-five first, then take a look at the others,' Beth said, glancing up and down the stairwell for any sign of life. There was nothing and it was very disappointing.

Reaching the top, they crossed the landing to Flat 35.

'That tape over the bell looks like it's been there for ages,' Beth said. She lifted the small metal doorknocker and rapped twice, the metallic twang echoing eerily into the emptiness. They waited.

'There's no one living here,' Matt said, taking a step back.

Beth rapped the doorknocker again, then tried to peer through the letterbox but something on the inside was stopping it from opening. 'I think you're right, although it's not like John to be wrong. Stay here and I'll go down and see who's living in that flat on the ground floor.'

'Shout if you need any help,' Matt called after her.

Beth retraced her steps down the two flights of stairs to Flat 1. Faded curtains and grubby nets hung at the windows, making the flat look as abandoned as most of the others, apart from what sounded like a radio coming from inside. She pressed the bell, a dog barked, and then a male voice shouted, 'Hold ya horses, I'm coming!' Beth took a step back.

It was a minute or so before bolts could be heard sliding and then the door was opened by a man Beth guessed to be in his eighties. Unkempt with thick stubble covering his double chin, his shirt and baggy trousers held up by braces were food stained.

'What d'ya want?' he demanded. 'I told that last social worker I'm not moving. It's me home and I'm not leaving it.' A mixed-breed dog, badly overweight and as old as its owner waddled to his side.

'I'm not from the social services,' Beth said, as she

showed him her identity card. 'I wanted to ask you about your neighbours upstairs.'

'What neighbours? I ain't got none. There's no one left here but me. They've all been re-homed like stray dogs and cats.'

'Is there no one living in Flat 35 on the top floor?' Beth asked.

'Oh, that lot. Yeah, sort of, but they don't live there proper. They're squatting. I keep out of their way. They're a bad lot.'

'Who's using the flat? Do you know?'

'Lads. Three of 'em. I've watched 'em come and go from behind me curtains but I don't have anything to do with 'em.'

So John was right! Beth thought. 'When was the last time you saw them?'

'This morning. Nah, later. About an hour ago. They went out in one of those white vans workmen use. But don't tell them I told you. I don't want no trouble.'

'I won't. That's helpful, thank you.' She hesitated. 'But what have you got against being re-housed? I'm sure it would be a lot nicer than living here.'

His eyes narrowed, suggesting that never in a million years would she have understood. 'Goodbye then,' he said gruffly, and closed the door.

Beth returned upstairs.

'It's the right flat. Three lads have been using it,' she said as she reached the top step. 'The old boy below said they've been squatting. They were here earlier but he says they all left an hour ago. Do you think that door would give if you leant on it hard? It looks pretty flimsy.'

Matt pressed his shoulder against the door and gave it a good shove. It moved and creaked but it didn't give. He tried again with the same result. 'Pretend you haven't seen this,' he said, and took a bank card from his wallet.

Beth watched with interest as he inserted the card at an angle into the crack in the door and then ran it up to the lock. On the second attempt the lock opened.

'Now I am impressed!' she said. 'Where did you learn that?'

'Mate at school. His dad was a burglar; it was his party trick.'

'Illegal but useful.'

Matt pushed the door wide open. 'Bloody hell, it's dark in there,' he said, going in first. 'And it stinks!' He squinted towards the small bare light bulb at the far end of the hall and giving hardly any light at all.

'Why would squatters paint all the walls, floor and ceiling black?' Beth asked, looking around.

'Cover the dirt?'

She pushed the front door to so she could see what had been stopping the letterbox from opening and started.

'Shit! Those scared me.' Halloween masks hung from hooks on the wall behind the door.

'They weren't expecting any mail for sure,' Matt said, bending to examine the piece of wood nailed over the letter box.

Now the door was shut the hall was even darker. Beth

took a few steps and tentatively opened the first door on the left. It led into a small kitchen – relatively normal-looking after the hall. Some natural light struggled in through the grimy window above a filthy sink. The small Formica table and all the work surfaces were covered with empty pizza and sandwich boxes, bottles and crushed beer cans. Matt followed her in and their shoes stuck to the gunge as they crossed the vinyl floor and began opening and closing the cupboard doors, all the time listening out for any sign the occupants might be returning.

'That accounts for some of the smell,' Beth said, referring to the takeaway containers overflowing with stale ash. A partially smoked joint of crack cocaine lay beside one of the cartons.

'At least one of them is a registered drug user on the needle exchange programme,' Matt said, examining a chemist bag containing boxes of new needles and syringes.

They quickly checked the other cupboards, but apart from some old chipped mugs and cracked plates they were empty. Leaving the kitchen they went into the next room, the bathroom.

'Typical squatters,' Beth said, grimacing, 'used a lot but never cleaned.' It was disgusting and with nothing of interest they came out.

They paused in the hall and listened again for any sound coming from outside suggesting someone might be returning. They didn't want to be caught off guard. Beth crossed the hall, where she opened one of the two doors on the other side. A haze of drug-laden smoke greeted

347

them from a recent joint. The room had clearly been a bedroom once. A wardrobe with a door hanging off was against one wall and two badly stained mattresses were in the centre of the floor. Between them was a plate overflowing with ash, matches, silver foil, and the ends of more joints. Dozens of plastic bags and bin liners overflowing with rubbish were propped against the walls. Ripped floral curtains hung at the grimy window.

'They've been using this flat for some time then,' Matt said, crossing to what was left of the wardrobe. A pile of clothes lay in the bottom. 'Well! What do you know!' he said, holding up a *Watching You* T-shirt. 'We'll take this with us.'

With nothing else in the room they returned to the hall. Another quick listen to make sure no one was approaching and then to the other door on the right, the only room they hadn't been in.

'We'll check this room then report back to the station,' Beth said, trying the handle.

'It's bolted top and bottom,' Matt said, spotting the metal bolts in the dim light. 'What have they got in here, a horse?'

He slid both bolts and eased open the door. His hand shot to his mouth. 'Jesus! This is where the smell's coming from. It's like dead dog.'

The room was even darker than the hall and lit by a low-wattage candle bulb on the wall behind a computer. The desktop computer was standing on an old table with a single chair in front of it. Matt made his way towards it. The rest of the room remained in a thick, cloying darkness.

Beth took out her phone and using the torch, shone it around the walls. Like the hall they were all painted black. What had once been the window had been boarded over and painted black too. She moved the beam slowly around the ceiling. 'It looks like Halloween in here with those model bats and giant spiders hanging from that netting.'

'Part of their online game, I suppose,' Matt said, glancing up from starting the computer.

'But where's that smell coming from?' Beth said. 'It's not drugs.'

'Dead rats?' Matt suggested.

She lowered the beam and ran it across the floor. There was no rubbish in here as there had been in the other rooms but models of ghoulish creatures – some very realistic. John had said they were playing a sadistic inter-active game, and their evil intent was obvious from the way they'd decorated the room. The putrid smell added to the atmosphere and Beth thought it wouldn't take much to believe you were in hell.

The light from her phone fell on some tombstones presumably stolen from a cemetery, then to what looked like the entrance to a cave. A model gremlin, teeth bared and ready to bite, sat on a rock as though guarding the entrance. She flicked her torch around as Matt concentrated on the computer. A mound covered by what looked like an old brown blanket lay ahead of her and as she approached the smell grew stronger.

'The smell is coming from whatever is under that blanket,' she said and shuddered. What dead and mutilated animal had played a part in their sadistic games?

Bracing herself for what she would find, Beth tentatively lifted a corner. The smell intensified but it was impossible to make out what she was looking at. Shining her phone directly onto the object she pulled off the rest of the blanket. The full force of the smell hit her.

'Jesus! Matt, quick! Come here. It's a person. Call an ambulance.' She dropped to her knees and looked closer. Matt rushed over, taking out his phone as he came. 'I think it's Derek Flint,' she said. With his face bloody and swollen and tape covering his mouth he was virtually unidentifiable; only his glasses were familiar. 'My God!' Beth gasped. 'What did they do to him?'

'He's dead,' Matt said joining her, and confirmed the address over the phone with the emergency services. 'We're too late.'

But as Beth looked, her fingers on his neck feeling for a pulse, she saw the slightest twitch at the corner of his eye. 'No, he's still alive!'

She began peeling the tape from his mouth. He groaned but his swollen eyes remained closed. 'Derek, it's Beth Mayes. Stay with us, an ambulance is on its way.'

Matt untied the cord cutting into his ankles and wrists and as he did dead skin fell away. 'Jesus! How on earth is he still alive?'

Beth stayed kneeling beside him, trying to avoid breathing in the foul smell; a combination of faeces, urine, vomit and rotting flesh. The only time she'd ever smelt anything similar was when she'd been called to the flat of an elderly woman who'd been dead for a week at the height of summer. The acrid smell had been overpowering and had lodged in her throat and nose and stayed with her for days after.

Derek's lips began moving as if he was trying to talk.

'It's all right, Derek. Lie still, we know what's been going on,' Beth reassured him. 'The ambulance is coming.' She tried not to retch but the smell was gut-wrenching. He surely wouldn't make it, but his lips were moving again. She put her ear as close to his mouth as she dared.

'What day is it?' he mumbled.

'Monday.'

He coughed and groaned, his claw-like hand reaching up. He was trying to tell her something.

'What is it, Derek?'

'Ashfield School. Nicole.' He paused and fought for breath. 'They're going to rape her. Stop them.'

'When?'

'Today. Now.' And he lapsed again into unconsciousness.

'I'm onto it,' Matt said, bringing his phone again to his ear.

Chapter Forty-Six

Ashfield Girls' School had already been dismissed at the end of the day and the girls were leaving in small groups, pairs and alone. The secondary school of approximately eight hundred students was at the end of a single-track lane along which they had to exit. There was no other way out. Three unmarked police cars were now parked at various points along the lane, hopefully blending in with the other cars waiting to pick up pupils. The coaches that took the pupils who lived in the outlying villages had already left. The rest of the girls either walked home or to the bus stops at the end of the lane. It was about a ten-minute walk. Nicole should be walking to the bus stop but there was no sign of her yet.

Nine police officers were waiting in the three cars but it was like looking for a needle in a haystack. Any one of the girls drifting past could be Nicole. They knew from the call that had summoned all vehicles in the area to the lane that the target was a girl called Nicole, but that was all they knew. There'd been enough time to discover that there were three Nicoles in the school but not enough time to identify which one was the intended target. Had they had more time they could have also staked out the road better, but now all they could do was watch and hope. Any of the cars parked along the lane could be hiding the abductors and so far there was no sign of the white van the station had told them to look out for.

The girls continued to stream along the lane, laughing and chatting, some listening to music, others on their phones, but all oblivious to the evil that lurked close by. Perhaps the rapists had got wind the police had been tipped off and had aborted their plans? If so there were more police staked out at the flat in Bushmead Close they'd been using, waiting for them to return. Keeping their presence as inconspicuous as possible, the officers in the cars remained vigilant and in contact with the other cars in the operation and the station. The crowds of girls began to thin as some left in waiting cars, a couple on the backs of motorbikes and the rest walking slowly towards the end of the lane and the bus stops.

Ten minutes later all that remained were the late leavers and there was still no sign of a white van. The DSI was updated.

Nicole King put in her earbuds as she came out of the school gates, then turned into the lane. She was usually with two friends but today she'd had to stay behind to see her science teacher, Ms Wilkins, so she'd told them to go on without her as she didn't know how long she'd be. Nicole was happy. Ms Wilkins had told her she would be running extra biology and chemistry lessons for those who were hoping to pursue careers in medicine; the budding doctors, nurses, paramedics and pharmacists. Competition was fierce to study medicine at university and Nicole knew this would give her a better chance of getting the grades she needed to be accepted. Starting on Wednesday, the classes would run for an hour after school and continue until they'd taken their exams the following year. Not only was Nicole pleased but she knew her parents would be too. They were both doctors and had been overjoyed when she'd said she wanted to follow in their footsteps and study medicine.

With her gaze concentrated on the pavement and listening to her music, she was completely unaware of the white van that had pulled out of the school gates behind her. Even when it drew level she gave it no more than a cursory glance. She continued along the lane, lost in her music and plans for her future. The van passed and then drew into the kerb a little way in front; the lane was more or less deserted now. As she walked by, the side door of the van suddenly opened and two figures wearing bala-clavas grabbed her and pulled her in. Her screams were silenced by a gloved hand clamped over her mouth. It was all over in a second. Roughly thrown on the floor in the back of the van, she was pinned down by the two men while a third stayed in the driver's seat.

Wide-eyed with fear, Nicole struggled and tried to thrash out but it was hopeless. Much heavier and stronger than her, they sat effortlessly on her arms and legs. Only their eyes and mouths were visible through the slits in their balaclavas. One produced a knife and held it to her throat; she felt the cold steel press against her skin.

'Keep still if you know what's good for you,' he snarled, then turned to the other and nodded as if giving him the go ahead.

Nicole stared in horror, rigid with fear, as he began towards her, undoing his trousers.

Further down the lane an officer in the last police car had just spotted the van.

'Shit! It must have been hiding in the school grounds!'

Starting the car, the driver swung out and accelerated towards the van; the other two police cars followed. The driver of the van spotted them and quickly starting the van's engine, drove towards the cars. They tried to block its path. With a screech of tyres the van swerved, clipped the first police car, sending it spinning, then accelerated, missing the second car but hit the third full on.

The officers poured out of their cars and surrounded the van. Batons raised and stun gun at the ready, they wrenched open the doors and rushed in, overpowering the abductors. Sobbing, Nicole was helped to her feet and out of the van. An officer draped a blanket around her shoulders and led her towards one of the police cars to wait for the ambulance. As they went, Nicole saw the three men being led to the other police cars, now unmasked and handcuffed. She paused and cried out in disbelief.

'I know that man!' she said, pointing. 'It's Paul Mellows. He came to our house to fit our CCTV. He's been dating my sister.'

And the horror and deception played on her would stay with Nicole and her family forever.

Chapter Forty-Seven

One month later, Derek sat propped up on a mound of pillows in his hospital bed while his mother sat in the chair beside him peeling an orange. Both his hands, feet and head were heavily bandaged, but after a week in intensive care and massive doses of intravenous antibiotics he was in a ward and finally starting to recover.

'Are you sure you won't have to go to prison?' his mother asked, not for the first time, her face growing serious again.

He stifled a sigh. 'No, Mum, I've already explained. I'll be cautioned but I won't be given a custodial sentence. I did wrong watching those people but I didn't actually harm anyone as the police now know. And what they've found on my computer together with what I've told them can be used as evidence against Mellows and his accomplices. Some very nasty people will be locked up for a long time.'

'Good,' she said, popping a segment of orange into his mouth. She waited while he ate it. 'But you won't do any more spying on people, will you?'

'No, I promise.' He chewed and swallowed. 'No more surveillance. I'll leave them to make their own mistakes. Lying in hospital has given me plenty of time to think. I've been given another chance and I intend to use it. Your sister was right when she said we needed to get out more. Once I'm well enough I think we should go away for a few days.'

Elsie Flint's face lit up. 'Yes. We could go to Broadstairs. My sister goes there and she says it's really nice. I'll ask her for the address of the guest house where she stays. It's right on the sea front. The sea air will do you good. We might even paddle in the water.' She chuckled and then looked at the small television suspended over his bed. It was nearly 1pm. She needed to keep an eye on the time.

The television had originally been for her benefit so she could keep up with the soaps during the many hours she'd spent by her son's bed when he'd been too weak to talk. But lately Derek had become nearly as involved in the plots – the ups and downs of people's lives – as she was. Like mother like son, he'd said which had pleased her immensely.

However, today it wasn't the soaps she was interested in but the local news.

At exactly one o'clock as the theme tune for the news began, she pressed the button to raise the volume. The main news headlines came on in brief, followed by the local news. The first item was about a house fire; thankfully, everyone had been rescued.

'I hope you won't mind, Derek,' she said, 'but I had to set the record straight.'

He looked at her questioningly but her attention was on the screen.

Derek watched open-mouthed and incredulous as an image of his house filled the screen. The reporter his mother had previously spoken to was walking up their front path.

'In an amazing turn of events,' she began, 'local man, Derek Flint, has gone from being vilified, accused of a number of heinous crimes to becoming our local hero. Derek is now recovering in hospital after a shocking ordeal when he was held captive and repeatedly beaten by his captors. But his selflessness and bravery have saved a young girl from being raped and possibly saved her life. His mother, Mrs Flint, has asked to speak to us and has a heartfelt message.'

'It was recorded earlier,' Elsie said to Derek, glancing nervously at her son.

The camera went to his mother, standing outside their front door, which looked as though it had been given another coat of paint. With her shoulders drawn back and standing tall, she was looking very smart in a dress he'd never seen before. He watched with a mixture of awe and apprehension. What was she going to say?

'I'm not allowed to talk about the actual case,' she began, addressing the camera in a steady, confident voice, 'because it hasn't gone to court yet and it could jeopardize the outcome. But I want you all to know how proud I am of my son, Derek. I haven't been the best mother in the world and I was far too quick to believe bad against him. That was very wrong of me.' She paused and took a breath.

'I should have had more faith in my son and known he would always do the right thing. He has looked after me for many years since my husband left and has never once complained. Recently he went through a dreadful ordeal when he nearly died. He showed incredible courage and was able to give the police the information they needed to save the young girl. She can't be named for legal reasons but I'm sure what he did, his bravery, will be revealed in court. I am sorry I ever doubted my son and I want you all to know how proud I am of him. It's never too late to say sorry, and I am.'

As the reporter wound up Derek turned to his mother, tears in his eyes. 'Thank you, Mum, that was nice of you.'

'No need to thank me. It's true. You are a good son. I just didn't appreciate you, but it will be different in the future.'

'Likewise.'

Chapter Forty-Eight

Sixty miles away, Jackson Clark sat in his bedroom in his mother's flat, bored and disaffected. Fed up with the homework he was supposed to be doing and fed up with life in general. His only interest, indeed his passion, was in computer programming. He loved working with HTML, Javascript, Linux and all the other languages of the world of programming and the Internet. One day he'd make a name for himself like the founders of Facebook and Twitter. He could picture himself as the next Zuckerberg.

Jackson would be the first to admit he didn't have friends in the real world. He'd never found the key to instigating and maintaining friendship and had more or less given up. Other fifteen-year-olds wanted to talk about girls, football and fast cars, of which he knew little and cared even less. Similarly, they failed to share his passion for coding and referred to him as the geek or the nerd.

His online friends were very different. Although he'd never met them, they understood and shared his devotion and excitement in the power of coding.

With them he could be himself.

Jackson picked up his pen, wrote one more sentence in his English essay, then, closing the book, pushed it to one side. Seven-thirty; his mother wouldn't be back for at least another hour. She always came up to check on the progress of his homework when she returned from work. She wanted him to do well, for her life had been a struggle, and was probably even duller than his. As a single parent, she had two jobs to make ends meet, serving in a shop during the day and cleaning offices at night. She knew he wanted a career in programming and had saved up to buy him a decent laptop for which he should have been grateful. But the knowledge that she'd slaved away serving disrespectful customers and cleaning up other people's mess had taken the edge off it. He'd make it up to her one day for sure.

Seated at the small desk she'd bought for him as a child, he opened his laptop and logged in. Immediately he felt his spirits lift and the angst and tedium of the day fall away.

This was his world, where the online community he was part of were all computer geeks or nerds like himself. They talked online not only about coding – sharing their stories, tips, experiences and achievements – but also a little about their personal lives. They were a brotherhood, although some of them were female, a secret online community united in their desire to take coding to its limits. So competent were they at breaking code that they popped in and out of most secure websites as if visiting a neighbour. Yet even this was starting to bore Jackson. He knew so much that it was rare to find any new challenges or surprises.

His best pal Lee initiated a pop-up chat box and they exchanged a few messages about their days. Lee's mother had remarried and the new baby demanded an unreasonable amount of attention so wanting to make it up to Lee (read: ingratiate himself) his stepfather had upgraded Lee's computer and then left him alone. Their community was full of TBIAs: teenagers bribed into absence.

Having chatted with Lee, Jackson said hi to a few others he knew and then another message from Lee appeared. *We've just lost a member, you interested?* Attached was a piece of code that Jackson recognized as coming from the dark web.

Yes! he returned straightaway.

I'll tell the group to expect you. Go in the main gates and you'll be shown to The Charter of Secrecy where you need to sign. See you on the other side!

Thanks, man. On my way!

Jackson felt his pulse quicken as he copied and pasted the code into the browser, working on a specially adapted external drive to get around the security controls on the laptop itself. He knew such organizations existed, buried deep in the dark web; he also knew they were by invitation only, and you didn't speak about them to anyone outside. He felt very privileged. This was where cyberspace met the real world and fantasy and reality collided. Once you were in, there was no going back and he was more than ready for the challenge.

Suddenly his computer screen filled with an interactive image of a massive iron gate, beyond which lay a Transylvanian type castle. The sound was on and he heard the gate creak open. An avatar appeared with his name on it. Cool. His excitement and anticipation increased. He began moving the avatar up the path towards the castle, flanked by barren and desolate graveyards. Dead rats, snakes and other half-gorged animals littered his path. Nothing lived here but ghouls and ghosts – the avatars of other members. Their faces matched their names: Devil, Demon, Vampire. They appeared suddenly out of nowhere from his left and right, trying to scare him into turning back. They snarled, bared their teeth and tried to halt his progress up to the huge wooden doors of the castle but he persevered. This was the test, a chance too good to miss. He might not be invited again.

Finally making it to the castle door, he pulled the bell cord and the doors creaked open. He shuddered as two poltergeists appeared: the transparent souls of dead children. Screeching, they flew in his face and he instinctively ducked out of their way. Then an arrow appeared, pointing to a crimson velvet curtain like the one surrounding a coffin in a crematorium. As he approached, the curtains parted and he entered a small chamber. In front on the lectern, a large book lay open titled *The*

Charter of Secrecy. He had to sign it by typing in his name. He heard applause.

'You are now ready to complete your first challenge,' a disembodied voice said. 'Once complete you will be awarded your new undead identity. The price of failure is your demise. Do you understand?'

'Yes, I understand,' Jackson said, his voice faltering.

The room vanished and the screen filled with a scroll.

Level one and to gain membership

Hack into the CCTV in a store of your choice (the bigger the store the more points).

You have one week to observe, then break in to the store and take an item or items to the value of at least £5000.

Other members will be monitoring your progress on the live footage and will decide how many points you will be awarded.

Once complete you will be given your next task.

When you reach level ten and have proved yourself you will be able to meet other members for the ultimate real-life challenge.

Jackson smiled to himself as his fingers flew over the keyboard and his spirits soared at the thought of what lay ahead. He'd meet the challenges head on, quickly prove himself and move up the levels to the ultimate real-life event. He could picture the praise and adoration of the other members when he met them for the first time after he'd set new records for completing the tasks. Yes, he'd impress them all right. This was his 'calling', his vocation. Here he was valued, in charge and his life had meaning and purpose. Without it he'd be nothing – a nobody – but in this he would excel.

Five minutes later he was in, looking through the CCTV cameras of Rumans, the biggest store in town. He watched and waited, and at closing time he saw Susie, the cashier, collect the day's takings from the tills and take them to the safe in the back room. He zoomed in as she entered the code to the safe and took a snapshot of the screen.

All that remained now was for him to choose a day and time to break in. He'd steal a lot more than the minimum of £5000. In the meantime he'd get to know Susie. She was really pretty, sexy, and not much older than him. As she left the store he launched the software that allowed him to look through the lens of her phone, and followed her home.

Author's note

This story is fiction but the technical details and the dark web are true. Sophisticated interactive games are freely available, many are violent and there are cases of people having killed after watching them. The software and technology is already on the Internet that allows spying through phones, CCTV cameras, laptops and tablets. This story could happen. It might already have.

To learn more about Lisa Stone and her books, please visit www.lisastonebooks.co.uk

Suggested topics for reading group discussion

What effect did Derek's father leaving have on (a) Derek and (b) his mother?

How had this affected their relationship?

Why do you think Derek's role online of watching and controlling his clients is more appealing to him than the real world? Would you describe him as manipulative?

How would you describe his sexuality?

Disaffected young people are drawn to violent online games. Why do you think this is and what, if anything, can be done to stop it?

The Internet generally needs better controls. Discuss.

What has been the positive and negative effect of the World Wide Web? What changes would you like to see?

Do you think Derek really has learnt his lesson?

Loved *Stalker*?
Try Lisa Stone's first crime thriller,
The Darkness Within

His death was just the beginning. . .